RENEGADE STORM

STAR BANDITS UPRISING BOOK 3

JENNIFER M. EATON

Renegade Storm
Star Bandits: Uprising Book 3
© 2022 Jennifer M. Eaton
R4

Published by Galactic Razor
Cover design: Covers by Julie
www.coversbyjulie.com

For Grandma Eaton.
My biggest fan.
Hi Darlin'

A MOLTEN-BLACK SECURITY ship locked its weapons on the *Star Renegade*. Cal clutched the armrests on his command chair as more ships charged them from every angle.

How did they always manage to get into spots like this?

The *Star Renegade* trembled as a spray of laser fire skipped over the top of the main viewscreen and riddled their hull.

"Report!" Cal banked the ship right.

Ty swiped back his blond hair as he adjusted the shields. "People are shooting at us!"

Cal glared at him. This, he already knew.

They'd dropped Dania's former commander off at Neptune 9 station after taking him on a rescue mission to save one of his people. Kile had promised to give them a solid ten-minute lead before the enforcer sent ships to chase them down. But the filthy liar had called the *Star Renegade* in the second he'd had the chance. Now it looked like the whole galaxy was coming down on them.

"How many ships are out there?" Cal asked.

Alanna leaned closer to her navigation screen, casting a blue glow over her face that made the pink highlights in her hair look purple. "It looks like thirty-six."

It seemed more like a thousand.

The doorway to the bridge slid open. Dania frowned at the viewscreens as she entered.

The enforcer they'd rescued—the annoyingly perfect Alexander—stepped in behind her. His long, silvery-blond hair flowed about him like he was in Zero-G.

"Having difficulty?" the enforcer asked.

"I don't need any lip right now." Especially from a six-foot-four walking doll. Even one with ridiculous powers at his beck and call.

Cal looked over his shoulder at Dania. "We were supposed to have ten minutes to get away."

She nodded. "I think ten minutes passed before the first guards fired on us."

Great. Kile was nothing if not precise. "Alanna, can you jump us?"

She shook her head. "There are too many ships. I'll hit one."

Alexander pointed through the window. "They're using spiral attack patterns to ensure you don't have a clean exit trajectory."

"How in the blazes would they know to do that?" Ty asked.

The enforcer folded his arms. "This ship is known for skipping space at phenomenal distances. The king's technologists on Keveron have placed a call of interest on the *Star Renegade* for that very reason. They'd like to take a look at your engines." He glanced at Alanna. "Or is it something else?"

Cal gritted his teeth. He'd be dammed if he'd put another target on a member of his crew. There was no reason their new resident pretty boy needed to know anything more about Alanna than he already did.

"We have special tech on board," Cal said. "Ethan is annoying, but he's a genius with stuff like that." Cal sent the ship into a spin, avoiding fire. "And I'll be damned if your king gets his hands on the *Renegade*, or anyone in it." And that was the truth. They'd been running for far too long to get caught now.

A blast roared over the top of the ship. Sparks shot out of a panel to Cal's right. Heat riddled the room as the wiring sizzled.

Cal jumped to his feet. "Ty?"

"I got the controls! Just keep anything else from getting fried."

Cal ran to the sparking panel as Ty took full control of the ship. If Cal were being honest, Ty was a far better pilot than he was, anyway.

Ethan's voice came over the speaker. "You guys okay up there? I'm reading a fire."

Cal hit the com on the wall. "No fire. Just sparks. It's the silver panel with the blue striped edge around it."

"Hit the white button above it," Ethan said.

Cal pressed the button, and the sparking stopped. "It worked. But what does this panel do?"

"Nothing that we need in a fight," Ethan said. "I'll fix it later."

Outside, a huge ship sank into view. Royal insignias shimmered on its sides.

"We got a really big bogey!" Ty shouted.

Alanna held one hand over her ear, probably listening to

the comm chatter. "I can't navigate around it. There's too much traffic."

Which meant they were screwed. Cal sat back in his seat and ran scans over the oncoming ships' flight patterns. There had to be a hole in their attack strategy. And if there wasn't, then one of those ships were bound to make a mistake sooner or later. If Cal could pick up on it before they corrected themselves, Alanna could jump the *Star Renegade* and they might just be able to get out of this in one piece.

Cal glanced over his shoulder to Alexander. It would be a little hard to keep Alanna's ability a secret from the enforcers with Mr. Perfect standing right there. He caught Dania's gaze.

She looked at Alanna, then the screens before giving Cal a quick nod and taking Alexander's hand. "Cal's right. The engines on this ship *are* formidable."

The enforcer quirked a brow. "So I've heard."

"Would you like to see the engines? Maybe even try to increase their efficiency?"

Cal narrowed his eyes on her. He didn't want an enforcer touching his ship. Especially *that* enforcer.

Dania glanced at him in that way that always seemed to settle his mind. Her beautiful brown eyes softened before turning back to Alexander. "If you help us out of this, you'll get your chance."

The enforcer pursed his lips.

She moved closer to him. "You said yourself how many Kever engineers have been postulating about this ship. You'd be the first to see what the *Star Renegade* can do. And why."

"The captain will never allow it." Alexander cocked his

head. "Unless you plan on returning to your old self and forcing him to comply."

Cal flinched. Dania used to be an enforcer. Maybe one of the worst. She played for team *Star Renegade* now, but he didn't like the reminder of who she'd been.

Dania looked at Cal. Her still-darkening brown hair made her look more human every day, but her face was enforcer-stern and as unreadable as ever.

"Incoming transmission!" Alanna said.

A firm male voice filled the room. "*Star Renegade, you are outnumbered and outgunned. Shut down your engines and prepare to be boarded.*"

Cal gritted his teeth. This was it. Do-or-die time.

He leveled his gaze on the annoyingly handsome enforcer. "Can you get us out of this mess or not?"

Alexander stared at him before a wry smile crept over his lips.

Cal wanted to knock the cocky grin off the guy's face. Was he enjoying the fact that Cal had asked for his help, or was he simply relishing the chance of getting his hands on the *Renegade*'s innerworkings?

The always-broken light on Ty's panel flashed yellow.

Seriously? Now?

Ty hit the button three times until it stopped. "Sorry. Ignore it."

The ship jolted, taking a hit to the left side. Cal grabbed his chair as Dania and Alexander stumbled a few steps.

Ty tapped on the screen in his console. "Shields still look good!"

"Not for much longer, though," Alanna said.

The enforcer's grin faded before he turned to Dania. "I

will not harm any of our own people. Nor the law enforcement of this loyal planet."

Dania placed her hand on his chest. "Of course not. But you could, maybe…move them out of the way?"

He pursed his lips and looked through the viewscreen as the largest ship loomed nearer. "If this smuggling ship lives up to its reputation, they shouldn't need my help. There are no enforcers on that cruiser."

"Huh?" Ty leaned closer to the screen. "Those markings sure look royal."

"The king's legions are mostly unranked, unpowered Kevers," Dania said. "The enforcers are the elite."

Cal grimaced. This wasn't new information for him. The problem was, he had no way to tell one ship from another. All he knew was that they all pointed guns at him.

Still, he'd take whatever good news he could get. He looked at Alexander. "Does that mean you can take them out?"

Ty started a spiral roll over the larger ship. "Heck, if it's not enforcers, I'll try to take them out myself."

Alexander whispered, "Fool," under his breath before raising his palm. A burst of shimmering light left his hand, passed through the *Star Renegade*'s hull, and engulfed the royal ship. The smaller crafts backed off as the larger cruiser started to list.

The enforcer lowered his hand. "They will regain power in about three…" He grunted and grabbed his head before stumbling back.

"Alexander!" Dania ran to him as he slammed into the wall. "What happened?"

He blinked repeatedly. "I-I'm not sure."

Cal gritted his teeth. *Pathogen depletion.* He'd seen it

several times with Dania when her own powers had started to fade. Thing was, he cared about Dania. He didn't give a shard of meteor rock about this guy.

"Three what?" Cal asked. "Seconds? Minutes? Hours?"

"Minutes." The enforcer winced, grunting with his eyes closed.

Dania pulled him toward her. "Let me get you to the med bay."

She started walking him to the door.

Ty pointed at the screen. "It looks like we're about to get our clear passage out of here."

Cal nodded, waiting for the door to close behind Dania and Alexander. He wasn't thrilled to see Dania leave, but he was more than happy to get rid of the enforcer.

He turned to Alanna, but she was already standing, a set of blue, glowing light-dials already spinning in the air. "Hold on, everyone."

She pressed the center of the dial, and the room took on a pink and purple haze. Cal didn't know where she was taking them, but at this point, anywhere was better than here. He wanted to be as far away from Kile as he could get now that the enforcers were after them again.

The problem was, they still had one of them on board, and Cal wasn't sure they'd ever be able to run far enough away to be safe.

THE MED BAY lights cast glowing highlights in Alexander's hair as he glared at Peter. "Your medicine makes no sense."

The doctor held a syringe, looking unimpressed by Alexander's anger and slights against his treatment plan. "In case you haven't noticed, your general is standing beside you, looking quite well. She's not getting by on her good looks alone, I assure you."

Dania touched her friend's arm. "Alexander, he really can help you if you trust him."

"I don't need treatment. I'm tired. I need sleep, not whatever he's hiding in that syringe."

It was more than simply needing sleep, and Alexander was a good enough healer to understand that. Her friend had never been good at admitting when he didn't know things, though. Right now, he was probably thinking about ways to get to a computer so he could research why he was weak, even though it should have been quite obvious, having been away from his sponsor for so long.

Peter lowered the syringe. His angular, yet kind face

remained placid, but she could sense the annoyance hidden in his dark eyes. Had Dania been so uncooperative when he'd tried to treat her?

Ridiculous question. Of course, she had. But she'd learned so much since then.

She turned to Alexander. "We can't get you fed any time soon. You've been through far too much, and you're more than just tired."

Her heart twisted as his gaze remained stoic. If Alexander continued to refuse treatment, his health would progressively fail, just like hers had. Without his power, he would always be a target for the pirates roaming the galaxy looking for pretty enforcers to sell as trophies. She hated to admit it, but he would have been safer returning to Keveron with Kile.

Alexander stood, blinked his eyes hard like he couldn't see, and headed for the door. "If you need me, I will be resting in my assigned quarters."

Why did he have to be so difficult? "Alexander!"

Peter waved him off. "Let him go. If he passes out, he won't be able to refuse the electrolytes."

Dania waited for the door to close behind her friend. "He needs more than electrolytes."

"I agree." Peter walked over to the comm station and tapped the pad. "Cal, we need to head toward Sector Z8. It looks like I'm going to need double the supplies if I'm going to start treating two of the king's finest."

A sigh permeated the line. "Dania is the priority. Don't waste her supplies on the other one."

Dania frowned. The *other one*?

Peter tapped the comm. "That won't be an issue for a while. He wouldn't even let me give him a general treatment. But I'd like to have the pathogens ready for when he drops."

For when he drops. Dania closed her eyes. Alexander had always been so strong. She couldn't imagine him weak. He'd been through something horrible, being captured and tortured, but he'd bounced back, becoming strong on his own. But it appeared to be short-lived. She couldn't bear to think of him weakened again.

"All right," Cal said. "We'll head down to the supply sectors. That's as good a place to lie low, anyway."

That was actually a good plan. By "supply sectors," Cal meant the areas known for trafficking illegal materials. Kile probably wouldn't expect them to head to the more illicit sectors of the galaxy with Alexander on board, so it was a reasonable place to avoid capture as well as gaining needed supplies.

Still, Kile had a vested interest in keeping the crew of the *Star Renegade* alive, so he'd been willing to overlook several instances of illegal behavior. Alexander had no such restrictions. If her friend saw criminal activity, Dania would be the only thing standing between the crew and the death sentence Alexander would be forced to carry out.

Alexander certainly wasn't as judgmental as Kile, but she needed to find a way to ingratiate the crew to him. It wouldn't get them exonerated, but it at least might buy them some time.

She stepped up to the comm. "Cal, do you have a moment to meet me in the lounge?"

The line crackled slightly before he answered. "Yeah, I'll be down there in five."

Good.

Exactly what she would say to him, she didn't know,

but he seemed like the best person to start with to try to figure something out.

She made her way through the halls toward the lounge. The blast marks on the walls seemed darker than normal. Maybe the lighting had been affected by the recent skirmish. She still hadn't heard the whole story about how the interior had taken such visible damage. Not that it mattered. Everything this crew endured seemed to make them stronger. Hopefully, having a new enforcer onboard would be no different.

Alexander's refusal to be treated was troubling. He had to know that he'd become weak the longer he was away from Geron. Had he figured she would change her mind and return with him right away? Had he not thought his own health would be an issue?

She shook her head, tapping the panel to gain access to the lounge. With any luck, he'd agree to some kind of care from the doctor, or at least treat himself before he got too weak to stand.

The doorway slid open. Cal stood on the far side of the room beside Rachel. The petite auburn-haired former stow-away sat on top of the long crew table hugging her knees and looking out the window.

Cal dragged his fingers through his dark hair. "Look, Rachel, I don't know what to tell you, but no one on this ship thinks any less of you."

She curled in on herself. "How couldn't they? I'm a total, complete fool!"

Dania stepped into the room. "What's going on?"

Cal turned toward her, a look of relief on his handsome face. "Rachel is...umm..."

"A complete dimwit. I couldn't see a galaxy even if it

were right in front of me." Rachel covered her face with her hands.

"I didn't say that!" Cal said.

"You didn't have to. You were thinking it."

A plate slipped off the table on the far side of the room. Dania stared as the dish clanged to the floor. There hadn't been anyone over there to knock it over.

Cal shook his head, ignoring the plate like any other quirk in the ship, and turned to Dania again. "A little help here, please." He gestured to Rachel with his palm.

Dania smiled and placed her hand on the woman's back. "Why do you think you're a fool?"

Rachel wiped her eyes. "Because I thought he loved me. I thought he'd stay."

Dania pursed her lips. Rachel had fallen in love with Dania's commander, Kile. However, the relationship had been doomed from the start. Kile was still beholden to Prince Geron, and not just by an oath. Geron had infected him with a pathogen that acted like a drug. It gave Kile—and all enforcers—phenomenal powers, but at the same time, their bodies needed to be refueled. Without their sponsoring prince, they would die.

Dania had been dependent on her prince as well until she'd been weakened by Palian steel and time away from her sponsor. As her mind slowly cleared, the *Star Renegade* crew had gained her trust, and their doctor had treated her with synthetic pathogens to help keep her alive.

So far, it was working. She was free. However, it didn't appear that she would ever get her enforcer powers back.

Taking a deep breath, Dania collected her thoughts. "I think he did care about you in his own way."

"Then why did he leave me?"

He hadn't left only her. He'd left all of them. Ethan and Ty had hoped that his relationship with Rachel would be enough to make him cut ties with his prince. None of them understood what it was to be an enforcer.

"In Kile's mind, he didn't leave you. He returned to his sponsor."

"It's the same thing."

"Not really. You need to understand that his dependence on his prince is something out of his control."

Rachel spun toward Dania, then hugged her knees to her chest again. "He could totally control it. He could have just stayed. It's not so hard. All he had to do was not walk out that door. But he did because he doesn't love me." She dropped her head on her knees. "I can't believe I fell for that. I was nothing but a way for him to get his rocks off."

Dania frowned. "Rocks off?"

Rachel looked up. "Oh, come on, Dania. How naïve are you? He used me and then took off before it got too complicated for him—just like every other man in my life."

Dania's lips parted. She was not quite that naïve. She knew exactly what they'd been doing in Kile's closed quarters. She just had trouble picturing her commander, or any enforcer, engaged in personal gratification.

"I'm trying to explain that he *did* care about you. It's unlike him to..." How should she put it? "It's unlike him to spend so much extracurricular time with someone."

Rachel snorted. "You're an enforcer. Why didn't you leave when your dear-old princey-poo called?"

Dania lowered her eyes. The sad truth was that she had tried. Luckily enough for the crew, she'd come to her senses moments before it was too late. Rachel probably wouldn't understand that, though.

The woman stood and pointed at her. "See? You stayed. You had a choice, and you decided to stay with Cally."

With Cally? Yes, Dania had stayed on the *Star Renegade*, but to be with everyone, and to be free. Why had Rachel singled out Cal?

Rachel slid along the tabletop, stood, and bounded for the door. "All I'm good for is to be taken advantage of and then dumped like yesterday's cargo containers. I'm a trusting simp and completely useless!" The door opened just as she reached it and started to slide closed behind her. Just before it sealed, it jumped back like it had hit something, tried to slide closed again, shimmied, and then sealed shut.

"I guess that's something else I'll have to get fixed." Cal dragged his fingers through his hair again. "Thanks for your help with Rachel. I definitely wasn't prepared to deal with something like that."

Dania nodded, although she wasn't sure how much help she'd been. She looked back at the door. The opening and closing mechanism appeared fine. However, many things on the ship seemed fine, until they failed.

Of course, this might be a way to help introduce Alexander's positive traits to Cal. "I can ask Alexander to look at the door if you like. He's really good at fixing things."

His jaw tensed. "Thanks, but no thanks. I don't need his help."

Dania's stomach sank. This might be harder than she'd anticipated. "You don't like Alexander, do you?"

"He's an enforcer."

"So was I."

Cal shook his head. "And when you were an enforcer, I

wasn't all that fond of you, either, if you'll remember. And I sure as hell wasn't unhappy to see Kile go."

That much, at least, was true. "Alexander is much more analytical than Kile. I think, in time, he might come around to our way of thinking."

"Maybe, but until he does, he's still an enforcer. He's a threat to you, and a threat to this crew."

Dania shook her head. "He would never hurt me." And she hoped he wouldn't hurt the crew, either. Unlike Kile, Alexander's default programming was not to kill. That left him one step closer to humanity by happenstance. However, that certainly didn't mean Alexander wouldn't enforce the king's law if faced with evidence of a crime.

Cal's cheek ticked. "I think your opinion of him is a bit jaded. He made it perfectly clear that his sole mission is to bring you home."

"But he's not dragging me there. That gives us time for you to show him everything you showed me."

Cal choked out a laugh. "Are you kidding? That guy is fully charged. He just proved that on the bridge by knocking out the power on one of his own ships and all he did was lift a hand." His cheeks reddened. "I'm not bringing him anywhere where he can start passing judgment on my friends."

Dania closed her eyes. He was right. Well, not right about Alexander being fully charged. Her healer was badly drained but still a serious threat to a human. She would have thought Alexander would have been in rougher shape after being separated from Geron for so long, especially after being floated in that liquid that kept him barely alive, hanging suspended and on display as a living piece of art for an eccentric collector.

At one time, Peter had cracked part of the pathogen code by matching Kile's DNA to hers. Maybe she should suggest he look at Alexander's genetic code as well, if her friend would allow it. All of this, though, required Alexander to stay on board, and for him to possibly become a member of the crew, as Dania had.

However, that would take Cal's approval, and something about Cal's posture made him look like a feral animal about to pounce. It was like he was on the defensive, and this change in demeanor had started when she'd mentioned her friend's name.

"Why do you have such a distaste for Alexander?"

Cal huffed out a laugh. "That should be obvious."

Maybe, but it wasn't. And it killed her inside.

She felt such warmth with Cal, a sweet familiarity she wanted to explore, but being in the same room with Alexander seemed to sweep all the kindness from Cal, replacing the captain she'd grown to trust with a man filled with a swirl of emotions that she couldn't sort out.

Yes, Alexander was still an enforcer, but he was so much more than Cal knew. If there was any such thing as a kind, caring enforcer, then that was her friend. She wished Cal could see Alexander how she saw him, but Cal's hatred for the enforcers ran deep. His distrust sparked from something more personal to him than simply being a man on the run from the law.

She'd thought having Alexander here would allow her to see her best friend and also remain free. But if she couldn't break through Cal's hatred, then having the best of both her worlds might be an unobtainable dream.

CAL LEANED against the back wall of the lounge as Ethan ran his fingers over the doorframe. Dania stood behind him with Mr. Perfect at her side. Cal wasn't really all that concerned about the door glitching, but for some reason, Dania really wanted it to be looked at.

If anyone was going to inspect something on the ship, though, Cal wanted it to be a member of the crew. Dania hadn't been all that happy when Cal had called Ethan, but she'd have to get over it. Even if her enforcer-buddy could fix the door, that wouldn't make Cal trust him.

Cal tapped the comm on the wall beside him. "Ty, everything still look good up there?"

The comm pinged back. "Yup. Just me, a bunch of pretty stars, and a big-ass asteroid to keep me company. It's kinda relaxing, if I'm being honest."

"Good. Don't jinx us." Cal shut down the comm.

Ethan pushed against the edge of the door and then scratched the edge of his disheveled red hair. "You're saying it bounced back?"

"Yes." Dania shifted her weight. "Alanna mentioned

that the same thing happened to Rachel's door this afternoon. It could be an entire systems issue."

If it was, it hadn't started until that enforcer had come on board. If Cal found out their new walking liability had messed with the ship, maybe so he could fix it and look like a hero, there would be hell to pay.

On the other wall, one of the food compartments lay open with a single ration bag inside. He'd have to talk to the crew about being more careful. They couldn't take a chance at anything being left out and spoiling.

Ethan shook his head. "I don't know. It looks okay to me."

Alexander folded his arms. "What, exactly, are your qualifications to claim the mechanisms are *okay?*"

Ethan shrugged. "I'm good at what I do?"

The enforcer quirked a brow. "Are you?"

"Yeah, I get by." Wiping his hands on his pants, Ethan turned. "Do they train you guys to be holier-than-thou or something? Because you sound so much like your commander."

Alexander's lips thinned. "I am *nothing* like my commander."

"Don't take it as an insult. The big guy was a major badass. When I think of an enforcer, I think of him. He definitely has that whole 'intimidating' thing down pat."

"You know nothing about what it is to be an enforcer."

Ethan grinned, beaming with Ethan-ness. "Aww, don't undersell yourself. I bet you're pretty badass, too." He punched Alexander in the arm.

The enforcer roared. His hair took flight and a bright yellow glare flashed around him. Ethan lifted off the ground and flew across the lounge, slamming into the door.

"Alexander!" Dania's voice filled the room as the enforcer charged Ethan holding a ball of swirling flames in his fist.

The air seemed to suck out of Cal's lungs as he lunged for Ethan, trying to push him out of the way, but Dania jumped between them. She hissed, a barely human sound, followed by a whimper that cut through Cal as if it had reached into his soul.

Her head was turned to the side as the ball of fire in Alexander's hand scorched her skin, blistering her flesh.

Behind her, Ethan hung splayed against the door, breathing heavily with wide eyes. The enforcer's hand reached over Dania's shoulder and held Ethan's neck, the fireball still swirling in his other fist, only inches from both their faces.

Alexander stood frozen, gaping with wide eyes.

Cal blinked away the shock and reached for Dania.

"No," she whispered. "Stay back."

Easy for her to say. Two people he cared about were about to get their faces burned to cinders. But she was right. He needed to keep a cool head...at least until he knew what was going on.

"Ethan," Cal said. "Don't move."

Ethan gulped. "Already ahead of you, boss."

The enforcer swayed, and the fireball winked out. He choked out what sounded like a combination of a sob and a cough before he fell to his knees.

"What the hell?" Cal grabbed Dania and pulled her back as Alexander held his temples and screamed like his head was exploding.

"What did you do?" Not that it mattered. Cal didn't care about the enforcer, as long as the guy wasn't hurting the people he cared about.

Cal tilted Dania's chin and grimaced at the red, swollen sores.

Still standing against the wall, Ethan barely breathed as he stared at the screaming enforcer.

Cal reached out and touched Ethan's shoulder. "You okay?"

The engineer nodded, rubbing the handprint on his throat.

Dania covered her mouth, tears filling her eyes as her friend screamed again. "He hurt me."

This, Cal could see for himself.

She turned to Cal. "You don't understand. He *hurt* me."

Alexander's cries stopped. He doubled over, holding his stomach.

Dania took a deep breath and reset her footing. It almost looked like she was getting ready for a fight. "I need the two of you to get out of here."

"But..."

Alexander took a deep breath and shakily huffed it out.

Dania slapped the panel beside the door and pushed Ethan through. "Get out. Now."

"What about you?" Cal asked.

She shook her head. "He won't hurt me again. Trust me."

Cal eyed the blisters on her cheek. She might feel differently if she could see her face. She needed medical treatment. The sooner, the better.

Alexander's breathing started to normalize.

She pushed Cal to the door. "Please. I need you to go."

Every part of him wanted to stay and make sure this ticking time bomb didn't hurt her again. But Alexander hadn't burned her on purpose. She'd only gotten in the way.

Her eyes pleaded. "He won't hurt me. I need you to believe that and go."

Cal grimaced. No matter how much he wanted to stay, he was no match for an enforcer. "Be careful."

She took a deep breath before she turned to Alexander. "I will. Now, get out while you still can."

The enforcer raised his eyes and glared at her. It took every ounce of Cal's resolve not to walk back inside and stand between them.

Luckily, Ethan closed and sealed the door before he could change his mind.

"What the hell?" Ethan said. "I was only talking to him."

"I saw." Cal sprinted down the hall to the med bay and slapped the panel, pushing through the door before it had completely opened.

"Where's the fire?" Doc handed Alanna a data pad.

"Almost in my face." Ethan stepped in behind Cal, rubbing the back of his head. "And I think I have a concussion." He lowered his hand, showing Doc bloody fingers. "Huh. That can't be good."

"What? Ethan!" Alanna grabbed a cloth from a box on the counter and put it on his head. "Apply pressure on that."

"Doc, I need your big brain." Cal tapped into the cameras and played a live feed from the lounge.

"What's up?" Peter moved beside him.

"Mr. Perfect just blew a gasket. He nearly burned Ethan and Dania's faces off."

On the screen, Alexander stood, waving his hands at Dania as if he were shouting.

"Where's the audio?" Cal asked.

"That's strange." Doc fiddled with the controls.

Great. Now the video systems were on the fritz, too.

"He looks pretty mad," Alanna said.

The enforcer's hair shifted like a breeze blew around him. Cal wished he had Dania's confidence that the guy wouldn't be able to hurt her even worse.

A tone sounded in the back of the room, and a round tray of hanging test tubes spun a quarter turn and sank into a machine. Neither Doc nor Alanna even seemed to notice.

Doc glanced at Ethan. "What did you do this time?"

Ethan shrugged. "I was just messing with him. I kidded a lot harder with Kile and he never tried to kill me."

"What happened right before he lost it?" Doc asked.

"I cracked a joke." Ethan adjusted the cloth Alanna had put on his head. "And then I punched his arm. You know… like, messing with him."

Doc turned to the engineer. "You punched an enforcer with PTSD?"

Ethan frowned. "No. I punched him with my fist. And not all that hard."

Doc shook his head. "He's already shown signs of post-traumatic stress. That was dumb. Even for you."

Alanna grabbed an ice pack and shook it. "You think the PTSD set him off—that he felt threatened, even if it was just Ethan?"

"Hey." Ethan removed the cloth as Alanna handed him the ice.

That was exactly what happened. And this didn't bode well for any of them.

Doc pressed a few buttons. "Here comes the audio."

"You could have killed me!" Alexander shouted.

Dania kept her stance level, showing no sign of concern. "I had no choice. You were about to execute the engineer. And for what? What crime had he committed?"

Alexander's eyes darkened. "He's a member of this crew. I'm sure it wouldn't be hard to find a crime."

"But what crime were you passing judgement on, Alexander? What had he done in that moment to warrant execution?"

The enforcer stared at her, his hair swirling about his head.

Had Alexander just said that Dania had almost killed *him*? He was the one holding the fire ball.

Ethan held the ice pack on his head as he looked at the screen. "I'm telling you. I didn't do anything. Even if I threw an actual punch, it would have bounced right off the guy. He's a walking wall of muscle, just like Big Bad was."

Doc tapped his lips with his finger. "But you did actually punch him. You might have not hurt him, but his captors back on Cerberus sure did." He looked at Cal. "It happens to soldiers all the time. They get triggered by what others think are trivialities, but those small, everyday things poke the memory centers." He looked back to the screen. "Our new friend might not even remember what they did to him, but his body does, and a small recess of his mind lashed out to make sure it didn't happen again."

Cal folded his arms. "Is that your clinical opinion?"

Doc shrugged. "I'm not a psychologist. Hell, I'm barely a doctor. But that's sure what it sounds like to me."

On the screen, Dania pointed at Alexander. "You will back down. Now."

He stared at her for a moment before turning away. "My direct orders were to protect you. You *made me* hurt you, and you knew what it would do to me!"

Doc gaped, glancing at Cal. Was that what she'd meant when she'd said he wouldn't hurt her? Was this programming-stuff strong enough that hurting her had caused him actual pain?

Dania pointed at him. "You gave me no choice!"

Alexander pressed his palms on his temples. "You have no idea what that did to me."

"What would you have had me do? Let you kill Ethan?" She held up her palms. "Think this through, Alexander. I am not in the wrong here. You are!"

Alanna folded her arms. "She shouldn't be yelling at him. That's not what he needs. He's been through some really bad stuff." She sighed. "He needs her to be his friend."

"I disagree. She's right. He nearly killed Ethan." Cal turned back to the screen. "Besides, he's backing down. He needs his general. He needs structure until he gets his head back on straight."

Alanna shook her head. "Whatever. I can't watch this." She headed for the door and left the room.

"Do you think he really would have killed me?" Ethan asked.

Doc rubbed his chin. "It's hard to say. If he did, he'd probably feel really bad about it afterward."

Was he serious? "That wouldn't do Ethan any good while we were loading his body into a casket."

On the screen, the doorway slid open, and Alanna entered the lounge.

Cal stepped closer to the monitor. "What in Jupiter's moons is she doing?"

Alanna waved at Dania and Alexander. "Hi. I was a little hungry. Do you two mind if I get something to eat?" She walked past them to the freeze-dried food cubbies and started rooting through the bags. "I don't know about you two, but I'm pretty tired of meat sticks. Don't you wish they'd think up another way to make protein last indefinitely?"

Alexander glared at her.

Cal grimaced. If that overwound pretty boy blew another fuse and hurt Alanna…

Doc grabbed Cal's arm, and he realized he'd taken a few steps toward the door.

"Dania's there. Alanna is her friend. She won't let him hurt her," Doc said.

Cal wanted to believe that, but right now that enforcer was both the biggest power on this ship and the biggest threat—and it seemed like he was just as unhinged as Doc thought he might be.

"You are not here to eat," Alexander said to Alanna.

She continued to sort through the packages. "What makes you say that?"

"Your digestion ratio is twenty-five percent. Your body is not done absorbing your last meal."

Alanna turned to him. "You can tell that by looking at me?"

Cal gritted his teeth. The guy could probably tell her

what she'd eaten, too. They all needed to get it into their heads that these were enforcers…not regular people.

"That's a little creepy," Alanna said.

Alexander folded his arms. "You are here at the behest of your captain."

Ethan snorted. "Behest? Who in the galaxy says 'behest' anymore?"

"Shh." Doc shoved him.

Alanna shrugged. "Cal doesn't even know that I'm here."

The enforcer turned his head and looked directly into the camera lens. "Somehow, I doubt that."

Ethan cursed. "That's impossible. That's a prime-one-grade military camera. It's the size of a pinhead."

Cal gritted his teeth. Once again, they underestimated the enemy. He wasn't sure how to get through to them that Alexander, and even Kile, were more like machines.

Alanna held up her palms. "Okay, you got me. They're watching from the med bay. But Cal didn't know I was coming. And if I know Cal, he's freaking out right now and probably on his way down here, so we have less than a minute before he barrels through that door like a crazed Trellen jungle boar."

Cal flinched. "Hey!"

"She's not wrong," Doc said.

On the screen, Alanna stepped toward the enforcer. "You almost killed Ethan. If he committed a crime, okay, that's your job to pass judgement. But what did he do?"

Dania straightened, lifting her chin. "I've been trying to discern that."

Alanna held up her palm to Dania. "I know you're his

boss and all, but can you give me a second?" Dania gaped as Alanna turned to the enforcer. "What did Ethan do?"

He stared at her for a moment before looking down. "I don't know."

"Do you think it's a problem that you don't know?" Alanna asked.

Sweat beaded Cal's brow. "What is she doing?"

Doc turned up the volume. "Hold on. I think she's onto something."

The enforcer looked up. "Yes, it is a problem."

Dania opened her mouth to speak, but Alanna held up her hand again, stopping her.

The enforcer's gaze lowered, maybe digesting for the first time that he'd almost taken a life unwarranted.

Alanna moved toward him. "You're a healer. Do you know much about the brain?"

"No." He continued to stare at the floor. "My specialty is mostly in healing injuries of the body, like those received in battle."

"No one on board is a psychologist, but my understanding is that a big part of the healing process is working through everything." She took another step. "Floating around in that tank for so long must have been horrible. Do you want to talk about it?"

"No." He looked back to the camera. "Is this why your captain sent you here? To try to soften me? To try to convince me to not bring my general home?"

Cal cringed. Alanna was walking on shaky ground, and if Doc's hand hadn't already shot out to grab Cal's arm again, he might be doing exactly what she'd expected him to—barreling in there to pull her out of harm's way.

Alanna kept her cool far better than Cal would have. "Well, none of us want Dania to leave. She's our friend. But you're really important to her, so that makes you important to me."

Mr. Perfect narrowed his eyes. "What?"

"Why do you think I sat by your bed and read to you every day? I wanted you to get better. Any friend of Dania is a friend of mine."

He stared at her. "I am an enforcer."

"And I'm the navigator on a smuggling ship. If you can get over my idiosyncrasies, I can get over yours."

The enforcer laughed. It changed his entire stance, losing the cadence of a weapon cocked and ready to fire.

Alanna held out her hand. "How about we take a walk? I know the places on the ship where there aren't any cameras."

"Is she crazy?" Ethan asked.

Alanna took a step closer. "We don't have to talk if you don't want to. But the quiet time might give you the opportunity to think about what happened today. So maybe the next time Ethan annoys you, you won't try to kill him." She took the enforcer's hand. "Because believe me, our beloved engineer will eventually do something to annoy you again. That's just who he is."

"Hey!" Ethan said.

"She's not wrong," Doc and Cal said in tandem.

On screen, Alexander nodded. "That would be agreeable."

"Is this okay with you, Dania?" Alanna asked.

Dania gaped. She stood frozen, like the feed had stopped.

Cal wondered what she was feeling, having Alanna walk in there and butting in on her general duties.

"Yes, I suppose," Dania finally said.

Alanna triggered the door, and she and the enforcer left.

Dania stared at the exit before she looked right at the camera. Cal could read the look on her face: *What the hell just happened?*

And moreover, would talking be enough to stop Dania's friend from killing one of them the next time someone pissed him off?

DANIA PACED THE SHINY, white floor in the med bay. "I barely even got through to him. He was so angry."

"So we saw." Peter poured some liquid onto a white fabric pad. "Luckily, our girl talked him down." He grabbed her arm, stopping her stride. "Now, will you please stand still so I can treat these burns?"

She nodded, closing her eyes as he dabbed the medicine on her cheek.

Her wounds were superficial, and nowhere near as important as the problem at hand. "*I should have been able to talk him down.*"

Cal leaned against the wall with his arms folded, watching her. The monitor beside him displayed a picture of the empty lounge, still showing the feed the crew had been watching when she and Alexander had fought.

Ethan adjusted an ice pack on the back of his head, his eyes darting toward the screen. No doubt they could tell Alexander had been angry, but they wouldn't have been able to feel the heat radiating off his skin or seen the glow threatening just beneath his eyes. That kind of rage was very unlike her friend, especially when he'd been so clearly in the wrong.

She turned from the screen. "It was like he couldn't even hear me."

"It wasn't that he couldn't hear you. He just didn't *want* to hear you." Doc pointed the back end of his pen light at her. "It's like when a teenager fights with their parent after getting caught doing something they shouldn't, you know?"

How was she supposed to know what a teenager acted like with a parent? Still, she nodded. "It was disconcerting."

"Alanna just played good cop, bad cop. She said all the same things you said, but nicer."

Dania cocked her head. "Nicer?"

"Our girl definitely has the *nicer* thing in her skills wheelhouse. Cal sends her to talk us into doing things we don't want to do all the time."

Cal pushed away from the wall. "I do not."

"Yeah, you do." Ethan removed the ice from his head. "She told me once you bribed her with chocolate."

Cal laughed. "Only when I really needed to."

Dania rubbed her arms. It wasn't the fact that Alanna had helped that bothered her. She shouldn't have needed to help at all. Dania was used to her enforcers complying without question.

Cal touched her shoulder. "Hey, Alanna is safe with him, right?"

Dania nodded. "I felt nothing from him to make me feel otherwise. Even when he was speaking to her, his anger seemed directed at you, not her." Which was odd in itself. It seemed like Cal and Alexander's aversion to each other was rooted in more than just one being an alleged murderer and the other an enforcer.

Ethan raised his hand. "Umm, I'm all for wanting to make sure Alanna is safe, but more importantly, since I'm the one with no feminine assets to help me out, I need to know… Am *I* safe? Because I'm kinda fond of my face being, you know…not burned to a crisp."

It was a valid concern. One Dania needed to rectify. "I will order him not to harm anyone in the crew without my permission."

Cal gaped. "You didn't do that already?"

"I didn't think I needed to. Hurting people without cause is not normally his way."

Doc laughed. "Yeah, well, we all need to keep in mind that Ethan tends to bring out the worst in people."

"Hey!" The engineer placed his hands on his hips.

"Is he wrong?" Cal asked.

Ethan's ears turned red. "No. I guess not."

A ping sounded, and Ty's voice came over the comm. "I hate to disturb the party, but I'm getting some weird chatter up here, and I can't find Alanna."

Cal tapped the comm. "She stepped off the grid for a minute. What's up?"

"Maybe you better come up here."

Cal tensed and his temperature spiked, then cooled before he tapped the comm. "I'm on my way." He turned to Ethan. "You okay to get back to engineering, just in case we need you?"

"Yeah, I'm good."

Peter shined a light in the engineer's eyes. "Just try to take it easy and get some rest as soon as you can."

Ethan waved his hand and headed to the door. "Yeah, yeah, I know, I know."

Dania doubted he'd be resting any time soon.

She slipped through the door and followed Cal to the bridge. The lights in the hallway dimmed, but Cal didn't comment. Either he'd expected it or he didn't want to alarm her.

His gaze carried over her cheek as he tapped the controls beside the doorway. "You okay?"

She reached for the burns. The ointment had deadened the pain some. It was odd that Alexander had been so angry that he'd forgotten to heal her. "It's not so bad."

His frown and slight temperature spike told her he thought otherwise, but he gave her a quick nod before they stepped inside the bridge. A bright display of stars glistened in the viewscreen. The auto-pilot indicator flashed on Cal's console while Ty sat tapping the screens on Alanna's station.

"What's up?" Cal walked up behind him.

"Look at this." The pilot pointed at two hazy lines on the screen. "These are long-range tracers."

Cal frowned. "You think someone is tracking the *Renegade*?"

"No, or they'd be on us already. It's more like someone throwing out a net and hoping to catch something."

"But are they looking for us?" Dania asked.

Ty shrugged. "Dunno. I also can't tell who it is, but the tech seems pretty advanced. I've never seen anything like it."

Which probably didn't narrow down the options too much. The king was looking for them, as well as the people they'd saved Alexander from. The Carteks had also tried, unsuccessfully, to extort information on Dania's prince. And there were also the pirates. It could be almost anyone.

Ty pointed to the screen as a third band appeared. "See? It's pretty localized. It definitely looks like they think there's someone out here. I just have no idea how to tell if they're looking for us or it's something completely unrelated."

Cal straightened, shaking his head. "The way our luck has been running…?"

"I agree. I've been dodging when the beams pop up, but they're shooting pretty wild."

"Could they have tracked Alanna's jump?" Cal asked. "Maybe they didn't have a jumper of their own to follow."

It was a good possibility. When someone skipped space, or "jumping," as Cal's crew called it, there was a short time when the location could be tracked if the follower had the right equipment. However, if a ship did not have someone with the jumping ability on board, they would not be able to follow. That most likely ruled out the king, or a ship would have already materialized.

Cal tapped the comm button on the navigation panel. "Alanna, if you can hear me, I'd love it if you'd join us on the bridge. Preferably alone."

"You want to jump again?" Ty asked.

"I just want to be prepared. Start looking for other options, just in case." He hit the comm again. "Ethan, any luck with the spatial inhibitor the Carteks gave us?"

"Slow and steady wins the race."

Cal shook his head. "Slow and steady in space makes you dead. Aren't the instructions helping?"

"Yeah, a lot. But it's written for a squid using squid tech and tools. If you hadn't noticed, I'm not a squid."

Cal rubbed his eyes. "You and Doc got it working once."

"Yeah, well, we kinda got lucky. Also, it's portable and all, but I don't really want to hook Cartek technology into the ship's systems without making sure we can disconnect it manually. Just in case."

"He makes a good point," Ty said. "The last bit of Cartek equipment nearly crushed us."

Cal seemed to ponder that before he answered Ethan. "Keep working on it. We could really use some speed right about now."

The front viewscreen lit up with a blinding light.

Cal shielded his eyes. "What the hell?"

"That one nearly hit us. Taking controls." Ty moved to his own station and steered the ship away from the light.

Dania grabbed the back of Ty's chair, staring at the beam of energy that seemed to be chasing them as Ty banked up and over the long cylinder of light.

Was it Kile, or worse…Prince Geron himself? Had Kile told their sponsor it was unlikely Alexander would succeed? Had Geron decided to take the initiative and come after them both on his own?

Another beam appeared. Dania held out her palms, willing the light away from them. She pressed her strength out, calling to the energy in her core—but nothing happened. No tingle. No warmth. No spray of power to help defend herself and her friends. She stared at her useless hands. How could she be a part of this crew when all she could do was stand there?

"They're not playing nice!" Ty swerved the ship down, away from the light.

The door slid open, and Alanna entered, taking in the bolts of light shooting across the main viewscreen. "Scan beams, huh?" She shook her head. "Will you boys please stop getting yourselves into trouble every time I take a break?"

"Where's your boyfriend?" Ty called over his shoulder.

She glared at him. "If you're asking about Alexander, I dropped him off in his quarters to lie down for a bit. He's had a bad day."

Cal shook his head and muttered, "Probably not as bad as Ethan's."

Dania closed her eyes. Alexander had made a huge mistake, which was unlike him. It might be a long time before the humans on this crew gave him their trust, and with good reason. Luckily Dania had been there to stop the worst from happening.

Alanna sat at the nav station, rubbing her temple as she stared at her screen.

"You okay?" Ty asked.

She blinked twice. "Headache. And I'm a little dizzy, which probably has everything to do with the way you're flying."

"We're in space. You can't feel gravitational changes."

She rubbed her forehead. "So you say."

Ty spun the ship again, the stars outside spiraling. The ship felt stationary under Dania's feet, but she still found herself grabbing the back of Cal's chair to keep herself steady. Maybe Alanna was right.

Cal leaned around Ty, looking at his navigator. "Can you jump us?"

Alanna held up her hand and a light-blue dial appeared. Dania stared into the odd, spinning glow. She'd seen the high prince and the king skip space on multiple occasions, but the intricate gears of light were something new to her.

She'd love to puzzle out Alanna's strange ability, but it never seemed like the right time to ask.

The gears winked out, and Alanna leaned back. "I can't. I'm sorry." She held her head again. Her eyes seemed red and swollen.

Dania crouched beside her. "You look exhausted."

"Yeah. Long day, I guess."

Cal turned back to the screen. "Okay, jumping is off our list of escape plans."

Alanna squinted into her screen, still pressing her palm to her forehead. "I think we have another scan coming in. It's a huge burst of energy in a five-point rotating pattern."

"Five points?" Cal asked.

"Yup."

Dania wasn't sure what that meant. Normally, her technicians would simply point her in the direction of danger, and her enforcers could thwart most threats.

"Should I get Alexander?" Dania asked.

"No way," Cal said. "I've had enough enforcer ego for today."

Maybe *enforcer* ego wasn't their problem. Alexander wasn't the only one who needed to get over his preconceived notions.

She opened her mouth to speak, but Ty stood, pressing a button on the panel above his head.

"I have an idea." Ty returned to his seat. "But you're not going to like it."

"I rarely like your ideas." Cal flipped a similar switch above his own head. "But tell me anyway."

The *Star Renegade* spiraled, heading for a stray mass of floating rock.

"Alanna, can you give me the trajectory and size of that asteroid out there?"

Holding her right temple with one hand, she looked into her screen. "It's a big boy, and it's going way too fast. What else do you need to know?"

He turned and looked at her. "Is it big enough to land on?"

"Land on?" Cal spun his chair toward the pilot. "Have you completely lost your mind?"

"It's definitely big enough," Alanna said. "Landing will be a risky bit of flying. It's definitely moving. It won't be like landing on a satellite or trading station."

If Dania still had her powers, she could have willed the *Star Renegade* to match the asteroid's speed for a few seconds, allowing them to land safely.

She'd been able to do that and more when she'd been an enforcer. But all she could do now was stand there, taking up space. She wanted to back up and leave the bridge, giving them more room, but she didn't want to call attention to herself and distract the crew.

Ty turned to Cal. "There's no rotation on that asteroid. If we land on the broad side, we can go for a little ride and be completely hidden from those beams. It'll take us right out of here."

Dania frowned. She didn't need a computer to see the obvious. "It's not going in the same direction we are."

"No, but it's not going the opposite direction, either. It's close enough." He turned to Cal. "I'll need you to take the controls for a sec while I make some calculations."

Cal took in a deep breath, then released it. "Can you do this without killing us all?"

"Would I suggest it if I thought otherwise?"

The expression on Cal's face told her he wasn't so sure. Still, he hit the comm. "Ethan, I'm going to need all available power to the shields."

The speaker crackled slightly before Ethan's voice filled the chamber. "Is Ty gonna do something stupid?"

"What do you think?"

Ethan laughed. "I think I'm going to shut down all unnecessary systems and juice up the shields."

"Do it." Cal switched off the comm and looked at Ty. "I'd like to be alive when this is over."

His eyes didn't leave the screen. "You worry too much, boss."

But from what Dania had seen, Cal's worries were more than justified. The pilot was skilled, but he took risks she never would have allowed on her own ship. Then again, that may have been another reason the *Star Renegade* always evaded capture.

"Here come those scans," Alanna announced.

"Taking controls." Cal maneuvered them slightly to the right, away from the searching lights but still heading toward the asteroid.

"You two watch the beams," Ty said. "I'll be ready to save the day before Cal even breaks a sweat."

"Too late," Cal whispered.

"Focus, boss."

Cal's temperature spiked as numbers and symbols flickered on Ty's screen.

The younger pilot whispered to himself, pulling trajectories from one screen and programming them into another.

Dania held up her palms, willing visual acuity and accuracy into the pilot. She'd heard humans calling it *positive vibes*. If there was such a thing, she'd try to send it to him.

Alanna looked up. "Here comes that scan!"

A flash burst across the main screen. Cal slammed his panel and the ship tilted down. Ty's screens flashed and the numbers started scrolling again.

The pilot punched the edge of his console. "Not cool, Cal! Now I'll need to start over!"

"If we get hit by a beam, it won't matter."

"But you overcompensated!"

"Stop fighting!" Alanna shouted. "We have a thirty-second window before the next beam gets near enough to hit us. I suggest we take it."

Ty typed in some numbers and nodded to himself. "I got it. Taking back controls."

Cal held up his hands. "All yours."

Ty leaned to the right, as if he could feel the non-existent inertia as the asteroid centered in the viewscreen. "Bringing her in."

The *Star Renegade* shuddered as he lowered the ship toward the mass of rock. A thud rattled the flooring as the hull clanged and scraped.

Ty winced. "Oops." The ship raised up again.

"Fifteen seconds," Alanna said.

Cal gripped his armrests. "Ty?"

"I got it, boss." He lowered the hull between two large ridges. "Ethan, reinforce the shields on the aft right section as fast as humanly possible." The landing gear clanged against the rock, scraping again. The shriek of rock on metal reverberated through the bridge.

"Ty!"

The ship slipped into a high formation of rock, slamming to a stop. Dania gripped Cal's chair as the ship jolted.

"Aft shields holding," Alanna said.

"Sending out a few tethers," Ty said.

Something clunked beneath them.

"Secure!" Alanna said.

Ty spun in his chair and clapped his hands. "Ladies and gentlemen, that's how it's done!"

Alanna's fingers slowly tapped on her panel. "I'm sending out sensor bursts every two minutes to warn us if our new asteroid friend is about to run into anything."

"Good call." Cal exhaled, swiping his fingers through his hair.

Sweat beaded his brow, and his elevated heartbeat eased somewhat. His temple pulsed. He probably had a headache worse than Alanna's. Dania needed to speak to Alexander about that—if Cal would even agree to being treated by an enforcer.

Cal closed his eyes, took a deep breath, and tapped the comm. "Okay, people, we have a short reprieve. Let's get some rest and then get repairs done." He pointed at Alanna. "Especially you. You're a notoriously bad patient. Don't make me sic Doc on you."

She stood, rubbing her eyes. "You won't get any flak from me this time."

She grabbed the edge of the doorframe as she walked through, hesitating as if the wall were holding her up.

Ty jumped from his chair. "Tell you what." He grabbed her arm. "I'm heading to my room to get some shut-eye. How about we walk together?" The door closed behind them.

Dania frowned. "She's ill, isn't she?"

Cal rubbed his face. He was also unusually pale. "I think we're all exhausted. It's been a long time since anything has been normal."

Dania's chest tightened, wondering if he meant since *she'd* been on board.

He lifted her chin and gazed into her eyes. "Hey. We're going to be okay."

She nodded, looking away. She hoped that was true. But a darkness seemed to hover over her that got heavier each day, and it had everything to do with an angry prince who would never stop looking for her.

CAL RUBBED his face as he walked down the hall toward engineering. Eight hours of rest hadn't done much to relieve the drumming in his skull. Ty and Alanna had set up sweeping sensors to keep track of where their new best friend the asteroid took them, making sure they didn't hit anything while they hitched a ride away from the laser scans. He trusted his crew's abilities, but he'd never be comfortable riding on something powered by inertia.

Hitching a ride on a rogue asteroid shouldn't have been necessary. The Cartek equipment was supposed to level the odds between the *Star Renegade* and everyone else. If it had been installed and working, they would have been able to soar away from those energy beams without even breaking a sweat. Cal had gone through hell to get the alien tech, and he'd hoped Ethan would have had it up and running by now, especially since Cal had put them all at so much risk just to get the directions to make the damn thing work.

He stepped into lower engineering and grimaced, hearing Alexander's tenor from across the room. "Why would your engineer cross wires like this?"

"I think he said it made the ship go faster." Alanna squinted, looking up at a panel over both their heads.

"That makes no sense," Alexander said. "It looks like it's drawing power away from the systems."

Alanna adjusted the thin belt of tools around her waist. "There are a lot of things about this ship that don't make sense." She patted the hull lovingly. "She's a strange old girl, but we love her."

"Your emotional attachment makes no sense. It's just a ship."

Alanna laughed. "That shows how much you don't know. You'll learn."

The enforcer continued to scan the wiring. "I highly doubt it."

Cal shook his head. The enforcer responded just like any enforcer would have. He was a cold, calculating weapon. Nothing more. Dania needed to wake up and realize this before she made a mistake that none of them would be able to live through.

Alanna placed her hands on her hips, staring at the panel above. "Now that you mention it, though, if we added a little more balance to the wiring, we might be able to tweak the efficiency."

"Not with those wires. They're far too old." The enforcer narrowed his eyes. "Unless you had a heat-sensitive malleable conductor, but that's unlikely."

"We have lots of strange stuff on board. You might be surprised."

"I doubt you have this. It's sold as a polymer in some parts. But it's far too unstable, and most people don't know how to harden it."

"How do you harden it?"

"You have to heat it and then super cool it."

Cal gaped. It couldn't be…

Alanna's eyes widened. "Hold on!"

She ran to the supply shelves and grabbed a small canister of what Cal guessed was the mystery polymer that Ethan had picked up on Triton. That strange goo had saved their hides when a piece of space junk had ripped a hole in their hull. But other than that, they'd been using it as glue for non-essential components.

"How much do we need?" Alanna asked, removing the lid.

The enforcer stared at the canister before he grabbed it from her, replacing the lid. "Only a drop. Be careful with that."

Alanna bit her lip, her gaze on the jar. "Only a drop? We usually use a lot."

The enforcer mumbled something under his breath, shaking his head. It sounded like, *How are you all still alive?* but he said, "This will be more than enough."

Cal turned for the hallway. He'd talk to Ethan about the alien tech later. He didn't want to spend any more time than necessary with their new passenger, but it would be dumb of him not to allow a few repairs, especially if Alanna was watching and making sure Mr. Perfect didn't do anything to tag the ship or undercut efficiency.

Still, he'd need to ask Ethan to review any modifications when the enforcer wasn't looking. If Alexander was sabotaging them, they'd have to take care of it delicately.

Dania stood in the hallway outside engineering. "He's starting to get along with the crew, isn't he?"

Getting along with the crew? Was that seriously what she was worried about?

Cal glanced through the scratches in the engineering window. The enforcer and Alanna were still working on the plate in the ceiling. "He's not killing anyone, if that's what you mean."

"He won't. He's not that kind of enforcer."

Cal ground his teeth. "Tell that to Ethan."

Her brow pinched. "*I was* that kind of enforcer, but you still took a chance on me."

This again? "That was different."

"Only if you let it be."

What galaxy was she living in?

Cal pointed at the window. "That guy has said on more than one occasion, including right in front of you, that his only objective is to keep you safe and bring you home."

"Yes, and always in that order. Which means number one outweighs number two."

"What does that even mean?"

"It means that as soon as he realizes bringing me back to Geron is not the best thing for me, then goal number one will outweigh number two. An enforcer will always honor their first directive."

Cal rubbed his eyes. He'd seen this in action. All enforcers had orders to bring Cal's head, and only his head, back to prince Geron. However, Kile had overlooked this directive, at least temporarily, because his primary goal had been to find Alexander. Cal still wasn't completely sure how he'd gotten off the hook, even if only for ten minutes once that goal had been achieved.

Dania ran her fingers over her cheek...her *perfectly normal* cheek.

"Your burns are gone."

She nodded. "Alexander healed me. He's very good with

battle wounds." She looked down, hopefully realizing where those battle wounds had come from in the first place. Him healing her didn't change the fact that Alexander had nearly killed both her and Ethan.

"Cal." Dania touched his arm. "It would really mean the world to me if you gave Alexander a chance. As much as he couldn't stand the idea of leaving me behind, I can't stand the idea of letting him go."

Cal flinched. Every time she talked about the guy like that, Cal wanted to hit something.

"He's really the only family I have. If I can be free and still have him in my life..." Her eyes were wide and glassy when she looked up. "Do you understand?"

Cal gritted his teeth again. Yeah, he understood. That didn't mean he had to like it...or how ready she was to forgive him...or how touchy-feely the two of them were.

He shouldn't really care about that last one. It wasn't any of his business.

Except he couldn't get the thought of that over-sculpted pretty boy touching her out of his head.

Why in Jupiter's moons did it piss him off so much? He needed to realize that they'd both grown up in another culture. An inhuman culture. It didn't make it any easier to watch.

Inside, Alanna left their new passenger and climbed the ladder to upper engineering. The enforcer remained downstairs, swirling a small, pin-like needle in the polymer.

The overhead comm pinged. "Calling all generals," Doc's voice said. "I have a little matter in the med bay that I could use some assistance with."

Meaning... *It's time for your pathogen treatment, Dania, and we don't want Alexander interfering.*

Cal pointed down the hall with his chin. "Go ahead. You need to keep to your schedule."

"Will you at least consider giving him a chance?"

There were those eyes again, melting him.

Consider? "Sure." He'd considered it several times, and always came to the same conclusion. It certainly couldn't hurt to consider it again.

Her smile beamed. "Thank you. That means a lot to me." She gave him a kiss on the cheek and walked toward the med bay.

Cal froze in place, the warmth of her lips lingering on his skin like a brand.

She'd never kissed him before. What would even make her consider doing that? Of course, she acted that way with Alexander all the time. Maybe that was how Kevers expressed friendship.

His heart clenched, and he wiped the thought away. She wasn't an enforcer anymore. She even looked normal, wearing one of those short jackets and deep-pocket cargo pants like Alanna wore. Her hair hung in soft, not-moving waves, showing no sign of the eerie enforcer power that used to run through her. Hopefully, Doc's treatments would keep working, and she'd never have to go back to that blasted prince to stay alive. And maybe, one day, she'd want to consider Cal as more than just someone who could teach her how to cook.

The sound of the engineering room door opening and closing above hummed through the floor. Cal blinked, snapping himself out of his daydream, and bounded up the stairway to find Alanna in the hall, tapping buttons on a side panel.

"I don't like the enforcer being left alone down there," Cal said.

She snorted. "Then why don't you keep him company?"

"Because I don't know enough about engineering to tell if he's doing anything to screw up my ship."

She closed the panel and turned toward him. "Which is kind of strange, don't you think? Why don't you learn?"

Because one time Ethan had thrown him out after he'd cut the wrong wire and severed the power supply that pushed water to the showers. "I'm just not good at this stuff like you all are. You know that."

"That doesn't mean you can't take the initiative and learn. That's what my mom always taught me." She turned back to the panel. "I have a funny feeling you didn't just break out in a sweat running up here to complain about me leaving Alexander alone." She tapped a few buttons. "After all, he did help us get away from Kile, and he's got a good head for repairs."

"He's still an enforcer. We need to be careful."

Her cheeks flushed, and she bit back a smile, closing the panel.

Cal leaned down, catching her gaze. "I need *you* to be careful."

"Me? Why me?"

Couldn't she see the look on her face? Okay, maybe not, but she had to know that she was blushing.

"I'm not a child, Cal."

"I didn't say you were. But you seemed to take a good, long look at his assets back in the med bay when he was unconscious, and I wanted to make sure you stay focused on reality."

She put her hands on her hips. "I did *not* look at his 'assets.'"

Cal quirked a brow.

Her cheeks flushed. "Okay, maybe I took a little itty-bitty peek, but that kind of stuff doesn't affect me. I'm not going to get all starry-eyed over a pretty face, and washboard abs, and ice blue eyes, and long, flowing hair."

Cal snorted.

She slapped him on the shoulder. "You know what I mean."

Yes, Cal knew exactly what she meant. The enforcer had been sculpted to near perfection. His prince probably meant to use Alexander's looks as a weapon as much as his powers. Cal just didn't want that perfection aimed at anyone who he cared about, which meant anyone on this ship. But part of him knew it was already too late.

Maybe part of this enforcer's superpowers was infiltration. If it was, he might already be doing too good a job, and Cal wasn't sure how to stop him.

CHAPTER 6

DANIA

DANIA FLINCHED when the doctor removed the needle from her arm. This had been the first treatment she'd endured on her own. Normally, Cal was at her side, but today he was preoccupied, keeping an eye on their new passenger.

Peter placed a small bandage on her arm. "Just apply a little pressure there, like usual, and you are good to go." He wiped his hands on a towel and tossed it into the recycler. The folded cloth shot out the other side onto a stack of identical towels. "How do you feel?"

She sat up and rolled her shoulder. "The same, I suppose."

"I guess that's good, as long as you aren't feeling weak." He pointed to the screen beside her bed. "I don't see any more cellular degradation. I'd say we found your secret sauce."

"Secret sauce?"

He smiled. "We found the magical recipe to make you well."

She did feel better. It had been some time since she'd felt weak or dizzy. Of course, she no longer had powers, but that was a small price to pay to be her own person...to be free.

"Do you think it will work for Alexander?" she asked.

"I have no idea. Once he's feeling a bit more trusting, we'll have to convince him to let me take a look at him."

That was going to take some doing, but Alexander wasn't the only one who needed to learn trust. "Can you talk to Cal? He seems to listen to you."

"You mean about Alexander?" He shook his head. "That kind of trust is something we need to develop over time. To be honest, I'm surprised Cal learned to trust you so fast. There's too much history there."

"What do you mean by that?"

He stared at her for a moment. "Let's just say Cal has been on the receiving end of enforcer judgement from a very young age. Just like your friend has issues he needs to work through, so does Cal." He pushed the bag hanging from a pole farther away from Dania's bed. "There is an old saying that time heals all wounds."

"That's ridiculous. Most wounds cannot be healed."

He pointed at her. "Most enforcer-inflicted wounds cannot be healed, and I believe that's by design."

He picked up some of the folded towels and placed them on the table beside the gurney she'd been reclined on.

"That's not what I'm talking about, though." He pointed to his temple. "The mind is the most advanced computer in existence. There have been leaps and bounds in medicine over the centuries, but we haven't even touched the tip of what the mind can do."

"I don't understand your point."

"Cal and your friend Alexander have lived through traumas that their brains have to figure out how to deal with. I think you have done wonders for Cal, but he still has trust issues. Which, frankly, I'm okay with. It's kept us out of trouble more times than I can count."

"But those trust issues are keeping him from seeing Alexander for who he truly is."

Peter cocked his head. "Sweetie, I think you also need to see past who you *think* Alexander is and look at who he is *now*. I'm sure deep down, he's a great guy, but we all saw what happens when we forget to treat him like the weapon all enforcers are."

Dania nodded. Ethan was avoiding Alexander, and she really couldn't blame him.

She couldn't deny what had almost happened. Maybe she was the one who needed to step back, take stock, and allow things to happen over time.

On the table next to them, the recycler hummed, spitting out a folded towel behind it.

Peter stared at the machine. "Did you put a cloth in there?"

Dania shook her head. "No. Was that the towel you placed in there a moment ago?"

He frowned. "I did toss one in there, but it usually pops out instantly." He looked at the pile of towels beside the recycler and the ones he'd placed beside the bed. "I'm not sure how many were here to begin with."

Dania took a towel from the top of the pile, shook it out, and threw it in the recycler. It hummed and the clean towel popped out the back, adding a clean, folded towel to the pile. "It looks like it is working fine."

Peter nodded. "Yeah, I guess it was nothing."

But he continued to stare. Obviously, he thought it was far more than nothing.

AFTER BREAKING free from the asteroid, it had been a clean run straight through to Ebuda. Cal relished nice, slow runs like that. It reminded him of simpler days, when only the enforcers were chasing them, instead of half the galaxy.

Now that they'd safely landed, Cal sat in his command chair and stared out the main observation window, scanning the trade station's dusty metal landing platforms. People whisked in and out, and the ship docked beside them had changed eleven times since they'd arrived. His left hand tapped on the top of his knee as he checked the entrances and exits on the far side of the platform.

On Cal's far right, Ty sat at Alanna's station, flipping through screens. The guy looked as calm as ever. That was never a good gauge of his mood, though. Cal had seen the kid smile in the middle of a fistfight.

"Any word from Alanna and Doc?" Cal asked.

"Not since the last time you asked five minutes ago." He glanced up. "Relax, boss. This is a simple trade run. Nothing to worry about."

But he did worry. He always worried. "You are aware

that we've had to fight our way out of the last several trade stops we've made, right?"

"Yup, so, statistically speaking, this one should be as easy as eating one of Mel's homemade pies. Smooth and sweet."

Cal sure hoped so. Still, it seemed like they'd been out there a long time.

Ty stopped his scanning and leaned his chin on his fingers as he stared at a single screen. His brow pinched.

"What's up?" Cal asked.

"I'm not sure." Ty tapped on the panel and read another screen. "It's weird. From the comm chatter logs, it looks like there's an increased enforcer presence at Teson Minor."

"Teson Minor? That's pretty far from Bane space." Which was never good. "Can you tell why?"

"No. The chatter looks confused. Lots of people asking questions, but no answers."

Cal didn't like the sound of that. "Do the enforcers look aggressive?"

Ty shook his head. "From what I can tell, it's just being called *a presence*. Weird." He flipped through a few more screen pages. "Huh."

"*Huh* what?"

"Our friends in the Trillian Cluster are also reporting ships with royal insignias."

The Trillian Cluster was a bit too close. "Could they be looking for us? We've been in both those areas since we picked up Dania."

"I don't think so. If they were looking for us, they'd be on the planets. All these mentions are talking about ships, not actual enforcers."

Cal's fingers tapped faster on his knee. Why those planets? They were nowhere near the outer rims, so they couldn't be worried about the Carteks.

But if not the Carteks, then what?

A light flashed on Alanna's panel.

"Message coming in." Ty tapped the screen on the right. "Alanna is sending us an all clear. They're on their way back."

Cal gripped his knee, stopping his fingers from tapping. "Good." Because every cell in his body wanted to get off this world and back out into open space as fast as possible.

———

Cal headed to the med bay. According to Alanna, Ebuda had been the easiest trade in months. Which wasn't saying much, with the way their luck had been going lately. Still, it was nice to leave a port without running for their lives for once.

They'd returned a little over an hour ago with several floating carts brimming with supplies. Cal hadn't looked much further than the food Alanna had purchased, but from the long list of medicinals on Doc's card with names Cal couldn't even pronounce, it looked like they'd both gotten a pretty nice haul.

Hopefully, Doc had everything he needed to keep Dania healthy for a long time. If the enforcers were hanging around common trade ports, it might be a while before the *Star Renegade* would be able to stop for supplies again.

Cal tapped the door controls and stepped into the med bay. A chill itched over his skin as Doc held up a small vial of clear fluid toward Alexander. "This is the hardest thing to find. It helps mix things so they don't get all globby-like."

The enforcer nodded. "It's a fluidic medicinal separating agent used in vaccine generation."

Doc nodded. "That's what I said."

Cal steeled himself and walked the rest of the way in.

"Hey, boss." Doc wrapped the vial in a cloth before placing it in a box. "Alanna and I hit the jackpot. They'd just received a shipment of medical supplies at the station."

The enforcer folded his arms. "No doubt they are *stolen* supplies. There is no reason for an outlier world to have even a fraction of these rare medicinal reagents."

Which was why Cal had hoped the enforcer—a man charged with stopping the trafficking of illegal things like medical supplies—hadn't found out about this.

Doc picked up a box and glanced at the writing on the back. "Relax, boss. I've just been showing my new friend Alexander here all the research I've been doing into curing the Castian flu."

Cal nodded. Curing the flu had been a plausible enough explanation to fool one of the top scientists on Themyscira as to what Doc had been really doing with all these rare and costly ingredients. If Alexander found out the real reason, Cal was sure he wouldn't be pleased.

The enforcer picked up a vial with blue liquid in it. "You are using this to heal a virus?"

Doc considered the vial. "It's one of the things I've been tinkering with, yes."

Alexander placed the vial down. "Your overly-exaggerated generalities may have been enough to fool my commander, but not me. What are you really doing with these supplies?"

Sweat beaded on Cal's temple. Kile had been nothing more than a battering ram. It had been easy to get things by him. This new enforcer had been Dania's healer, a doctor. Doc was the smartest person Cal had ever met, but was he smart enough to fool a person with actual medical training?

Walking across the room, Doc tapped on a panel and a picture appeared on the largest screen. Little red ovals swirled through a pink-tinted liquid.

Doc pointed to the darkest of the ovals. "This platelet is dying. It's used to being refueled regularly by a biological agent that is no longer available."

Cal held his breath. That blood sample should have been hidden. What was Doc doing?

The enforcer walked up to the screen. "Whose platelets are these?"

"Dania's." Doc folded his hands behind his back. "I know what your prince did to her. We're setting her free."

Cal shifted his footing, readying for a fight, although he wasn't sure what he'd be able to do against a guy who could bend the laws of gravity.

The enforcer looked back at the table of ingredients and narrowed his eyes, as if calculating how they could be mixed together.

"Interesting." He looked back to Doc. "But it won't work."

"Really?" Doc tapped a few buttons. A flush of new fluid rushed onto the screen, and the dark oval turned a bright red.

Alexander considered the ovals moving across the

screen, now fluttering as if they'd been jolted with caffeine supplements. "Very interesting. How did you get past initial cellular decay?"

Doc's eyes widened, like he was surprised by the question. "Biocellular renumeration."

Alexander shook his head. "That's only theoretical."

Doc stood taller. "Not anymore."

The enforcer stared at the screen for a few more minutes. "I do see the possible applications for dealing with viruses. With proper engineering, this could be modified to protect cells from the Castian flu." He turned to Doc. "Your work so far is exemplary, but it won't work as intended. You cannot break the enforcer bond."

"Why not? It's been working so far. She was dying, and if you hadn't noticed, she looks pretty good these days."

Alexander ran his fingers along the edge of the screen, as if appreciating the increasing energy of the cells. "You will fail for the same reason my commander left—because you are talking about more than healing her body. The bond is still there, and I assure you, it is just as strong."

Cal stepped forward. "I disagree. She's barely even thinking about your prince anymore." She was having fun, playing games, learning to cook… "She's her own person. She's making friends. Smuggler friends, I might add."

Alexander leaned against the wall. "Tricking the cells to make them think they are independent is quite inventive. To be honest, I'm impressed."

He was?

"Your navigator and I have been doing research on the mind." The enforcer perused his nails. "Our brains are smarter than I think you realize. Dania's brain knows what it really needs, and when she sees the chance to get real healing, rather than these temporary treatments, she will reach for the cure that she truly needs."

Cal moved closer than he probably should have. "I think we have a difference of opinion on what she really needs. Dania wants to be free."

He nodded. "There have been others like her, enforcers who have developed a mindset, even a personality separate from the one prescribed by their sponsor."

Prescribed? So, this prince controlled who they were, as well as what they did? Doc twitched and glanced at Cal. Had he realized this?

Alexander continued. "I have seen several enforcers engage in relationships similar to that of my commander and Ms. Quirky. But they always end the same way. When Geron calls, they go to him. They do not question. They do not argue. They drop any misconceived notions about a different life, and they return to who they truly are."

Who they truly are? This pompous ass had no idea, no conception of who Dania really was. She'd been a tool. A weapon of war. An automaton. Now she was so much more.

Cal's hand curled into a fist. "You can't have her back."

Alexander stared at him for a moment, similar to the way Dania did when she was about to mention a change in someone's temperature. "Her time here has always been temporary. I am a healer. I have been trained with and have dealt with enforcers my whole life. This is not a battle you can win, no matter how hard you try."

Doc tapped the panel, shutting down the display. "Well, then, I consider this my greatest challenge because right now, I think she's cured." He stared the enforcer down with more bravado than Cal had ever seen from the self-taught doctor. "I'm going to keep her that way."

The enforcer shrugged. "You will fail." He held out his hand to the supplies. "And this extravagant expense will be for naught."

Doc narrowed his eyes. "Does the phrase 'game on' mean anything to you?"

Alexander smirked. The expression reminded Cal of a teacher he'd once had, after Cal had tried to convince him that water wouldn't evaporate on a muggy day.

The enforcer's long hair floated about him as he inclined his head slightly. "Give it your best effort. I look forward to watching you try."

CHAPTER 8
DANIA

HUMIDITY HUNG in the air over the boiling pot of water in the kitchen. Dania leaned over the crockpot, taking a whiff of the deep red sauce. "Are you sure we used enough oregano?"

Cal smiled and placed a clean towel on the counter. "Yes, I swear. Stop worrying."

She stood, looking over the pots. Had they been boiling too long? Or maybe boiling too hard? "I just want it perfect. It's my first meal. I want it to be spectacular."

Cal placed his hands on her hips and drew her nearer. The closeness was oddly soothing. "You're doing great, and the crew will love it."

She hoped so. She did her best to help out where she could, but overall, she'd felt so useless. Everyone seemed to have their place on the crew but her. Even Alexander had been working on repairs, while Dania wasn't much better than an extra set of hands to hold tools and supplies.

She eased out of his grip. "Should we take the pasta out now?"

He looked down, sighing before he answered. "Give it another minute."

His temperature had spiked, then righted, lowered, then raised. It would be indiscernible to a human, but her training taught her to notice confusion and... Was that disappointment?

"Have I done something wrong? I cooked everything like you've shown me."

The air about him warmed as he laughed. "No, you're fine. I told you, it's going to be great."

The door to the dining room swung open, and Ty poked his head in. "Need any help in here?"

Cal's skin paled, then flushed as he took a full step away from her.

What was wrong with him? He almost seemed...embarrassed?

He reached for a pot, clearing his throat. "No help needed. You can tell everyone to get seated. We'll be right out."

Could Cal be as nervous about the meal as she was?

Her heart fluttered as she turned off the sauce and handed Cal the first plate.

He picked up a ladle. "I always like to place a tiny dab of sauce on the bottom of the dish and add a little grated cheese." Cal demonstrated. "Then you add the pasta, and a scoop of sauce on the top." He handed her the plate. "This is the way my mom used to serve pasta when I was growing up."

The aroma of the sauce wafted up, the tang of the tomatoes swirling with the spices. "It smells amazing."

He tapped her nose with his finger. "All credit to the cook."

Dania's cheeks heated before she pushed through the door. The crew sat in their normal places, except Alexander sat in the seat beside where Dania would be, with Alanna seated beside him. Ethan sat on the other side of the table with Peter and Rachel, while Ty sat on the end opposite of where Cal would sit when he came out.

Dania placed the plate in front of Alexander. "Here you go. Cal says guests first."

Peter shook his head. "Is there ever a world where Doc gets fed first? Because I'm hungry over here."

Ty snorted a laugh. Dania held in her smile as she and Cal served the rest of the crew before sitting down with their own servings. Dania shifted in her seat as the crew started to eat. Had she remembered to put the garlic in the sauce three hours ago? A chill ran down her spine. She couldn't recall. Or maybe she had added it twice by accident. Had she ruined the sauce?

Alexander poked at the meal with his fork. "You made this?"

Too much garlic. She knew it!

Dania gulped. "Yes. I've been working on it since this morning."

He looked at her, then back to the food. "That seems like an inefficient use of your time."

Cal put down his fork, but Dania placed her hand on his knee under the table, stopping his retort.

She rustled up an unsure smile. "I don't think it was a waste of time. I enjoyed it."

Rachel held up a fork filled with pasta. "And I enjoy eating it." She shoved the fork in her mouth, then began scooping up more.

Alexander stared at Dania. Annoyance shone in his

eyes, but he managed to regulate his temperature. "You enjoyed cooking, like one of the king's appointed chefs?"

She nodded. "Yes. I've found that creation gives me joy."

He quirked a brow. "Creation gives you...*joy*?"

She nodded again, but she understood his confusion. All their lives she'd been taught the thrill of slaughter. She was to look for reasons to find people guilty and then feel no remorse for ridding the galaxy of wrongdoers. In her case, the bigger, the more public the executions, the better. The galaxy was a safer place if people were too afraid to break the law. At least, that was what she'd believed—or been forced to believe.

She mixed the pasta and sauce and lifted it on her fork. "There's a list of ingredients that are added at different times. They each taste different. Some even taste bad, but they blend into something special."

Alexander tasted the food. He seemed to chew for longer than necessary before placing his fork down. "It's palatable."

Dania's heart sank. "Just palatable?"

She stared at him for a moment. What had she expected? That her cooking would snap him out of Geron's hold? Even the idea was ridiculous. Still, she'd hoped he would at least enjoy it.

"Well, mine is outstanding," Cal said. "There's a hint of something new in there. Did you tweak the recipe?"

Dania cringed. The truth was, she'd grabbed the wrong spice and hadn't realized it until she'd sprinkled it into the sauce. She'd done her best to scoop it out, but she'd already stirred some in.

Cal's smile dazzled. "What is that flavor?"

Dania looked down. "Cinnamon."

He perked up. "Daring choice."

Ty spun his fork in the air over his plate. "I think this might be better than yours, Cal."

The captain nodded. "I think you're right." He leaned toward Alexander. "And I'd say it's far better than *palatable*."

Dania sat a little straighter. He really thought it was good?

Rachel grunted, nodding, her cheeks full as she cleaned her plate.

Across the table, Doc cut his pasta up into smaller pieces. "I love that you were able to experiment and not follow the recipe to the letter." He looked at Alexander. "My treatments have given Dania a chance to live a new life. A *real life*, you might say. She's found that she enjoys things she never dreamed of trying on her own."

There was a spot of defiance in his voice, like he was proving the most important point in history to someone who would never believe it. When speaking of freedom to an enforcer, that was probably exactly what was going on.

Alanna leaned toward Alexander. "You seem to be enjoying helping fix up the ship. Maybe that's your version of cooking? Like a normal hobby that doesn't involve the law."

Alexander nodded, staring at his plate. "Increasing the efficiency of machines has always been an interest of mine."

Ethan pointed at him with his fork. "And he's pretty good at it. I've been watching—you know, from as far away as I can—but he seems to know his stuff." He took a bite of his meal and swallowed. "In fact, I'm hoping we can get some of those fake pathogens into you, too. That way, you can stick around for a while, and—you know—not want to kill me anymore. Because I can sure use some help with some of the new tech."

"As interesting as additional mechanical duties may sound," Alexander said, "I assure you that I will not be polluting my blood with artificial stimulants anytime soon."

Peter gave an overexaggerated grimace. "Well, I hate to tell you this, but while you were unconscious, after we first picked you up, I gave you a first dose of the artificial pathogens. It's probably why you're in such good shape as you are right now." He leaned back in his chair. "After floating around in that fish tank for so long, I wasn't sure if I'd be able to save you. The treatment seemed to do the trick."

Alexander pushed his plate back. "You actually think your artificial concoctions are keeping me alive?"

Peter nodded. "To some extent, yes. They jump-started your healing. It certainly wasn't the result of your prince. *That,* I can guarantee you."

Peter spoke the truth. Her friend's recovery had been remarkable, though. He seemed to take to the pathogens far better than Dania had.

Alexander's gaze locked with the doctor's before a slight smile touched his lips. His hair took flight a fraction of a second before all the dishes on the table levitated, spun once, and then set down gently back to the surface.

All sound seemed to suck from the room as everyone sat silent, staring at their now-inert plates.

Alexander leaned on the edge of the table. "I assure you, your inconsequential treatments had nothing to do with my recovery. My powers are intact, and my blood still flows with the strength of my sponsor."

Dania flinched. His powers weren't quite intact, or he wouldn't have appeared tired at times. However, he was obviously not as encumbered as she was. Not yet, at least.

It seemed odd, though, that he still seemed to have such good control, even after being so depleted. She'd expected him to have been drained after disabling the royal cruiser, but it seemed that he'd been correct, that he'd only needed sleep. If that were so, though, why hadn't sleep helped Dania?

She'd been drained by Palian steel, which could have been the issue, but Alexander had been drugged and who knew what else by the people who'd held him captive. He'd been a shell of himself when they'd found him, but now he seemed just as strong as ever.

Ethan cried out, pushing his chair back as something clanged to the floor. He looked at Alexander. "Seriously, dude, why is it always me? I am over here minding my own business."

Alexander stared at him, cocking his head.

"Oh, don't give me that," Ethan said. "My plate just slipped off the table all by itself. The last time I checked, you were the only one in the room who likes to show off like that."

Alexander folded his hands. "Are you sure you didn't push it off by accident? From what I've seen, you humans can be a bit clumsy."

"No, I..." Ethan looked at the plate on the floor. "Well, I don't *think* I hit it."

"Well, I assure you, this time, it was not me," Alexander said.

Cal leaned down and helped pick up the food. "It's okay. I'll get a cleaning bot out here when everyone leaves. No harm done."

Ethan looked under the table. "Where's my roll?"

"Are you sure you didn't eat it?" Cal asked.

Ethan scratched his head. "I don't know. I'm not sure of anything anymore."

Rachel stood. "Well, this has been interesting as usual, but I'm going to head back to my room. I need a little me-time." She walked toward the doorway and stood inside the arch as it opened. "I'm going to leave. So, umm, goodnight, everyone. Thanks for the great eats, Dani." She waved at Cal. "Thanks again, Cally." She looked at the floor, then continued through the door.

"She is so odd," Ethan said.

That she was. Dania hoped she was not still pining for Kile because the truth was that she'd probably never see him again.

CHAPTER 9
CAL

CAL RUBBED his eyes as he headed up the stairs toward the bridge.

He didn't even remember sleeping last night. He'd put his head down, and his alarm seemed to go off minutes later. He wasn't sure if that was good, or really, really bad.

Rachel's voice came from around the corner. "It's just not a good idea."

Cal rounded the turn to see her looking down the empty hall. "Who are you talking to?"

She jumped, grabbed her chest, and spun toward him. Her eyes were wide.

"You okay?" he asked.

Rachel lowered her hand and stuck out her chin. "Of course, I'm okay. Why wouldn't I be okay?" She stepped toward him. "Are *you* okay?" She barely waited for an answer. "Well, are you?"

Cal massaged the back of his neck and turned back toward the bridge. "I'm seriously not up for this right now."

"Well, fine, then," Rachel shouted from behind him. "Just remember what we talked about here."

Cal was sure he'd forget because he honestly had no idea what they were just talking about, anyway. Which was pretty common for a conversation with Rachel. Still, he needed to remember to have Doc screen her for deep space dementia.

He rubbed his sore eyes again. He really needed to find a way to get some better rest.

At the end of the hall, he hit the entry pad beside the door, walked onto the bridge, and stopped, rubbing his eyes again.

Nope, it wasn't his imagination. There really was a tall, blond guy sitting in his chair.

Ty stood and pointed at Cal. "Don't blow a gasket."

Cal narrowed his eyes. "I'm not blowing a gasket."

"Says the guy who obviously can't see the look on his face."

Alexander shifted in his seat but didn't turn. "Your captain is showing a slight elevation in temperature and change in breathing, and he's shifted his weight twice since entering the room. These are all signs of extreme agitation."

Cal gritted his teeth. They'd just gotten rid of one enforcer and ended up with his younger carbon copy, albeit this one was a little more polite.

Except for the part about sitting in his chair. That was definitely not polite.

"Alexander is doing a little research," Ty said. "I figured you'd be okay with that since you were sleeping in again," Ty said.

Cal cocked his head. "Sleeping in?"

Ty sat down. "Yeah, it's nearly ten-fifteen standard time."

Cal glanced at the pad on the wall, where the digital time meter switched over to 10:14. How many times had he snoozed his alarm?

"Anxiety or depression?" Alexander asked, still facing the screen.

"What?" Cal was about ready to kick this guy out of his chair. Enforcer or not.

Mr. Perfect finally turned. "The most common causes of oversleeping are anxiety or depression. Which is it?"

Cal took a deep breath. "I have an enforcer onboard my ship."

"I'd call that anxiety," Ty said.

"I'm fine," Cal said. But he'd be better if Dania's favorite pretty boy was somewhere else.

Alexander looked at Ty. "Does my presence give you anxiety?"

"Nah. I kind of go with the flow."

Cal stepped closer. "Can I ask what we're researching?"

Alexander swiped through some screens. "*You* are not researching. You are standing beside me, asking questions. *I* am researching the ships registered in the vicinity during the attack on planet Opanus."

Cal scanned the screen. "The Opanus attack? When you were taken prisoner?"

The enforcer looked over his shoulder at Cal. The guy had a way of making you feel small without even standing up. "Please tell me that was a rhetorical question, and you are not really as daft as my commander said you are."

Cal gritted his teeth. "I don't know. Are you really as much of a pompous ass as the commander said you are?"

Kile hadn't actually said that, but he'd alluded to it. Or maybe that was just what Cal had wanted to hear.

The enforcer chuckled and turned back to his screen.

Cal watched the ships go by. Most were pirate cruisers, banged and dented from fighting. Three of them were dinged, but without blast patterns.

"Those are your guys," Cal said.

"How do you know?"

"Maybe I don't. I'm daft, remember?"

The enforcer raised a brow at him. Cal had never wanted to punch a guy this much in his entire life.

Instead, he looked past him and pointed at the screen. "Most of these ships have seen heavy battle. Those three were just made to *look* like they'd seen battle. Those dents are self-inflicted."

The enforcer nodded. "No scorching or signs of repair. The marks are superficial. That is very observant, Mr. Espinoza."

Alexander tapped a few keys on the screen, entered some codes faster than Cal could comprehend, and pictures of people scrolled past. He pulled out one photo, then another, then two more. The enforcer tensed, leaned back, and glared at the pictures of four men. Alexander's right hand formed a fist, and Cal found himself stepping back.

"Friends of yours?" Ty asked.

Alexander rubbed his annoyingly perfect chin. "Definitely not." He looked down and seemed to contemplate the brown cargo pants they'd given him. "I wanted to save that family. They'd been so kind to me. But these men cut them down." He slammed his fist on the edge of the console. "They were helpless, and they died trying to protect me."

Kile had told them that after Alexander had passed out from exhaustion, he'd been cared for by a local family on Opanus. The slavers had rewarded their generosity by cutting the family down when they'd tried to protect Alexander.

Cal resisted the urge to move closer. "There wasn't anything you could have done. You'd worked yourself nearly to death protecting that planet and then healing the injured." Why he was trying to make the guy feel better, Cal had no idea. He should try to make him feel worse, even if it was just so he'd get out of Cal's chair.

The enforcer stared at the pictures on the screen. "I had no reinforcements, and they knew that. They took advantage."

"That's what pirates do," Cal said.

The enforcer clenched and unclenched his fists, like he wanted to reach into the screen and strangle those men. His hair lifted and floated a little higher around his head. The screen blinked, and names and last-known-locations appeared beneath each photo.

Cal didn't even want to know how he'd extracted that kind of information so quickly. "What are you going to do?"

The enforcer shook his head. "I'm not sure yet. Logically, I need to calm down. But…"

"But what?"

The enforcer took a deep breath and let it out slowly. "These people are out there, targeting enforcers who are trying to help people. They have to be stopped." He stood but continued to stare at the screen.

Cal had never really thought about it like that. Alexander had been helping those colonists when the slavers had taken him. Cal had only had the opportunity to see the bad that enforcers do…the punishment for crimes that really shouldn't be crimes. But they were supposed to defend the people as well as the law.

He'd seen so much bad that Cal still couldn't comprehend that maybe some enforcers worked for good.

The comm pinged, and Doc's voice filled the room. "Boss?"

Cal hit the glowing button. "Talk to me."

"I found something interesting on the intergalactic relay comms."

The enforcer's eyes narrowed. "Those communications are restricted."

"We have permission," Cal said.

"From whom?"

Doc's voice came over the comm again. "Tell Tall, Blond, and Beautiful that he'll want to hear this, too. I think he'll forgive me."

Cal didn't like the sound of that. "We'll meet you in the lounge in five minutes."

"Make it ten," Doc said. "And make sure everyone is there."

Cal rubbed his eyes. Whatever this was, it wasn't going to be good.

CHAPTER 10

DANIA

DANIA SETTLED into her chair at the larger table in the lounge. Cal sat at the head of the table to her left. Alexander sat at her right.

"Anyone know what's going on?" Alanna asked, taking the seat next to Alexander.

Dania had the same question. There was an odd foreboding in the air, and on this ship, her intuition usually served her well.

Ty leaned back in his chair at the opposite end of the table. "I think Doc heard something in a transmission. He called for all-hands-on deck."

Which was concerning. Whatever this was, he wanted everyone to know rather than just telling the captain in private.

Cal was supposed to be in charge, but the entire crew seemed to take a hand in the decisions. Sometimes, the open nature of this ship still seemed strange to her.

Rachel and Ethan came in and took seats on the other side of the table, Rachel sitting in the middle next to Doc's vacant chair, while Cal paced the center of the room.

"Walking is not going to make your crewman arrive any faster," Alexander pointed out.

Cal glared at him but continued to pace. Dania shifted her weight. She'd hoped that they would get along better by now, but the continuing hostility seemed to come from both sides. She wished she understood why so she could try to do something about it.

The doctor entered, holding several data pads. "Sorry! I zeroed in on a little more chatter, and I figured the more info, the better." He settled into his seat opposite Dania.

Alexander folded his hands on the edge of the table. "I hope you have a good reason for tapping into restricted communication channels."

Peter quirked a brow. "Yeah, I do. I was listening to make sure there were no enforcers on our trail. It's called self-preservation."

Dania prepared to intervene, but Alexander kept his calm. He had orders not to harm anyone, but his demeanor seemed... Was that *amused*?

Cal gripped the back of his chair. "Can you get to the point, Doc?"

Peter nodded and tapped on one of the data pads. "I had to break through a lot of static. The enforcers are still trying to make sense of it, but with a little ingenuity, I was able to clear it up enough to confirm what they're still postulating on."

Rachel pulled up her knees and hugged them. "Come on, Doctor Pete. You're driving me crazy here."

Peter's eyes lowered before he turned away from her. "There's a huge, cloudy haze moving through the galaxy. It looks like a swarm of flies on the radars, which is confusing all of the enforcers' *very legal* systems."

Alexander cocked his head. "Does this mean that your *very illegal* systems know what that cloud is?"

Doc nodded. "The resonance is the same field that was around Elbus when we were there recently. It was an echo at the time, but it was the same technology."

Dania shifted her weight. The last time they'd been at the long-range comm station at Elbus, the Carteks had nearly destroyed the *Star Renegade* trying to get information about Prince Geron. Any semblance of similar technology was troubling news.

Cal seemed to grip the back of the chair tighter. "What are you trying to tell us?"

"It's a very sophisticated cloaking device." Doc's gaze settled on each of them. "It's not just a renegade storm. It's Cartek ships. From the size of the cloud, I'd say it's hundreds of them."

Alexander straightened. "Carteks? In free space?"

"It wouldn't be the first time," Cal said.

And it wouldn't be the last. This war had raged for far too long, and the Carteks wanted the territories back that they'd lost to Keveron when Earth signed the treaty that had made the Earthan cradle—and all its colonies—vassal planets of the Banes.

"Where is this supposed cloud of enemy vessels going?" Alexander asked.

Peter looked down. He was undoubtedly the most intelligent of the crew, but in some instances, he could be the most emotional. It was maybe why he was such a caring doctor.

He lifted his head. "The cloud is headed straight for Ephershia."

Rachel's feet slipped back to the floor. "I'm from

Ephershia."

Peter nodded, looking at the tabletop.

She sat on the edge of her chair. "Well, why are they going to Ephershia?"

Dania wished there were another answer. "There would be only one reason for them to go to Ephershia. It's an outlier colony, far from any other planets."

"Far from any help," Ty pointed out. "Could there really be hundreds of ships in that cloud?"

Peter nodded. "Easily. The only good news is they aren't moving fast. But they aren't moving slow, either. And the cloud seems to be getting bigger."

"Meaning there are more Carteks in free space than anyone was aware of." Cal pushed away from his chair and started pacing again. "This isn't good."

Rachel leaned on the table, her hands shaking. "Dani, the Banes will send help, right? I mean, that's what enforcers are supposed to do, isn't it? They help people in trouble."

An ache formed in Dania's chest. "Your people broke ties with Keveron. As far as the Banes are concerned, that colony doesn't even exist."

Rachel gaped. "What do you mean, *it doesn't exist?* My parents are there. My family. Everyone!"

"They made their choice," Alexander said. "They decided to fend for themselves, and the Banes will allow them to do that. Ephershia is no longer the king's concern." His brow furrowed, though, and he looked off to the side.

Ethan tapped his fingers on the table. "The royals are all a bunch of cowards if they're going to sit back and watch all those people die. It's not right."

They needed to understand this from the Banes' perspective. The people of Ephershia had asked to be left alone. The king would comply with their wishes, for good or for bad. "The Banes need to protect those worlds under their domain. They'll step back and use the time to fortify the colonies loyal to them." She tried to keep her voice steady. "Ephershia will be considered an acceptable loss."

Alexander leaned back. "Thirty-seven million people is not an acceptable loss."

He was right. Dania would usually argue with her healer, but now her thoughts were clear. Still, she understood why the Banes wouldn't help. This was no longer their fight.

Alexander's pinched brow worried her, though.

"Get that thought out of your head," she told him. "Trying to protect people in the outer rims is what got you caught by the slavers in the first place."

Alexander stood. "I need to try. I'm coded to protect, no matter the danger to myself. Maybe I can simply help the colonists rally their defenses."

"Yes, yes!" Rachel punched her fist in the air. "Rally away, oh big, overly-pretty enforcer-guy."

This was ridiculous. Dania needed to put a stop to this. "You cannot go to the planet. You said you needed to protect *me*."

Alexander looked to the side before meeting her gaze once more. "You are safe for now. I have every intention of returning after I've eliminated this threat."

A ball formed in Dania's throat, but she shouldn't have expected another response. "You are one man," she reminded him.

He lifted his chin defiantly, and with good reason.

Yes, he was far more powerful than any one *normal* man, and they both knew it. Alexander's power almost equaled her own when she'd been at full strength. No, he could not thwart hundreds of Cartek ships, but he could certainly slow them down, maybe even disable enough of them to give the colonists a fighting chance.

Then again, his powers were unpredictable if not unstable since his capture. He needed to take that into account.

She placed her hand over his. "I can't lose you again."

He grasped her palm. "Then join me."

"This isn't our fight. They aren't a Kever world anymore."

His eyes sparkled, just like they had when they'd been young and snuck into the royal kitchens, where they'd burned the counters trying to make sweet cakes. "When have we ever allowed laws to get in our way? You've always been one to see beyond the practical."

That had been true, when they'd been children—before she'd become a general. Before her choices had been systematically programmed out of her. But now?

She closed her eyes. Every time she thought she'd figured out who she really was, another impossible choice was thrown her way.

"Ephershia is only three sectors away." Ty turned to Alanna. "Are you up to doing your special kind of navigation?"

Alanna nodded. "Yeah, I'm good."

"There you have it." Ty put his feet up on the edge of the table. "We'll take Alexander to the colony."

Cal stepped toward him. His temperature started to spike again. "No, we won't."

Ty held out his hands. "I'm not saying we fly the ship into war, but if Alexander thinks he can help, we can fly him in and then disappear. It will at least give those people a chance."

Cal shook his head. "I don't want to be anywhere near a cloud of Cartek ships."

"We do have their tech," Ethan said. "The modifications are almost done. I say, let's use it against them."

Cal gaped. "Have you lost your mind?"

Ty held up his hand. "Everyone in favor of taking Mr. Perfect into the belly of the beast, say *aye*."

Most of the crew raised their hands. Alexander lifted his brow hopefully to Dania.

She wanted to say *no*.

She wanted to have more time to convince him that freedom was a viable option.

She wanted to reiterate that this was not their fight, that they needed to keep Alexander safe until he was completely well.

But even if Alexander had been free, he'd still want to save those people. It was simply who he was deep down, beneath his healer programming. Alexander was good, and she could not ask him to be something that he was not. He'd never backed down from a fight, especially if he was protecting the innocent. It was simply not in his nature.

But that didn't mean she didn't love him. That didn't mean she wouldn't do everything in her power to keep him safe, even from himself.

"I'm sorry, Alexander." Shifting her weight, she sat on her hands and waited for Cal to talk some sense into them all.

DANIA HAD ACTUALLY SAT on her hands. That was probably the only "no" he'd ever seen in a situation like this. It was nice to have someone thinking reasonably for once.

Still, this whole crazy situation might end up being the perfect chance to get rid of their new passenger. No matter how many times everyone sung this guy's praises, the enforcer had always been truthful about his intent. They couldn't have both Dania and Alexander. It was a sad truth they all needed to get used to. But since his crew was stubborn, and Cal knew they'd never listen to reason, he'd grab onto the only chance he had to get rid of a potential problem.

He raised his hand. "Aye."

Dania's eyes widened as she jumped to her feet. "Wait. No!"

Of course, she'd be upset. In time, though, she'd realize this was the best for her. Alexander may be her friend, but the guy had his own agenda, and that agenda landed her back with that stinking prince, no matter what Dania said or thought.

Cal headed for the door. "I need to get back to the bridge."

"Cal!"

He tried to pick up speed as he moved through the hallway, but Dania caught up to him. Not that there were too many places to hide on this ship, even if he had been able to outrun her.

She grabbed his arm. "Cal, what are you doing?"

"Going to the bridge?"

"You know that's not what I mean."

He dragged his fingers through his hair. She'd never agree with his reasoning. It wasn't even worth having this conversation again. "Dania, everyone else had already said *aye*. What I voted wouldn't have mattered, and I, for one, think we should let him go."

"But—"

"You're the one who told Kile that you'd let Alexander leave whenever he wanted. Was that a lie?"

She blinked, looking down. "You know I can't lie. I just didn't think..." She rubbed her face. "I can't lose him again." She walked to the end of the hall and turned back. Her brow pinched over her reddened eyes.

She had to be coming to terms with reality. After the guy had floated their plates, showing them all just how much power he was still capable of wielding, it was pretty obvious that there was nothing she could do to stop him if he wanted to leave.

She straightened and nodded, but it seemed more to herself than to Cal. "He'll be smarter this time. I think he'll be okay."

That was all well and good, but as long as he wasn't on the ship, he was no longer Cal's problem. And he was more than happy with that result.

———

On the bridge, Cal called up a map of the area surrounding Quirky's home world. Nothing but blank space bordered a few scattered stars. "There really isn't much out there."

Ty nodded. "That's probably why they felt safe. No one had ever bothered them before."

Alanna stepped onto the bridge and took her chair. "Do we have a game plan yet, boys?"

Cal leaned back. "Where is the cloud?"

Ty pressed a few buttons, and a golden glow lit up the right side of the screen. "Yellow is just to make our friends stand out. But don't be fooled, though. They are a void of black. To the naked eye, there is nothing there but intergalactic static."

Cal pointed to a light at the bottom of the screen. "What's that?"

"Refueling Station Millie 1921. There's not much there."

No, there wasn't. Which made it pretty close to perfect. "It's the only refueling station, and it's surrounded by open space. We can jump as close as we can get, drop off Alexander, and then jump back out before anyone even knows we're there."

Ty nodded. "Yeah, and there's enough useless space out there that we can jump in cleanly without any issues. It almost looks too good to be true."

Cal sighed. Hopefully, for once, it really was as good as it looked. "Let's keep on our toes, just in case."

"Shall we get to it, then?" Alanna asked.

Cal steadied himself in his seat. As far as he was concerned, the faster they got rid of their latest passenger, the better. "As soon as you have the course plotted, let's go."

She made a few adjustments to her console and tapped on the comm. "Everyone, hold on."

Alanna stood, raised her palm, and the lighted blue dial appeared at the end of her fingertips. The glowing gears spun as she waved her hand.

"Here we go," she said.

The door to the bridge slid open, and the enforcer stepped inside.

Alanna's eyes widened. Cal tried to call her name to stop, but her fingers were already inside the center dial. It was too late.

A pink and purple haze overtook the bridge. The enforcer gasped, taking flight and slamming against the wall as the ship spiraled through space at unfathomable speed. Cal held on to his chair, his mind spinning, until they shot out into regular space.

Ty cursed beside him. "Incoming!"

Cal blinked, shaking away the haze from the jump. "What?"

"You heard me. I said *incoming*. Lots and lots of incoming!" Ty pulled up, just missing a massive, dilapidated cargo cruiser.

"What in the name of Jupiter's moons is *that* doing out here?" Cal said.

Ty spun away, missing another smaller craft. "Probably the same thing this one is doing."

The enforcer pushed up from the floor. A line of blood ran down the side of his face as he narrowed his eyes at the monitors.

Craft after craft filled the screen, most banking down, others banking up, doing their best to not collide with other ships. It was mass chaos, like thousands of ships flying where there should only have been a few.

"What's going on?" Cal asked.

Alanna touched her earpiece. "Comm chatter sounds like they've seen the cloud and aren't waiting to find out what it is. They're evacuating the planet. They must be trying to get to Opanus."

Which would send them all flying past Millie Station. Cal shook his head. Couldn't anything ever go their way?

Ty looked into the screen on his console. "That makes no sense. Their passenger manifests say half those ships are at less than fifty-percent capacity."

Cal rubbed his jaw. "They're panicking, leaving while they can rather than saving more people."

The enforcer wiped the blood from his cheek. "Cowards."

Ty banked down, nearly hitting a skipper ship before spiraling around a freighter. "They may be cowards, but there are a lot of them."

He pushed the controls down again, breaking back into free space.

Ty sat back in his chair. "Well, that was exciting."

Cal checked their trajectory. "If we stay on course, it looks like we'll have a free run to Millie Station." For once, they'd gotten out of a bad situation without things getting worse...or had they?

The enforcer grimaced at the screen and then looked at Alanna. She kept working, either not noticing his scrutiny or trying hard to pretend that he hadn't just seen her jump the ship.

Alexander certainly didn't look happy. His silent stare continued until he turned and left the bridge.

Ty breathed a sigh of relief, and Alanna looked at the door. "Am I in trouble?"

"No. We're fine." The truth was, Cal had no clue, though. But now he wanted the enforcer off his ship more than ever. And then they needed to find somewhere to lie low where no enforcers would ever find them again.

CHAPTER 12

DANIA

CAL STORMED down the hallway toward Dania and skidded to a stop. "Alexander saw Alanna jump the ship."

Dania's breath hitched. "What?"

He started pacing the hall. "It was an accident. He stepped onto the bridge as she initiated the jump." He paused, staring at her. "Is he going to be a problem?"

Dania wished she knew. Alanna's ability wasn't illegal, but it *was* unusual. What would Dania have done if she'd been fully charged?

She gulped. She had no idea.

Cal pointed at her. "You need to make sure this is okay. We only have a few hours before we drop him off. I don't want any issues until then."

She cringed. Cal had always been protective of his crew, but recently, he'd been protective of her as well. She didn't like being treated like an enforcer again...like she had to watch over Alexander and give him orders.

Of course, she'd do that anyway. She couldn't believe that Cal thought she wouldn't intervene on Alanna's behalf. She closed her eyes, her head spinning. All these emotions clambering in her mind at the same time... How did humans handle them?

Taking a deep breath, she steadied herself. "I'll talk to him."

His temperature regulated. "Good. We'll be at the station in a few hours. Please don't give me any problems when we get there. For Alanna's sake, let him go."

She nodded. Oddly enough, it wasn't an answer that she needed to toil over. As much as she didn't want Alexander to leave her, she realized that she worried about Alanna more. Alexander was a good enforcer and an even better person, but she wasn't sure how he'd react to such an odd gift.

She made her way to the lounge. Peter had told her that Alanna got dizzy sometimes after jumping. Maybe she'd gone to get hydration. If she didn't find her there, she'd check her room at the back end of the ship. Once she knew Alanna was safe, she'd find Alexander.

She stepped inside the lounge and froze, finding Alexander and Alanna seated opposite of each other at the table.

"It's just something I've always been able to do," she told him. "I started small, jumping just me. Then after a while I started jumping a few people at a time."

Dania held her breath, hoping that Alanna would have the foresight not to mention that she'd been involved in pirating.

The navigator wrapped her hands around a steaming mug. "Then I came on board the *Star Renegade*, we got in a jam, and I tried it. I jumped the ship."

"We call it skipping space," Alexander explained. "It is a very specialized skill."

That was an understatement. Only high-ranking royals had the ability. Kevers…not humans. Dania was not aware of an instance, before now, where the ability had manifested outside of the chosen few.

Dania drew in a deep breath and released it. The *Star Renegade* was a formidable ship, but Alexander had just learned why they'd been so hard to catch, even for the most seasoned enforcers. The only question was, what would he do with this information?

Alanna looked up at her. "Hey."

"Hello." Dania took another step inside. "Is everything okay?"

"Yeah." Alanna stood. "We're almost at Millie Station. I guess I better get up to the bridge." She took a last sip from her mug and placed it in a recycler. "It was nice chatting with you, Alex."

He stared at his own cup, not answering.

Alanna bit her lower lip, turned, and left the room.

Dania slipped into Alanna's seat. "Are you all right?"

He continued to peruse the liquid in his cup. "She skipped space."

"I know." She tried to read his temperature, his stance, but he was stoic, more like an enforcer than she'd ever seen him.

Her own heart rate spiked. What would she do if she had to stand between Alexander and the crew?

Drawing his gaze from his cup, he frowned at her. "You don't find that odd?"

"It's definitely not normal. I've watched her, though. She's not strong like a royal. She tires quickly, and she can't jump far." Dania took a breath. "That's why we're still a few hours from your drop point. She was unable to take us all the way. She can only go short distances, usually with a rest in between." She stopped herself, realizing she was rambling.

He continued to stare at her. "It's still a power a human shouldn't have."

Dania had to agree. The king may not be pleased to find out that humanity had begun evolving. It would take thousands of years to harness primordial energy like the Banes had, but the royal family still might look at this as a long-term threat.

Her chest clenched. She should have thought of all these things before. Alanna's ability put her in danger. Not only her, but all of humanity. Allowing Alexander to stay was a huge risk that she never should have taken.

"Can she do anything else?" Alexander asked.

"Not that I've seen. I don't think it's power like we're accustomed to with the royal family or any of the Banes."

He looked down again. "I'm not sure that makes me feel any better about it."

Her stomach churned in agreement. "Alanna's not a threat. She's a good person."

Alexander smiled wryly. "She's a good smuggler."

"I've learned that smuggling doesn't mean you're bad. The galaxy isn't as simple as we've been taught. There are complexities that make everything..."

"Confusing?"

Dania sat back in her chair. "Yes."

He nodded. "Which is why we need to remain charged with our sponsor's strength. We need to keep our clarity in times like these."

Dania shuddered. That wasn't quite what she'd wanted to hear.

The overhead comm pinged. "We're approaching Millie Station," Cal's voice said. "I'd like to get in and out as quickly as possible."

Alexander stood.

Dania followed him to the door. "What are you going to do?"

"Nothing has changed. There are colonists who need my aid." He didn't even look at her before passing through the doorway.

"And Alanna?"

He stopped, finally looking back. "It was the best of times, it was the worst of times." His expression turned stony. "We had everything before us, we had nothing before us."

Alexander's gaze lowered to the floor, as if considering his words.

Dania had heard the odd phrases before, when Alanna had read to Alexander in the med bay while he'd been unconscious. But why repeat those words now?

The ship jolted. A rumble vibrated through the hallway, and Dania grabbed on to the wall.

Ty's voice came over the intercom. "We got incoming...again."

CHAPTER 13
CAL

CAL DUCKED as the edge of another cargotainer nearly skidded across their front end. "Why in the blazes are all these ships headed straight for us?" He pressed a few buttons, diverting what power he could to the shields.

Ty tapped the keys on his console. "It looks like they're evacuating Millie Station, too."

"How could there have been that many ships on that tiny station?"

A blast of laser fire shot over their hull. The lights blinked.

Cal ducked again. "Are they shooting at us? Why would refugees be shooting at us?"

A rumble rolled through the room.

"There go our shields," Ty said.

"How is that possible?"

Ty gritted his teeth. "You got me!"

Alanna slipped through the door and took her seat. "Why is it every time I leave you boys alone, you drive us into trouble?" She placed a device into her ear.

Cal leaned closer to the screen, hoping for a better view

to make sense out of the chaos outside. "Can you tell who's shooting at us?"

She shook her head. "There's too much chatter."

Another blow hit them. The main viewscreen winked out, turning into regular glass, showing ships spinning and darting around each other, fleeing from the advancing Cartek cloud. But why? This station was far enough out that the cloud would probably fly right past them.

Another blow hit them, and the power winked out.

That couldn't be good. "Ty, what's going on?"

"I don't know. It's like every hit takes out a system. Like whoever the hell is out there has studied a schematic of the ship or something. It's just not possible."

Yet here they were, sitting in the dark.

The lights came on.

Ethan's voice sounded over the comm. "This is your friendly neighborhood engineer, sending you emergency power thanks to our buddies the Carteks and their snazzy new tech. But I'd appreciate it if we didn't get hit again."

Cal gripped the arms of his chair. If Rgrythei had told the truth, then they had about thirty-five minutes before this extra power ran out.

Another blow jolted them, and the lights dimmed.

The comm engaged from engineering. "Maybe I should explain what I meant about not getting hit?"

Ty and Cal both yelled, "Shut up, Ethan," as they worked to keep the ship together.

Another jolt hit them, and the lights winked out again. So much for the superiority of the Cartek technology.

"Alanna," Cal shouted over his shoulder, "can you jump us out?"

"I can't see anything now, but last I knew, there were too many ships around us to take a chance."

She was right. There were far too many civilians that they might run into.

"Can anyone tell me who's shooting at us?"

Alanna's panel started to glow.

Wait. What? "Do you have power?" Cal asked.

The glow lit up her face. "Apparently, but I didn't do anything."

A voice crackled over the comm. "*Star Renegade*, your systems have been disabled. Prepare to be boarded."

"On whose orders?"

Cal's panel lit up, and the screen before him flickered to life. His stomach soured as the hazy image slowly formed into a familiar silhouette. *No. It couldn't be.*

Ty cursed as ridiculously broad shoulders clad in an opalescent enforcer uniform shimmered into view. As the rest of the transmission sliced its way through their defenses, the screen focused on a stern, clean-shaven face.

"You are being boarded under my orders, Captain Espinoza," Kile said. "Stand down and do not resist."

The communication went dead.

"That's not good," Ty said.

No, it definitely was not.

———

Cal stood on the lower deck, staring at the opening to the cargo hold. His mouth dried as the clang of metal outside told him the enforcers' ship had locked on to them—glued to the *Star Renegade*'s hull like a life-sucking leach. How in the name of Venus had Kile tracked them all the way out here?

Maybe even worse, if the commander had spent enough time studying the ship that he could disable the *Star Renegade* so easily, what other information had he found in their computers?

Dania jumped down onto the deck of the lower cargo hold, with Alexander right behind her.

Her brow furrowed as she approached. "Ty said it was Kile?"

"Yup." Cal was just glad that Doc was keeping Rachel busy, because her kind of nuttiness was the last thing they needed right now.

A boom sounded through the hold, like someone had hit the side of the ship with a fist the size of a planet.

Dania touched Cal's arm. "You need to open the door or they will cut their way in."

She was right, of course. That didn't make it any easier. Cal hit the controls, and the cargo door opened. Three enforcers, including Kile, stood on the platform of the larger ship below.

One appeared to be a woman, although her shoulders seemed wider than Kile's and her silver-white curls coiled tightly to her scalp. The other was a little taller than Kile, with a square face and short hair, also silvery white, like all enforcers.

Cal shuddered, realizing the *Star Renegade* was partway inside the enforcer ship. Trapped. He grabbed the side of the hull to keep himself steady. Once again, things had gone from bad to worse. He needed to keep his cool, though, and act like he was in control, even though it was brutally obvious to anyone that he was already at their mercy.

He lifted his chin. "I'd lower the landing platform, but we haven't had a chance to fix it yet."

All three enforcers raised their hands slightly before their feet left the ground, and they floated toward the opening.

Cal kept his expression steady, acting like three flying people was no big deal, and moved out of Kile's way as they stepped inside. "It looks like you're feeling better."

Kile walked toward Dania, not even addressing Cal. The other two followed him inside.

The woman picked up her pace. "General," she growled at Dania. "You should be executed immediately for your crimes."

"Whoa." Cal held up his hands. "No one is boarding my ship if you're already talking about executing people."

"I'm sure we can discuss this in a more civilized manner," Dania said, her gaze narrowed on the taller woman.

"She's right," Kile said. "Shivana, stay with the ship. This crew is comprised of imbeciles, but they are resourceful. I don't want any of them sneaking onboard."

The large woman bowed slightly and headed back out the door. She floated down to the deck as if the ship had only partial gravity.

"Let's head up to your lounge area," Kile said.

Cal really didn't want to let Kile or this new guy any farther into the ship than they already were. "How about we chat right here?"

Kile spun on him. His eyes darkened, and he seemed to loom over Cal. "The lounge. Now."

———

As they passed through the doorway into the lounge, the new enforcer wrinkled his nose like the room smelled bad before he turned to Kile. "I must agree with Shivana. We should take our former general into custody. She is no good to us until we return her to Geron so he can restore her to her rightful place. If we leave now, we may still have time to…"

Kile held up a hand, silencing him.

Cal wished he hadn't. *Still have time to…what?*

Alexander placed his hand on Dania's shoulder as she glared at the new enforcer, and Cal couldn't blame her. The guy was talking about her like she wasn't even in the room.

The door started to close, and Ethan slipped in. "Hey, Big Bad. How've you been?"

The commander grimaced. "What are you doing here?"

Ethan punched him lightly on the shoulder. "Aww, come on. I missed ya, you big balooka."

The other enforcer tilted his head. "What is a balooka?"

"Ignore the little one," Kile said.

Ethan waved at the larger, blocky enforcer. "Hi. I'm the capable one. Maybe you've heard about me?"

Ethan was just being Ethan, but his hands shook slightly. There was only one reason for him to be here, and that was to support Cal. He'd probably drawn the short straw. Either that, or Ethan was just crazy enough that he wanted to be here.

Cal shifted his weight, testing the placement of the small pistol hiding in his boot. Doc had manufactured the weapon when Dania first had come on board. It had been a touch of extra security, and Cal had started wearing it again when Kile, and then Alexander, had shown up. Doc was fairly certain it would take out an enforcer. They still didn't know for sure if it would work, though. Part of Cal still didn't want to find out because if Doc was wrong, whoever shot the weapon wouldn't get a chance to explain.

Kile narrowed his eyes at Cal. The guy had a way of making you think he was poking around in your head. Hopefully, that wasn't true.

"There are sensitive issues we need to discuss," the commander said.

The other enforcer grimaced. "What do you need to discuss with humans?"

Cal folded his arms. "Maybe he needs to discuss how he lied to us. We were promised a ten-minute head start. You gave us five minutes, tops."

Kile's visage remained stony. "By the time the ships reached you, it had been ten minutes. It is not my fault if you did not use your time wisely."

"We are wasting words," the other enforcer said. "We need to drag the general back to Geron or give her the execution she duly deserves." A ball of fire formed in his hand.

Kile's eyes narrowed on Dania as he walked over toward Ethan. "I agree."

The new enforcer took a step toward Dania.

She raised her hands, looking no less menacing without her power. "Miguel, stop. That's an order."

His eyes blazed as much as the flames in his fist. "You lost that right when you turned away from your sponsor. You are nothing."

Alexander pulled Dania behind him, his long, silver-blond hair taking flight. Cal reached out his hands, then drew them back, wishing he'd gotten to her first.

Miguel continued to advance. "Get out of the way, healer. Do you think I will not go through you to do my duty?"

Alexander's hair whirled like it was alive. "And I will do mine."

Kile raised his hand and a burning scrape sliced up Cal's leg. The gun flew out of Cal's boot and into Kile's grip. The commander fired, shooting Miguel in the back. The blocky enforcer froze, still staring at Alexander, before he slumped to the floor.

Alexander gaped. Cal stood frozen, his heart beating madly in his chest. His leg stung, and his sock seemed damp, but he pushed the pain aside.

Had the commander actually killed his own man?

Dania dropped to her knees beside the enforcer who'd just threatened her. "You..." She looked up at Kile. "You shot Miguel."

The commander pursed his lips. "Do not even pretend that you haven't thought about pummeling him more times than you're willing to admit."

Alexander blinked, still gaping. "But-But you actually did it. You shot him."

Dania looked back up at Kile. "That shouldn't be possible."

Kile harrumphed. "You know better, General. It is completely possible, if he had come between me and my mission."

Dania's breaths seemed shallow. "Your mission?"

Kile placed the gun in Ethan's hand. "Hold this."

Ethan gaped. "Umm..."

Cal's leg started to tingle and sting where the weapon had been tucked inside his boot. The only other person who'd known about that gun was Doc.

Kile tapped on the comm. "Doctor?"

Cal steeled himself, ready to defend Doc if the enforcer brought up the gun he'd engineered.

Peter's voice came over the com. "Did you just call me *doctor*?"

Then Quirky's voice piped up. "Is that the Big Guy?"

Alexander helped Dania stand as she continued to stare at the enforcer on the floor.

Kile's cheeks reddened. "Doctor, are you able to revive someone whose heart has stopped after a trans-miortic shock?"

"Yeah. Why?"

"Come to the lounge with whatever equipment you need. Immediately." Kile closed out the comm.

"What's going on?" Cal asked.

The overhead comm pinged. "Hey, boss?" Ty's voice rang from the speaker. "The big, scary enforcer lady is running down the hall toward you, and she doesn't look very happy."

Great. Just great.

"Now what?" Cal said.

Kile held up a finger, and the room went quiet. Then he held up his palm to Ethan. "You are actually the only one I like. So I'm sorry."

A burst of energy left his hand, slamming the engineer in the chest. Ethan flew back, hitting the wall before thumping to the floor, still holding the gun.

"Ethan!" Cal sprinted to him.

Kile held up his palm again, and Cal slammed into a

wall of…nothing. Cal punched the air, and his fist slammed against a barrier he couldn't see.

On the other side, Ethan's eyes were partially open. He didn't move. His chest didn't rise and fall.

Heat rolled over Cal's skin as he turned to the commander. "What did you do?"

The door opened, and the female enforcer entered. Her short hair shifted about her head as she zeroed in on Miguel. "What's happened?"

Kile pointed at Ethan. "The human thought himself a hero. He's been dealt with."

Cal's heart rattled in his chest as the woman's gaze trailed over Ethan's body, no doubt confirming his heart had stopped.

Kile pointed at Miguel. "Take him back to the ship. He's only knocked out. Our healers can revive him."

Her gaze fell on Alexander, still holding Dania.

Kile moved closer. "I cannot guarantee Alexander has not been compromised. Until I can confirm his allegiance to Geron, it's better to get Miguel back to the ship."

She nodded. "Agreed."

Dania stood, her face an odd twist of changing emotions as Miguel levitated and floated out of the lounge. The large woman followed him out the door, not looking back.

Doc blasted into the room, carrying a metal box. "I guess we're not worried about the enforcer-lady walking through the halls all by herself?"

"She will follow her orders," Kile said. "She will take Miguel back to our ship, and nothing more."

Quirky pushed in right behind Doc. "Ethan!"

They both dropped to their knees and opened the box,

laying instruments out on the floor. Alexander moved beside them.

Dania also fell to her knees and touched Ethan's face. "Is he dead?"

He better not be, or Kile will be right beside him. The wall of air around Cal abated. He shoved the commander in the chest. "What the hell did you do?"

The enforcer looked indifferent. "If you had used your weapon on Miguel, you may have missed, and then you'd be dead. Even if you hadn't missed, the discharge would have alerted Shivana to come, and then you would also be dead."

Rachel handed Doc instruments as he and Alexander worked on Ethan.

Cal glanced at the gun, still lying in the engineer's unconscious hand. "How did you even know I had it?"

"There is very little about you I do not know, Mr. Espinoza."

A chill ran up Cal's spine. The attacking ships had known where to hit them, disabling them far too easily. Kile had obviously been very busy learning too much about the *Star Renegade* when he'd been onboard.

A clang ran through the hull, probably the enforcer ship breaking free.

Cal hit the comm. "Ty, are the airlocks okay?"

"Yeah," he answered. "I watched her leave, or they wouldn't have been. She didn't even warn me before they disengaged."

Cal shook his head. Typical.

On the floor, Ethan drew in a deep, long breath and coughed.

Cal leaned against the wall and closed his eyes. Every

time he thought they might catch a break, things managed to get worse. Kile killing a member of the crew out of convenience was not something he was prepared to deal with. His head began to swim as pressure started to build behind his right eye.

Ethan's head lolled, and he moaned.

Doc breathed a sigh of relief and tapped Alexander on the shoulder. "Thanks for your help."

Cal blinked, the lights suddenly stinging his eyes. He drew in a deep breath and let it out slowly.

Ethan sat up, holding his head. "Why is it always me?"

Quirky rubbed his back. "You okay, Red?"

He nodded, coughing again.

"Good." She stood, walked across the room, shoved Cal out of the way, and then punched Kile in the chest. "That's for leaving." She punched him again. "Oww!" She shook her fist and then slapped the enforcer across the face. "And that's for Ethan, you jerk!"

Kile just stood, staring at her, his expression as stony as ever.

Cal grabbed his temples as they started to throb. "There is entirely too much going on at the moment and none of it is making sense." He glared at Kile, pointing at Ethan. "Why did you do that to Ethan?"

The commander leveled his gaze on Cal. "Because Miguel had been shot, and someone needed to be punished for it."

Had the commander lost his mind? "*You're* the one who shot him!"

Kile shrugged. "I anticipated that someone needed to die to satisfy Shivana's need for judgement. My death would have been far too inconvenient and only caused more problems for your crew."

This guy actually thought Ethan's death would be less inconvenient than his own? This was all Cal needed, a psychotic guy with crazy intergalactic powers. He drew in a deep breath through his nose and let it out through his lips, trying to ward off the headache, but the pounding deepened, as did the growing burn in his leg. Not that a superficial wound mattered, when Ethan had been dead a moment ago.

The commander glanced at Ethan. "You were the only one standing outside Miguel's line of sight, so you were the logical choice." Kile turned back to Cal.

"I checked to make sure your doctor could revive your engineer. It would have been unfortunate if you'd lost the only truly capable person on your crew."

Cal closed his eyes. No matter how long he lived with enforcers, he'd never be able to understand their reasoning.

"That doesn't matter." Rachel slapped Kile's arm again. "You're still a jerk." She shook out her hand. "Can you stop being so damn hard! You hurt!"

He glared at her. "Then I suggest you stop hitting me."

She folded her arms. "Yeah, well, you deserve worse. And as soon as I think of something worse that won't hurt me, I'm gonna do that too."

Cal shook his head. Hopefully, the commander still found Rachel's idiosyncrasies endearing and she wouldn't push any buttons to set him off, because this day obviously wasn't going to get any better.

DANIA NARROWED her eyes as Ethan took in several deep breaths, dragging his fingers through his coppery hair. She could sense the agitation rolling off Cal, and with good reason, after he'd almost lost his engineer. However, she understood Kile's reasoning. Ethan was luckier than they all knew. Any other enforcer would have considered him collateral damage and not worried whether or not there was anyone on board who could revive him.

Still, Dania glared at her commander. "I trust you plan on explaining yourself?"

Kile's chin lifted as he walked toward her. "I needed both Miguel and Shivana off the ship so I could speak with you privately, without their interference."

Dania tempered the twisting in her chest. "So, you facilitated this by shooting Miguel? And nearly killing Ethan?"

She inwardly cringed, knowing that not too long ago, she may have done the same, or worse, in the name of completing a mission.

"Miguel has always been a problem. You know that.

When the possibility arose of executing you, he was first in line for what he called *the honor* of doing his duty."

She looked toward the door Shivana had floated Miguel through. "Did he really hate me so much?"

"His concerns about you are not isolated." He took another step toward her. "They no longer trust you. You've committed a crime in forsaking your sponsor. Your execution would be a more palatable punishment for them than bringing you home for the forgiveness they know Geron will give you."

Dania sighed, looking down. Kile was right. Geron rarely reserved forgiveness for anyone but her. She'd seen others punished for far less. "So, Miguel wanted me dead. Is that why you shot him?"

Kile shook his head. "No. I shot him because your death, or forcing you back home prematurely, were both contradictory to my orders."

"And what are those orders?" Cal asked.

The commander kept his focus on Dania. "I am here on Geron's behest. He requires...no, he *asks*, that you do the right thing."

Interesting choice of words. Dania's eyes narrowed. "He *asks* me to return?"

"In time, yes. That would be the most beneficial."

Cal's temperature increased .0195 degrees as he shifted his weight, his gaze switching back and forth from her to Ethan.

She wished he wouldn't be so concerned. He should know where her loyalties lay. "That's not going to happen. I'm not going back."

Kile lowered his eyes. "I knew it was unlikely you'd come to your senses, but I thought I'd at least try."

Ethan shifted on the floor. "Big Bad, I'm still your favorite, right? The most capable one on the crew?"

Kile glanced at him. "Unless your captain suddenly grew a brain, then yes."

Ethan closed his eyes and continued to rub his head. "Okay, good. Because I was kinda starting to wonder here."

Kile's gaze returned to Dania, still blank and stony. There was more to his request. She could sense his trepidation, even though he didn't show it.

He'd said it would be beneficial for her to return *in time*. That meant he wasn't expecting her to return immediately, which would be more in-tune with Geron's impulsive and totalitarian nature. That meant there was far more to this mission than reinstating a fully-charged general.

Kile looked back up. "You are still highly trained, and even without your powers, you are a formidable leader. More so than I."

Dania gulped. No, she wasn't. She'd been a good leader because her enforcers had been under her control. She knew tactics and how to maneuver enforcers and weaponize them for the highest kill rates. Actually leading, as she'd learned from Cal, was something completely different.

But why did they need a leader?

"What's going on?" Dania asked.

"We were not in this sector by accident. We were sent here by Geron. He is in disagreement with his father." Kile strode toward the window. "The colony on Ephershia has called for help, and our sponsor was the only royal to answer."

Again, very unlike Geron. "Does the king even know you're here?"

Kile shook his head. "Of course not."

Geron had never been the most compliant of the king's children. For the most part, the king ignored the prince, instead focusing on the few of his children he'd groomed for positions of power. Still, it was unlike Geron to go out of his way for anyone unless the outcome was personally beneficial. "He's taking a terrible risk."

"On the contrary," Kile said. "Our sponsor is perfectly safe, most likely entertaining a few attractive guests within the safe borders of Kever space."

Well within his father's borders, and well out of range if anything were to go wrong.

"You're out here alone," Dania whispered.

Kile nodded. "Without our prince, and without our general."

Geron had never been one for understanding battle tactics. Did he even recognize that the odds could be stacked against his people?

Ethan rubbed his head. "So why shoot the stocky mean guy?"

Kile seemed to consider his answer. "Because the egos of Geron's enforcers are getting in the way of their clarity. We are no longer unified. We have not been since we lost Dania." Kile looked back to her. "There is something of great concern headed in this direction. I, for one, do not feel comfortable leading them into battle against an unknown of this caliber without you."

Dania flinched, taking a step back. Peter's surveillance equipment was probably experimental, if not already deemed illegal, and therefore may have been better than what the enforcers had. Kile only seemed aware of a threat, but what that threat was, he didn't know.

Doc stood, helping Ethan to his feet. "I've seen what the colony is afraid of. It's hundreds of Cartek ships."

Kile closed his eyes. "Then it is as Geron feared." He looked to Dania. "They are bringing our war back inside the borders of human space."

Dania's vision spun as she took a seat at the table.

Geron caring about the plight of a remote human colony was a shock in itself but sending enforcers against his father's will was unheard of.

Kile paced the opposite side of the table. "Our sponsor does not believe we should let the colony die just because they cut ties with their royal protectors." Kile glanced at Alexander as he took the seat beside Dania. "Geron isn't a military prince, so his resources were not called to protect the ally planets. Since his enforcers were free, he sent us here to assist."

Alexander tapped his fingers on the edge of the table. "Caring about anyone but himself is very uncharacteristic of Geron."

A swirl of rage built within Dania. "Do not speak ill of our sponsor."

Cal's eyes widened, and Dania eased back, pushing down her anger. Why had she even admonished him? She didn't even think of Geron as her sponsor anymore. Then again, maybe a small part of her still did—and always would.

Alexander shrugged. "I cannot lie."

"He's right," Kile said. "Geron's orders are odd, but this is an order I am happy to comply with." He glared at Cal as the captain took the head of the table, before returning his attention to Dania and Alexander. "I'm not fool enough to believe I'm anywhere near the leader you are, Dania. I don't have the programming. I need both of you back to help mount the defense and counteroffensive against the Carteks."

"I'm not coming back." Dania struggled to not grab Cal's hand beneath the table. She needed to stay calm and in control...every much the general Kile knew she was.

The commander growled, banging the table with his fist. "Our prince sent us here for a reason. You're going to let those people die?"

"Hey!" Rachel slapped Kile on the back of the head. "You don't have the right to come in here and yell at Dani like that. Apologize!"

"I will not..."

She slapped him again.

He stared at her, unblinking.

Alexander snorted a laugh, and Dania nudged him under the table.

Kile took a deep breath and released it more slowly than Dania had ever seen him do. "I'm sorry," he grumbled.

Dania rubbed her face, partially to collect herself, and partially to hide her smile. "Please understand that I want to help, but not by returning. And even if I said yes, we wouldn't have time to get back to Kever space to be recharged. The cloud would reach the planet before we'd make it back in time to help."

"That is why I said your return to Keveron would be the most beneficial *in time*. For now, all I need is for you to come back to our ship and command as you always have."

Cal slammed his fist on top of the table. "No way. I'm not stupid. If she steps foot on that ship, you won't let her come back."

Kile only stared at him. Dania wished she could read her commander's thoughts.

Cal scoffed. "Seems I'm not as daft as you think I am."

Alexander drummed his fingers silently on the edge of the table again…a curious and very human-like habit she hadn't seen from him before.

"This ship has an interesting piece of technology," Alexander said. "We can use it to bolster the communications equipment. She could verbally command our enforcers from the *Star Renegade* with ease."

That would work, but if her enforcers were lining up to execute her, communications were the least of her problems.

She returned her attention to Kile. "Will they still follow me?"

Kile sighed. "They are still coded to you, despite your crimes. If they believed an unlinked command was a temporary solution, if they thought you planned on returning to Geron, maybe."

Dania straightened. "You want me to lie?"

"Are you capable of lying?"

Dania shook her head. "I don't think so."

Ethan raised his hand. "Heck, I'll lie for you." He leaned on the table and smiled at Kile. "I'll even do it competently."

"You're dead, remember?" Kile said.

Rachel raised her hand. "I'm kinda good at lying, too." She pointed at Kile. "But I won't do it for you. I still don't like you. I'll do it for Dani."

"Hold up, people," Cal said. "Our plan was to fly in here, drop off Alexander, and get out before the cloud got here."

"We can't do that anymore, Cal." Dania rubbed her temples. "Those colonists are helpless. The *Star Renegade* alone might not have been able to help, but with the addition of enforcers?"

Cal's ears turned red. "This ship is built for running away from battle, not running toward it."

Alexander stood. "I'm staying."

"*You* can do whatever the hell you want," Cal said.

Alexander glared at him. "There are thirty-seven million people on that planet. Only a small fraction will be able to get off-world."

Rachel took the seat opposite Cal. "We have to help them."

Doc shifted his weight. "Should I call Alanna and Ty so we can put this to a vote?"

"No." Cal rubbed his temples. A small vein under his fingers pulsed.

Dania needed to have Alexander review the captain's medical history and see if he could help with Cal's headaches.

After a moment, Cal looked up. His eyes were slightly glassy and red. "Are you sure you want to do this?"

In many ways, Dania *wasn't* sure. She wasn't the same person who'd stepped onto Midway Station searching for criminals so many months ago. In some ways, she was better, but in the ways that mattered to an enforcer, she was decidedly less.

Losing her powers didn't change who she was at the core, though.

She took Cal's hand. "I'm free, but I'm still an enforcer. The Carteks are breaking the law. Innocents are in danger. I need to do the right thing."

His grip on her hand tightened. "But what if they don't let you leave?"

They both looked at Kile.

The commander pursed his lips. "My first directive is to save that colony. This is an agreeable solution to that end. If Alexander and your engineer can make it happen, Dania may command from the *Star Renegade*."

"Wait...your *first* directive?" Cal sat taller. "What is your second directive?"

He seemed to consider it. "To make sure Dania is safe."

Dania jolted. "What? Not to bring me home?"

"He did not actually say to bring you home. But he will, in time."

Cal leaned his arms on the table. "Does that mean that if we help you, you can give us more than a ten-minute head start?"

Kile sighed. "It means that I need to make sure Dania is safe. Once that is achieved, I will return to my prince for new orders."

Meaning he would let them go? Dania narrowed her eyes, looking for anything hidden in his words, but she could find nothing.

Cal nodded. It looked like he could live with that. "I don't like it, but it looks like you've got yourself a command ship."

THE AIR about Dania seemed to press in slightly. It was strange, how much lighter the air had seemed since Kile had been gone. She wondered if the energy change was real or all in her head. Kile had claimed he wouldn't try to bring her back to Geron after this conflict was over, but she knew better. Even if his next directive was to see her safe, from his perspective, she could only be safe if she was with her sponsor.

Laughter echoed through the halls. It was not an unusual sound on the *Star Renegade,* but the tone of one voice seemed deeper. She headed toward the open lounge door.

"Oh, please," Ty said. "I doubt Rachel is an anomaly. You probably have women falling at your feet all the time."

"On more than one occasion, yes," Kile said. "But unlike Alexander, I have only enjoyed the company of a single woman at a time."

"Wait, what?" Ethan's high-pitched voice carried down the hall. "How many?"

Kile's voice held an air of amusement. "Three."

"Three at a time? Are you kidding me?" Ethan said.

Alexander muttered something she couldn't hear. Probably setting Ethan straight. Enforcers rarely had time for trivialities.

The room erupted in laughter again before falling into a hush as Dania entered. Kile and Alexander sat opposite each other at the table. Ty sat at the head, while Ethan and Peter sat next to the enforcers. They each had a glass in front of them filled with a brown-tinted liquid.

"Oops," Ethan said. "The boss is here."

Kile held his hand out to an empty seat at the table. "On the contrary. Our general is always welcome."

Ty grabbed an empty glass and poured another drink. "We were just celebrating Big Bad's return to our happy home."

It seemed unthinkable, a criminal celebrating the arrival of an enforcer. Yet Ty and Ethan had always believed they'd be able to help Kile, as they'd helped Dania. Too bad they'd been wrong.

Dania eased into the seat beside Peter as Ty passed the drink to her.

"Where's Rachel?" Dania asked.

Kile took a drink. "She's still angry with me."

Dania doubted that would last long. She was probably trying to prove a point. "What about Cal and Alanna?"

"I gave Cal something to ward off a headache," Doc said. "I figured better safe than sorry with an escort of enforcers flying alongside us."

Dania nodded. Cal did seem to suffer more in high-anxiety situations.

Ty drew a line through the condensation on his glass. "Alanna's trying to sweet-talk Millie Station into giving us a landing site. Apparently, there are too many people evacu-ating to safely land a ship. Imagine that?"

"Landing is a waste of time," Kile said.

Ty pointed at him. "No negativity, and no enforcer stuff. You know the rules. Drink."

Kile glared at him, laughed, then tipped his drink back, swallowing until his glass was empty. The humans cheered him, while Ty refilled the commander's glass.

"I keep telling you, I don't get inebriated," Kile said.

Ty leaned over the table toward him. "Well, we'll see if that's true if you keep talking like an enforcer. I think that's the fifth time that you've had to down your glass."

Dania lifted her drink to her nose and sniffed.

"Spiced wine," Doc said. "Ethan's ridiculously strong blend."

Dania placed her glass down. Her eyes burned slightly from the scent.

Ethan leaned across the table. "Can we get back to Alexander's love life? I mean, I have trouble getting one woman, let alone three."

"Look at him," Doc said. "And I'll bet love had nothing to do with it."

Alexander shook his head. "Love is rarely an option for an enforcer."

"So, it was what—like recreational activity for you?" Ethan asked.

"Isn't that what Quirky was supposed to be—a tempo-rary distraction?" Ty pointed out. "She was just a little more tenacious than any of us expected."

Peter's eyes widened. His temperature spiked, and with good reason.

Ty and Ethan had procured Rachel's assistance to keep

Kile entertained during a recent outing. Rather than allowing him to leave after her job was done, Rachel had stowed away in the cargo hold. Luckily, her efforts hadn't ended in her execution. As far as Dania knew, though, her commander wasn't aware of the original arrangement.

Kile glanced at Peter. "No need for alarm. Ms. Quirky informed me that her services had been paid for in advance. Her subsequent attraction to me has not been an unpleasant experience." He shrugged. "It's saved me from seeking out companionship elsewhere."

Dania frowned. "You make it sound like you do that often."

"When my powers wane, and my direction is less centered, yes. If companionship is offered, I would normally accept."

Ethan shook his head. "I want to live in Big Bad's world, where women just offer up the goods for free, no strings attached."

Dania's gut clenched, remembering how easily Alexander had unfastened her uniform when she'd ask him to pretend he was using her. It had shocked her at the time, but could he have actually been practiced?

She turned to her friend. "Have you done things like this?"

Ethan snorted. "Yeah, apparently three at a time."

Alexander smiled and looked down at his drink.

Three at a time? Did that mean *three women* at the same time?

Kile leaned on the arm of his chair. "Oh, please, Dania, don't look so shocked. You are not what a human would consider unattractive. Certainly, you've indulged from time to time."

She stared at him. Seeking companionship hadn't even crossed her mind. Not once.

Peter cupped his mug between his hands. "Human men tend to be a little different from human women. A lot of women would look at the danger as a challenge. They know enforcers can't love, so they try to break you. Bagging an enforcer would be exciting for them. Where guys—"

"Don't wanna die." Ty held up his palms. "No offense, Dani, but I would have run in the other direction if I saw you coming with your hair all floating around like it was when we first met. Unfathomable cosmic powers would give me serious performance issues."

Ethan set his drink down and wiped his mouth on his sleeve. "Seriously! I mean, way too much pressure when the woman you're with can melt your face off if you aren't delivering the goods."

Alexander frowned, leaning toward her. "Human idiosyncrasies aside, I'm surprised that you never sought out human company. What did you do between missions?"

Good question. One she couldn't even answer. She'd usually looked for more criminals to kill.

Alexander's brow pinched as he stared at her. He tilted his head. "Not even once?"

Their stares pressed down on her, like weights attacking from all sides. Her hands started to shake before light burst around her, and all five men jolted back as if punched. She stood, grabbing the table.

"Whoa." Ethan held up his hands placatingly. "What gives, Dani?"

Dania's breath came quick and shallow. Had her power just flexed? Had she just pushed them all back like that?

Alexander and Kile both lowered their heads in supplication, as if she'd just admonished them for not following orders. Maybe she had. That burst had been primordial power. But where had it even come from? She'd thought it was all gone.

She looked down at her trembling fingers. Why did she feel… What did she even feel?

Alone? Lost? Less?

That was ridiculous. There were five other people in the room. How could she feel alone?

She tried to take in another breath, but her chest tightened.

Peter stood next to her. "You okay?"

"I'm fine!" But she wasn't fine, and she wasn't even sure why.

She pushed away from the table and ran for the door.

"Has she really never been with a guy?" Ethan asked.

Alexander stood and started after her. "Dania, wait."

She didn't want to wait. Even free, she was different. Maybe having Alexander here was a mistake. Things had been so much better when she hadn't felt like there was so much wrong with her.

"Dania!"

She stopped near engineering. She knew better than to think Alexander wouldn't keep following, and there were few places to hide on this ship.

He grabbed her arm, turning her to him. "I'm sorry. I didn't mean to embarrass you."

Her cheeks heated. "I'm not embarrassed."

His eyes looked over her, no doubt taking her temperature. "None of us intended to threaten you or make you feel trapped."

"I don't feel…" The word wouldn't come out.

"I apologize," Alexander said. "From the way the crew talked, I took for granted that you and the captain…"

She looked up. "Me and the captain what?"

He closed his eyes and looked down. "You really can't even comprehend what I'm talking about, can you?"

Her breaths became shallow again.

Alexander held up his hand. "Please don't feel trapped."

"I'm not…" She dragged her fingers through her hair. Did she feel trapped? In some ways, yes, but that was ridiculous. She was free. "I'm not sure what I am. I'm feeling… I don't know. Something's just…wrong."

He nodded. "I'm sorry. I had no idea the shunt was deep enough that it held even after your power waned."

"The…what?" She shivered like ice had rolled over her skin. "What did you do to me?"

He held up his hands. "Please don't say that like I had any choice. He controls all of us. You know that."

Yes, she knew that, but she'd thought she was free. "What's inside me?"

"Geron is aware that enforcers frequently enjoy human company between objectives. He didn't want you so easily distracted. He wanted to make sure you kept your focus." He rubbed his temples. "I didn't realize that it never waned between feedings, even now."

Dania rubbed her shoulders. While her people had been out seeking personal gratification, she'd been seeking more people to kill. Her focus had always been on enforcing the law, even between missions. "He made me into a monster."

"He called you a work of art. His prized possession." He looked down. "It always made me feel inferior."

Several times when she'd been with Cal, she'd felt a warmth from within, a sweet sense of serenity and desire to be closer that she'd thought had been friendship. However, whenever she'd focused on that feeling, it would wink out as if it had never been there.

Were those feelings intentional on Cal's part? Was the captain interested in more than friendship? Had she pushed him away without even knowing it?

"You're getting more confused."

She pushed Alexander away. "Get out of my head!"

"I wasn't reading your thoughts. I don't have to. Your temperature fluctuations are more erratic than I've ever seen."

Because Alexander had been right. Her body realized she'd been betrayed before her mind had. Even though she was free, Prince Geron was still controlling her. "Can you take it out? Can you fix me?"

He puffed out a breath through his lips. "Geron made you what he wanted. Do you really want to alter that?"

"That's him talking, not you. He's controlling you, Alexander. Even from this distance. Doesn't that anger you?"

He stepped back. His eyes turned stony. "I will *never* be angry at my sponsor."

"Because you aren't *allowed* to be angry at him. That alone should make you furious!"

He looked down. His temperature spiked a full degree.

"Wait a moment. You *are* angry."

He shook his head, but it seemed more like a refusal to comment than an actual denial. A pink flush coated his cheeks.

"It's wrong what he did to us, Alexander, and you know it."

His eyes turned stony as his temperature cooled. "I will never forsake my sponsor."

Yet he didn't deny his anger, or that what had been done to them was wrong.

It was a start.

Maybe they could get through this, together.

Or if not together, maybe she could keep Alexander away from Geron long enough to convince her friend to fix whatever he'd done to her.

CHAPTER 16
CAL

KILE WAS ANNOYED WITH HIM, but Cal didn't care. After a brief argument that Dania had stopped with a whisk of her beautiful hand, Cal had Ty land the *Star Renegade* on Millie Station for whatever fuel and supplies they could find. Cal wasn't going into battle short on anything if he could help it.

While Ethan, Doc, and Alanna headed to the industrial center for essentials, Cal headed toward the local markets, hoping to find some non-processed protein and vegetables, even if he needed to pay a premium during an evacuation. If the enforcers were starting to set up patrols around common supply stations, he'd have to pick up real food wherever he could.

He worked his way past people pushing to get out, while he was walking in. The sound of people's voices bounced off the stark, metal walls as the drumming sounds of footsteps on grime-coated steel floors echoed everywhere.

He didn't blame the residents for not being crazy enough to stay in this overblown metal tomb with a big, black blob headed this way. Cal wished that the *Star Renegade* were heading in the opposite direction as well.

Someone shoved him. Cal stumbled back, and a kid with dirty cheeks and ripped overalls ran away from him, looking over his shoulder. A sudden unease settled over Cal before he realized his comm band was no longer on his wrist.

"Hey!" Cal sprinted after the kid, weaving in and out of people toting large bags on their backs as they made their way to the evacuating ships.

The kid looked over his shoulder again, wide-eyed, as he darted into a building. Cal pushed through the door behind him and stepped into a large, vacant chamber.

A gravelly voice filled the room. "Greetings, Captain Espinoza."

Cal cringed. Apparently, the room was not as vacant as it had seemed. His comm band lay on a chair in the center of the floor, the only thing illuminated by a light hanging above. He considered abandoning the tech, but they didn't have many extras on the ship, and a replacement would be hard to come by in the outer sectors.

Pretending he hadn't heard the voice, he grabbed the band and headed for the exit.

His shoes tapped across the floor, echoing in the emptiness.

"You keep interesting company these days, Mr. Espinoza." The shadows shifted and a man stepped in front of the door.

Well, *man* was a relative term. The being before Cal wore a long, dark coat that shifted from black to brown to white. Its hair shortened and elongated, changing from light brown to gray and back again. Cal had only been in the presence of a Cartek once before, and this time was no less disturbing.

"Are you the same guy I spoke to last time?" Cal asked.

The creature made an exaggerated bow, a mimic of human movement that was right but very wrong all at the same time. "Rgrythei."

"How'd you know I'd be here?"

Rgrythei bared sharp teeth. It was probably supposed to look like a smile. "I believe on Earth you call it 'coincidence.' We were already here. As you know, we have business in the area."

Business? Yeah, attacking a defenseless planet. "What do you want?"

Cal tried to look relaxed, but he knew exactly what the creature wanted. They'd cut a deal. Or rather, they'd forced Cal to cut a deal or they'd destroy his ship and everyone on it. The Carteks had wanted him to hand over Dania, Kile, and Alexander. Cal had thought he could keep one step ahead of them. Apparently not.

"We had an agreement, Mr. Espinoza. Or maybe you've forgotten?"

Or maybe this squid had forgotten that they were in the middle of an evacuation?

"I don't have time for this. There are a whole lot of people trying to get off this station. If you hadn't heard, there's a big dark cloud headed this way."

Rgrythei smiled. "I assure you, it will pass this station by."

"And head directly for the planet?"

The creature nodded.

"Those people are innocent. They're just colonists."

"The Cartek Empire has no interest in the people. Only the planet."

"And you think they're just going to let you take it?"

The creature made a snorting noise that was probably supposed to be a laugh. "I assure you, they will have no choice."

Which was exactly why the colonists needed protection. Thank goodness the nutty prince had decided to grow a conscience for once and had sent the Ephershians some help.

The Cartek shifted, fading to black and then reappearing. "The colonists may leave, as many are in the process of doing. We will not hamper those smart enough to evacuate."

Which meant they planned on obliterating the others, just like they'd done to so many colonies before Earth had signed the treaty with the Banes.

Cal did his best to keep his voice level. "I can't let you do that."

The creature snorted a laugh again. "Back to the issue at hand. You did not meet the conditions of our agreement within our prescribed parameters. Therefore, the Cartek trade rules say that I can charge what you might consider *interest.*"

A chill ran down Cal's spine. He didn't like the sound of that.

The Cartek shifted right, then left…probably another poorly executed mimic of human movement. "There are now sixteen enforcers in the two ships in orbit," it said. "I know you are in communication with them. You will deliver them all to me."

"What? How am I supposed to do that?"

"This is for you to figure out."

This crazy Cartek expected Cal, a regular human being, to deliver sixteen enforcers, most of which were probably fully charged?

"What you're asking is impossible."

"Then your ship will be destroyed."

Maybe not. Doc had done something to trick the sensors. He'd said that the tech couldn't hurt them anymore.

"I see the way your eyes look to the side, and how your facial features change, Mr. Espinoza. Do not think your childish tampering will stop our technology. It learns. Whatever you did to stop it before, it has already undone. I can take your ship at any time."

Cal gritted his teeth. "So why haven't you?"

"I am an opportunist. And I am patient." Rgrythei began to saunter through the room, the color of his coat fading in and out. "And you did not disappoint. Now I will get sixteen enforcers, rather than just three."

Cal looked at the floor. The only way he'd gotten out of this last time was agreeing. Of course, that agreement was what had gotten him into this trouble in the first place.

The Carteks had lived up to their reputations. They knew what they wanted in a negotiation, and they always made sure that they had the upper hand before talks started. He couldn't win this. Not at the moment, at least. But maybe he could stall, just a little.

"It's impossible to get all of those colonists off the planet before the cloud gets to them. Does the Cartek Empire really want to kill all those people?"

Rgrythei held up his hands slightly higher than would have been appropriate if he were human. "We have no desire one way or another to harm the humans. We want only the planet."

Cal's eyes narrowed. "But you *are* willing to wipe out everyone on the surface."

"We do prefer a pristine world, free of complications."

They were psychopaths. All of them. "You guys are always trying to prove you're a better option than the Banes. Earth will look more approvingly on you if you give those people a chance."

The Cartek took two steps toward Cal. "Your point?"

"I need the enforcers to help get the people off the planet."

Rgrythei laughed, a sound akin to metal scraping against stone. "You don't need them to evacuate the planet. The more intelligent humans are doing that already. What you hope is to use the enforcers to fight the oncoming storm. I am not a fool." He walked toward the door. "You have forty-eight hours to comply, or we will destroy your ship."

"And then what? You'll still have to face the enforcers."

He made that gravelly sound again. "Mr. Espinoza, sixteen enforcers are no match for what's coming." The door opened. "Forty-eight hours, Mr. Espinoza. The Cartek Empire appreciates your compliance and will not ask again."

The door closed, leaving Cal alone.

Forty-eight hours.

How the hell was he going to get out of this one?

CHAPTER 17

DANIA

DANIA AND ALEXANDER leaned over the table in the lounge, scanning the data pads strewn across the surface. Ephershia was the most remote of the planets near the Cartek border, and as such, it had few places for the fleeing colonists to go, and even fewer allies to come to their aid. The colonists were innocent, whether they were officially under Bane protection or not. They should not have been in this predicament, and the odds did not seem in their favor.

"What do you think?" Alexander asked.

What she thought was inconsequential. There were lives at stake. Innocent lives. She needed to find a way to save them.

"Defending the planet will be difficult if the doctor's numbers are correct," Alexander said.

He was speaking the obvious—maybe trying to fill a void, since she hadn't spoken in some time.

"Do you want to take an offensive stance now, before they get any closer?" he asked.

Dania stood, taking one last look at the information.

Normally, she preferred an offensive position. However, this was not a normal situation. "Even the best offensive is a moot point with the number of enforcers we have."

"We've faced worse numbers and won."

Yes, but that was when she'd been connected to her enforcers. They had been an extension of her own hands, working as one solidified unit. A miniature army completely under her control. They'd had no free will. No questions. No fear. Only her own thoughts replacing their own. It had been perfection.

Dania closed her eyes.

The power of her prince no longer flowed through her. Even the small spark of strength that had flexed the previous day, pushing the men at the table, hadn't returned.

In her current condition she could command them from afar, but not from her mind. They might lose untold seconds before her orders reached each soldier, if they followed her orders at all.

As hard as this was, Dania needed to face the truth. "I don't think winning is our goal. We need to do what we can to get the people out."

He raised a brow. "You want to let the planet go?"

She grasped the edge of the table. "No, I don't want to let it go, but I'm not sure we have a choice. The numbers we have do not equate to victory."

Geron was not a military prince, but he wasn't a fool. He must have known this. So why had he sent enforcers at all?

She pointed to the data pad showing the cloud. "Luckily, they seem to be slowing down. That might give us enough time to evacuate large numbers of civilians." But to where? She called up the star map on the wall screen. The closest planets were Morak and Opanus, but Opanus had recently suffered an attack of their own.

She glanced at Alexander. His eyes darkened, seeing the planet he'd defended until he'd passed out from exhaustion, and from which he'd been subsequently taken captive. He'd go there if she ordered him to, but in his fragile state, that would be a last resort.

She leaned on the table again. "I need a report on how many people we can transport at capacity."

"Not enough."

Wasn't he listening?

She slammed her fist on the table. "Then we need to find a way to *make* it enough."

Alexander sighed. "Under other circumstances, I'd find this newfound compassion endearing. And then, of course, I'd send you to our sponsor for a proper feeding." He pointed to the data pads. "But right now, you need to understand that our best chance to save the most people is by stopping the Carteks from getting there in the first place."

She knew that, but with their small numbers, the casualties would be high.

Alexander's eyes seemed to plead with her. "They'd be no higher than if we tried to evacuate only what we could carry."

She nodded, pretending to ignore his invasion into her thoughts. As usual, Alexander gave good counsel. "I need a full tally of ships and munitions. We may need enforcers in small fighter crafts as well as hanging in space."

Alexander smiled. "It's good to see you analyzing your

situation and building your attack plan. This is what you were built for. I hope you realize this.”

She shook her head. “It’s not who I am anymore.”

“But it is, deep down.” He pursed his lips, running a lock of her hair between his fingers. “How can you stand it? Your hair, your eyes… You used to be so beautiful.”

“She still is beautiful,” Peter’s voice rang out from the doorway.

Alexander’s lips thinned. “You say that because you’re human.”

“So is she.” The doctor entered the room.

“Not anymore.”

Dania startled. Had Alexander just said what she thought he’d said?

She touched his hand. “Did you know I was once human?”

He glanced at her, then back to the data pads. “Of course. I’m your healer. I know everything about you.”

Her stomach sank. “Are *you* human?”

“No. I am an enforcer.”

Her hands trembled slightly. “But what were you before?”

He pursed his lips again, looking up. “All enforcers are at least part human. It’s not something the king wants to be general knowledge, so I suggest you keep that to yourself, or Geron’s first task will be to make you forget.”

Dania flinched. This was another reason not to return. She’d learned so much about the galaxy and even herself over the past several months. She refused to go back to that blank slate, not caring, not thinking.

Doc took a seat at the table. “Doesn’t it bother you to know that you were *created*? That you used to be a different person. That you used to have a family of your own?"

Alexander swiped through a data pad. "I have a family. My sponsor and my fellow enforcers."

Dania's stomach twisted. A year ago, she would have responded similarly. This most likely was not what Alexander really thought, but what he'd been programmed to think. Even though Alexander seemed to be waking up on some counts, Geron's hold still seemed stronger than ever on others.

Alexander looked up at Dania. "Now that my general is returning, my family will be complete once more."

Dania closed her eyes. She didn't know how many times she'd had to reiterate that her life as an enforcer was over. Either he wasn't listening, or he was not yet capable of understanding.

"Where is the commander?" Alexander pushed back from the table. "He should be reviewing this data with us."

Peter leaned back in his chair. "He and Rachel are still in Rachel's room making up."

Alexander frowned. "*Making up?*"

Dania sighed. They'd definitely been in there a long time. "I hope he doesn't hurt her again. She's been through enough."

Alexander reached for a new data pad. "If you are referring to her erratic emotional responses, there is no doubt that she will be hurt again. I have no doubt where the commander's loyalties lie, and you should not doubt him, either."

And Rachel knew that. However, if she opened her heart to him again…

"It will be her own fault," Alexander said.

"That's kind of cold," Peter said.

Alexander shrugged. "It's the truth. I'm sure the commander made no promises to her. He is incapable of lying."

That was also true. But perhaps Alexander didn't understand that humans sometimes heard what they wanted to hear, not what was actually being said.

Alexander folded his arms. "Then that will also be her own fault."

Peter frowned at Alexander. It wouldn't be long before the intelligent doctor figured out the special link between her and her healer. Once he did, he'd probably try to study it.

"I don't know," Peter said. "Maybe Big Bad came back because he enjoyed it here. I mean, Quirky aside, Kile made a home on the *Star Renegade*. He made friends."

Alexander glared at him. "Enforcers do not have friends."

His words sunk through Dania, cutting a hole in a place unused to feeling pain. "Aren't we friends?"

"That's different."

"I'm not so sure it is." Peter folded his hands on his chest. "I noticed you've made friends with Alanna. You two look like you've been having fun fixing up the ship." He paused, maybe letting that thought sink in. "My girl says you're a wiz with engine modifications."

A slight smile touched Alexander's lips, although he didn't respond.

"That would all be over if you returned to Keveron," Dania reminded him.

His smile faded. "Then I will have to enjoy myself while

I'm here. Amusements will never counteract my duty to my prince."

Unfortunately, that was probably true. Not only for Alexander, but for Kile as well. And both of them had plans of bringing her back with them when they returned home.

A slight flutter ghosted over her skin, and she stepped away from the table. In her current condition, she might not be able to stop them if they decided to force her to comply. And once she returned to Geron, he'd take away everything she'd learned. She'd be no better than Alexander and Kile.

No. She'd be worse.

THE SOLITARY LIGHT still hung above Cal as he paced the small room on Millie Station. He should have been out in the trading centers looking for supplies, but he knew better than to think he'd be able to focus. Not now that he was knee-deep in trouble with the Carteks again.

Doc had seemed certain the *Star Renegade* wasn't in any more danger, but could that tech really be intuitive enough to outsmart the *Star Renegade*'s resident genius?

Cal rubbed his forehead. The *what-ifs* were starting to chip away at what little hold he still had on sanity. The weapon the Carteks had installed into their sync navigator had nearly killed them twice. They needed to be careful not to accidentally set the thing off again. Maybe Doc and Ethan, or maybe even Mr. Perfect, could take a look at the tech and see if there was still a threat.

That was what he needed: more information. If he could confirm that Rgrythei was blowing ice crystals, then maybe they could still get out of this in one piece, and Cal could avoid making any more enemies.

A presence pressed in on him, like he was being watched.

That wasn't really a surprise. The Carteks probably wanted to make sure he went back to the ship. Little did they know that the *Star Renegade* was the best place for him to go to get out of this mess.

He nodded to himself, leaning on the chair. That was the plan. Get back to the *Star Renegade* and pull in people who were smarter than him and see what the facts were.

There had to be a way out of this. There always was. By now, he should know better than to trust anything that stinking Cartek said.

He walked toward the door, but a man in ripped military-green khakis stepped through and pushed him back inside.

So, he *was* being watched...just not by a Cartek.

"I'm not in the mood," Cal warned.

The guy held his hands to the side. "No one is. If you haven't heard, there's an invasion coming."

He had a short, shadowy beard, just like Chris Columbus. It must have been a trendy fashion for pirates. His clothes were thinner than military-grade fabric. Typical cheap knockoffs worn by felons who wanted to look tough and trustworthy. Cal knew better.

"What do you want?" Cal asked.

"Probably the same thing the squids wanted."

Cal sighed. He should have realized that this was no ordinary pirate. He was probably a slaver. "What makes you think that?"

"We've been doing a lot of business with the squids. Very lucrative." He held out his hand. "Name's Victor."

Cal stared at the offered hand until Victor lowered it.

"You know why they want the enforcers gone?" Cal asked.

"Divide and conquer. It's the oldest battle tactic in the universe."

"And you're helping them."

Victor shrugged. "Who am I to break the tradition? Those with an entrepreneurial spirit have been making money off war since the beginning of time."

"By catching people and selling them to collectors?"

He pointed at Cal. "No. By catching enforcers… Cold-blooded killers who should never have been allowed anywhere near the Earthan cradle to begin with."

A few years ago, Cal would have agreed with him. It didn't seem so cut and dry anymore.

Victor folded his arms. "You have a particularly beautiful enforcer onboard. We caught him on Opanus not long ago and sold him for an astronomical price."

Cal did his best not to react. This was one of the guys who'd caught Alexander? Not only that, but they'd attacked a peaceful, helpless colony to do it. It was all well and good to say the pirates were targeting enforcers, but not when they killed innocent people to catch them.

"Needless to say," the pirate continued, "we'd like to get him back. There are five collectors out there who keep outbidding each other to get him." He took a step farther into the room. "Apparently, his former owner showed him off at a party and caused a little jealousy among the collector community. In these circles, that's great for business."

Cal's stomach soured, realizing there was an actual community of these crazed people, and not just a few insane politicians with too much cash on their hands. "I'm not selling anyone into slavery, no matter who they are or what they've done." Cal headed for the door again.

Victor grabbed his arm. "I don't like the Carteks any more than you do. Help me out, and I may be willing to help protect the colony."

Cal glared at him. "It's going to take a hell of a lot more than you to fight off that cloud."

A smug grin covered his face. "I have friends. Lots of them. No one wants to see all those people die. We can help."

"For a price."

"Of course. Consider us soldiers for hire…another age-old practice from Earth." He released Cal. "I have several hundred ships all within striking distance."

One ship wouldn't help much, but a few hundred? That could tip the balance in their favor. "What do you want?"

"Something you probably already want to get rid of. The enforcers."

Had everyone lost their minds? "I already told the squid… I'm just a human. How do you guys expect me to catch and contain that many fully charged enforcers? You've seen firsthand what a single enforcer is capable of."

The guy's skin paled slightly. According to Kile, Alexander had bested over a dozen ships attacking Opanus. The only reason the pirates had caught him was because Alexander had gone to the planet and healed colonists, expelling every last bit of his energy until he'd passed out.

Victor cleared his throat and pulled a clear bag out of his right front pocket filled with what looked like coarse sand. "These are micro tracking chips. They're completely harmless and nearly undetectable unless you know what you're looking for."

"What do you want me to do with those?"

"Once they're ingested, they'll turn on and we'll be able to track the enforcers. More importantly, we'll be able to tell when they slow down and start heading back to Kever space."

"And that's when you'll attack."

The pirate nodded. "They seem to run home to daddy when they start to get weak. That's the best time to strike."

"They'll still be lethal."

"Yeah, we'll lose a few ships in the process, but we've found it's quite profitable for those that survive."

They're all insane.

Victor laughed. "Aww, come on. You're a smuggler. You can't be all high and mighty about things like this. You have no love for the king, either."

That much was true, but there had been far too much betrayal going on lately, and most of it done by Cal. "How about you do the right thing and stand and fight with us? Save that colony out of the goodness of your heart?"

The pirate snorted. "Personally, I would, but my friends out there still want a profit." He shrugged. "Deep down, I think I want a profit too."

Once a pirate, always a pirate. If this had been Chris Columbus, maybe Cal would have been able to talk him into it. Then again, the way things had been going lately, maybe not.

Victor held up the bag. "Come on, Espinoza. It won't even hurt them. It'll only track them. It will be on our asses to catch them."

"We'll need the enforcers to fight off that cloud, even with your ships."

"I don't deny that one bit. I don't mind fighting alongside them and then screwing them over. It's kind of my thing."

The pirate rolled the edge of the bag between his fingers. The crinkling sound filled the otherwise-silent room.

"Come on, Espinoza, think about it. When the dust clears, the *Star Renegade* will do what it always does. It will disappear. You'll be long gone, and hopefully, the colony will still be habitable." He shook the bag again.

It seemed like such a little thing. If Geron had charged up his enforcers before sending them, they'd probably beat the crap out of these pirates anyway. Maybe a little tracker might not even be an issue for them.

"I see your tow cables whirling around in your head, Espinoza. It's not much to ask to get a lot of firepower on your side."

This would have been true if he didn't have to betray the enforcers. Or worse, Dania. Did they even know about her?

"Come on, Espinoza, that cloud isn't getting any farther away."

No, it wasn't. And the *Star Renegade* was going to fly right into it. No one had any idea how much firepower was coming down on them in that cloud. It was a suicide mission, even with the enforcers fighting alongside them.

The pirate raised a brow. "Last chance."

Cal stared down the small bag. This was crazy. The enforcers would disembowel him if they found out he was even considering betraying them. But if he didn't do this, he'd probably end up dead anyway. Even worse, his crew, for all their bravery, wouldn't survive. That was even worse than Cal losing his own life.

He grabbed the bag.

The pirate rubbed his hands together. "Good choice. As soon as we see all sixteen enforcers on our tracking equipment, we'll join you in the fight." He smiled. "Hey, if we get lucky, half the Kever patsies will be burnt out by the time the battle is over. It will be easy pickings."

Cal's stomach turned. This was wrong in so many ways. But was turning away a few hundred ships the right thing to do, when so many lives, and an entire planet, hung in the balance?

He choked down the bile in his throat and headed back to the ship. One of these days, he was going to find a way to cut a deal with someone that didn't make him feel like galley refuse.

THE *STAR RENEGADE* seemed smaller as Cal trudged through the hallway. Somehow, the air seemed tighter every time he left the ship. Maybe that was because aliens and pirates had started manipulating him like a puppet. All these private ambushes were enough to make him never want to leave the ship again.

Cal pushed through the doorway into the med bay.

"You don't look happy," Doc said.

"I'm not." Cal's gaze carried over the empty beds and the flashing lights in the back area where Doc ran his experiments. "Where's Quirky?"

"Where she always is lately, giving our big, bad commander a house call." He picked up a test tube. "Don't worry, though. I checked her out. Believe it or not, she's fine."

Cal tilted his head. "What are you talking about?"

"Have you suddenly forgotten how strange she's been acting? Well, strange-er." He put a test tube into a container on the shelf and grabbed another. "She cleared the deep-space dementia test you asked for, though. She's just her normal old wacky self." He turned back to Cal and frowned, looking him up and down. "I have a funny feeling that you didn't come here to talk about Rachel."

Unfortunately, Quirky's idiosyncrasies were the least of their problems.

Cal sat on a gurney and rubbed his face. "I just had another run-in with the Carteks."

"What?" Doc gaped, putting down the test tube.

"Yeah. We're in trouble, and I'm not sure what to do about it."

Doc eased onto a rolling chair. "That sounds ominous. I'm all ears."

Cal pulled out the package of the coarse, sand-like microchips and handed it to him.

Doc held up the bag to the light. "Huh. The Carteks gave you this?"

"Not exactly."

How was he supposed to explain this in any type of way that didn't end with one of them shooting him again?

His head started to throb. It wasn't worth the effort of trying to sugarcoat anything. He was going to have to own up to this. He was royally screwed no matter what.

Standing, Doc walked to the back of the room and looked at the bag under a microscope. "Wow."

Cal joined him. "You're not kidding."

"This is some serious tracking tech. Ridiculously expensive." He leaned closer to the screen showing the enlarged chips. "It looks like they're rigged to attach themselves once triggered, and there's an acidic protectant overlay." He looked up. "Are these meant to be ingested?"

Cal nodded. "There's a small army of pirates. They say they have a hundred ships, and they're willing to help fight off the Carteks, but only if we implant these into the enforcers."

"Wow." Doc leaned away from the microscope. "And you agreed to that?"

"They said they would help as soon as they see the trackers go online. I was hoping you could find a way to either fool them into thinking they went online or find a way to turn the trackers off after they turn on."

Doc rubbed his face. "That's a pretty tall order. They'll expect the enforcers to be on their own ship, moving around doing whatever enforcers do when they aren't enforcing the law." He looked at the screen, then back to Cal. "I thought you said you had a run-in with the Carteks?"

"I did. Remember that alien tech you had to sever from the hull so we didn't implode?"

Doc raised a brow. "That's a little hard to forget. Especially since it's still partially attached to the ship."

Cal lowered his gaze. "They cornered me and threatened to use that tech to destroy the *Star Renegade* if I didn't give them the enforcers. They said what you did was only temporary, and they can still use it as a weapon."

Doc looked at the overhead lights and laughed, but there was no humor in his eyes. "Well, that sucks."

He didn't need to tell Cal that. "Is that tech still safe? Are they bluffing?"

"I'll have to take another look." Doc pointed at the microscope. "But this is going to be a challenge on its own." He turned back to Cal. "I know you're not fond of Tall, Blond, and Beautiful, but how about we assign him and Ethan to the sync navigator, to make sure the Carteks can't use it against us again?" He pointed to the bag.

"Alexander would be great help with this tiny tech, but it would probably be a very bad idea to let him know about the little deal you made."

Cal nodded. "Agreed." Now the even worse news. "I need a way to counteract this powder by the time the cloud reaches us. The pirates won't help unless they see the enforcers on their scopes."

"What's to stop them from not keeping their part of the bargain?"

"They need the enforcers weakened. They'll stick around to make sure that happens."

Doc drew in a deep breath and let it out slowly. "So, you need the antidote by the end of a big space battle that will probably be as distracting as hell and practically impossible to think during?"

"Pretty much."

Doc shook his head. "Just another day on the *Star Renegade*."

DANIA WARMED INSIDE, hearing Cal had invited her fellow enforcers to dinner. A "home-cooked meal," as her new friends called it, was a wonderful departure from food supplements, and a great time for the crew to bond. She only hoped that the enforcers could appreciate it as such, and not turn this nice, human custom into a reason to try to influence…or worse, *hurt* the crew.

Alanna and Alexander walked into the hallway in front of her. The navigator held Alexander's arm as they laughed about something.

Alanna smiled at Dania. "Ready for a good meal?"

"Always."

"I'm surprised you didn't help Cal cook." Alanna released Alexander's arm. "The two of you have been inseparable in the kitchen." The woman's cheeks still blossomed red from whatever they'd been laughing about.

Cal cooking the meal alone had seemed odd. He'd already prepared the meal by the time he'd sent the invitation. "He said he wanted to cook it himself. Something about an old family tradition of hospitality."

Alanna continued walking toward the front of the ship. "As long as it's not meat sticks and veggie pills, I really don't care who cooks it."

Alanna touched the side of the door leading to Cal's personal meeting area. The lounge table had been added to Cal's normal dining room, allowing the eating space to span most of the area in front of the window.

Rachel beamed, hanging on to Kile's arm possessively, speaking with Shivana and a slightly pale Miguel, who was no doubt still healing from being shot in the back. The doctor had lied, telling them that Kile had destroyed the weapon that had been used against Miguel. Kile, while not lying, didn't refute the fallacy.

Both enforcers shot daggers at the petite woman holding on to their commander. Rachel either didn't notice or didn't care as she rambled on about how she and Kile had met on Hedonaii.

Four additional enforcers congregated at the far end of the room, frowning and examining the walls, no doubt looking for possible threats. Other than the cameras, they would find none. Cal was nothing if not a hospitable host.

Peter fidgeted near the kitchen door, speaking with Ty. Both glanced at the enforcers, whispering to each other. She could see their lips moving but could not focus on their words with the other chatter in the room...another effect of losing her Kever pathogens.

Her stomach turned, and she rubbed her gut. She didn't like the thought of them keeping secrets. This was normal, though. Humans spoke softly so others could not hear them. Their secrecy was probably aimed at the other enforcers, not her. She just hoped that they knew that the enforcers would still be able to hear every word they spoke, even in their hushed tones.

Cal stepped out of the kitchen and seemed to survey the room. "Is this everybody?" His brow creased as he turned to Kile. "Don't you have more people on your ship?"

Kile nodded. "Of course. They are making plans and protecting our vessel." He held out his hand to the far side of the room, where the other enforcers glared at Cal. "Ms. Quirky tells me that this is a sufficient showing to not be rude."

Rachel shrugged. "One or two more would have been better, but that's okay. More for me to eat." She elbowed Kile. "Cally's a great cook. Your people may not want to leave after this."

Kile scowled. "I highly doubt that."

Cal bit his upper lip. The crease in his brow deepened before he dragged his fingers through his hair. "Well, I made a lot. I'd hate for it to go to waste. Maybe I'll make dishes up to send back to your ship, so no one is left out?"

"What a great idea!" Rachel clapped her hands. "I can help bring it over there. I've been wanting to see Big Guy's ship anyway."

Kile glanced at Dania. Technically, the ship poised just off the *Star Renegade*'s bow still belonged to her. She was sure that her commander was taking good care of it in her absence, though.

Cal looked at the floor. "Yeah, that will work. Why doesn't everyone take a seat? I'll be right out." He glanced at Peter before disappearing through the doorway.

The doctor's skin seemed a shade lighter than normal, and his temperature was elevated by five-hundredths of a degree. The presence of so many enforcers must have been causing a great deal of agitation. She was still technically a general. Surely, the crew had to know that she would protect them as much as was in her power. Then again, in her current condition, maybe they were right to be afraid.

Moving toward the table, Dania reached for the chair directly to the right of where Cal normally sat.

"No," Kile said. "You will take the head. You should not allow the captain to remain in a traditional seat of power."

She glanced down at her chair. "This is where I always sit."

Alexander's voice fizzled into her mind. *'He's right. You cannot look weak in front of your enforcers. They are aware of human traditions.'*

She tired of posturing, but they were probably right. At the moment, her people thought little of her. It would be best if they believed she had some modicum of control over the ship. She took Cal's seat.

Cal came out of the kitchen carrying two plates. He frowned at Dania, before glancing at Kile, pursing his lips. He probably knew this choice of seat hadn't been her idea.

Shaking his head, Cal placed one plate in front of Dania, and the other in front of Alanna.

Kile narrowed his eyes, taking the seat to Dania's left. "Only two plates?"

A stream of sweat glistened on Cal's brow. "I only have two hands. I'll be right out." He turned and disappeared back into the kitchen.

"The captain serves the crew?" Miguel said. "Another sign of his weakness." His gaze swept over Dania before returning to the door.

"We will be here for a considerable portion of the night if we have to wait for the captain to bring out every plate,"

Kile said. "He should utilize his crew for help. A true leader delegates."

"Cal has a very different leadership style." Ty took his normal chair at the far end of the table. "He likes to show his appreciation whenever he can."

Kile's stomach growled, and his cheeks reddened.

"Are you really that hungry?" Dania asked.

He glanced at her plate, a slight gleam in his eye. He'd only spent a short time on the *Star Renegade*. Did he miss the few times the crew had shared their food with him?

"Here." She pushed her plate toward him. "Take mine."

He leaned back. "I will not take yours."

Cal came back out, two more plates in his hands. He coughed, looking at the plate in front of Kile.

"My general apparently thinks I'm in need of sustenance."

Cal smiled in an odd way that seemed forced for him. "That's not necessary." He placed one plate close to Kile and pushed Dania's plate back toward her. "There's more than enough for everyone." He walked past Rachel and Doc and gave the next plate to Miguel. "Here you go."

"Hey, I'm hungry here!" Quirky said, reaching for a bean off Kile's plate.

Cal slapped her hand. "Are you really going to steal food from the Big Guy? I saw you in the lounge snacking less than an hour ago."

"A girl gets hungry."

He pointed at her. "Hands to yourself. I'll bring out your plate next."

Dania frowned. That was an odd reaction for him. Either he was trying to teach the odd woman human manners or trying to look more civilized in front of the enforcers. Either way, he'd probably failed.

Cal continued until nearly everyone had a dish in front of them. He hesitated at Alexander's place, his temperature spiking a fraction of a degree before he placed the last plate before him.

Sweat sheened Cal's brow as he sat beside Dania. Did he think Alexander might think less of him if the food was bad? What was he afraid of?

Down the table next to Rachel, Peter pushed the food around his plate, scanning the other meals before taking a tentative bite of his own.

Dania sighed. "There is far too much tension in this room. These meals are for enjoyment. You all look like a bomb is about to go off."

Rachel placed her fork down. "Well, Big Guy is fairly certain this is a bad idea, and someone named Miguel is probably going to blow a gasket and kill someone. My guy is hoping it's Cal, and he's trying to decide if he'll let it happen or not."

Cal stopped eating and gaped across the table at Kile.

Dania's commander quirked a brow and swallowed his food. "That is not exactly how I put it, but there is a reason Miguel is sitting so far away from our host."

Miguel cut into his chicken. "I am not a machine. I am not going to blow a gasket or anything else." He shoved the meat into his mouth.

Dania wasn't quite sure that was the truth. Yes, he'd been told Ethan was dead after Miguel had been shot in the back. But Miguel would have been happier if he'd been able to dole out the punishment himself.

Dania hoped the engineer understood the gravity of the

situation and stayed hidden in the back of engineering on the other side of the ship, as far away from this room as possible.

Shivana gulped down the last of her food and leaned on the edge of the table. "Now that we are done eating, I hope we can forgo any niceties and address the problem at hand."

Around the table, nearly everyone stared at her with full mouths and equally full plates.

"Which problem would that be?" Alexander scooped a few vegetables on his fork, not even turning toward Shivana on his right.

Alanna shifted nervously in her seat beside him. Dania wished she could reach across Cal to try to settle her.

Shivana glared at Alexander. "I certainly hope you have not been here long enough to be tainted by humanity. This ludicrousness of her staying onboard this antiquated vessel must end. We need our general on her own ship. Preferably linked for battle."

"Linking is no longer possible," Dania said.

Shivana's short hair began to shift on its own. "We could at least try. I would hope you are not completely useless in your current form."

Cal leaned over the table and pointed his fork at her. "That's uncalled for."

Shivana's eyes narrowed. "I will not speak to you, smuggler."

Cal shook his head. "Yes, I did cook the entire meal all by myself. It took a while, but that's okay. I like to be a good host. You're welcome, by the way."

Shivana's nose flared.

Peter held up his hands. "Whoa, whoa, let's not get all

hasty here, people." He placed his hands on his lap. "As Dania's doctor, I have to admit that her enforcer abilities are very diminished, but she's still quick as a whip. Her brain power and training are all intact. She just can't do all the magical mumbo jumbo."

"What is *mumbo* and *jumbo*?" Miguel asked.

Dania rubbed her temples. "It means I cannot link you, no matter how hard we try."

"But she can still lead us," Kile said. "Better than I."

"From *our* ship," Shivana said.

Dania knew location would be a point of contention. They wouldn't admit it, but they wanted her on their cruiser so they could take her back to Geron as soon as the battle was won. Dania would have done no less when she'd been an enforcer.

One thing was certain. She needed to act the leader now, or maybe never get her people back. "I can command from either ship. The *Star Renegade* is far more maneuverable. We can weave in and out of other ships, giving me the best view so I can relay orders."

Miguel shook his head. "Without you linking us, we will be severely hindered."

Kile stood. "But no more hindered than if I were commanding you." His gaze carried over each of the enforcers. "And for the good of our mission, I am required to admit that Dania is a better leader."

Dania wasn't so sure that was true. Kile had always been adept in the past. Her perfect second-in-command. Still, she was the one who'd received the triangulated training, turning her into a sharpened tool, no different than Prince Geron's own hand.

'*Only better,*' Alexander's voice sounded in her mind.

'Our prince never had an interest in war or fighting. You, on the other hand, are an artist.'

She nodded. This was the truth. Geron would point Dania at any battle and showed little interest in her reports when she returned, only wanting to know if she'd been successful.

She kept her face placid. "I will command from here. That decision is final. As you are all aware, this ship is highly modified, and some of the technology is quite formidable. The *Star Renegade* is the better choice, and we are all required to put the fate of the Ephershian colony first, above all."

Dania lanced Shivana with her gaze and then Miguel. They each nodded. At the end of the table, the others nodded as well, their programming forcing them to comply since she'd spoken the truth. Once the battle was won, though, she and the *Star Renegade* would need to make one of the miraculous disappearances this ship had become so well known for.

Dania scanned down the line of the table, waiting for any objections. "Tomorrow, we will spread our forces and make a wall between the planet and the advancing cloud. All enforcers will be assigned a fighter craft."

Alanna's eyes widened. "Even Alexander?"

Dania turned to her, being careful not to look directly at her best friend. "Especially Alexander. He's stronger than anyone in this room, including me."

"Why is that?" Miguel sat back and looked at Alexander from across the table. "The commander told us you were severely disabled when they freed you, and you did not return to Keveron for..." The word *feeding* hung in the air before Miguel corrected himself. "For proper healing."

Dania tensed. She'd wondered the same thing. Yes, Alexander had received a single dose of the experimental pathogens, but he'd healed miraculously, retaining his power, where Dania had continued to decline.

She glanced at Alexander, whose gaze shot to Peter, before turning to Miguel.

"The ship's technology is not the only formidable thing on the *Star Renegade*. I've actually learned quite a bit of very interesting healing techniques from their doctor."

Shivana slammed her fist on the table. "Better than Kever healing? I doubt that."

Alexander shook his head. "No, not better than Kever healing. I am not at my full strength as I would have been if I'd made it home." He looked at the table. "I will need to return for actual healing when this is over."

"As all of us will," Kile said.

Dania stiffened as his eyes met hers. She held his stare, doing her best to hide the spark of fear hovering within.

Cal rubbed his face. His skin paled as a new sheen of sweat touched his brow.

Dania touched his shoulder. "Are you all right?"

He nodded. "Yeah. It's just been a long day." He sighed. "What do you need from me to make sure you can command all your people?"

Good. Finally, a straightforward question. "Full access to the communications system."

"You got it," Alanna said. "I'm your girl."

"We should run some tests to make sure Dania's commands come through clearly," Kile said. "As we've already pointed out, we will be hindered. Since Dania's orders will not be instantaneous, we may need to make decisions on our own."

Dania flinched. He was only stating facts, but that still stung. Every moment they were here, she was reminded of who she had been, and how she was now something less.

Under the table, Cal rubbed his ankle against hers and smiled. Such a simple gesture, but she appreciated the support.

"Everyone should get some sleep," Dania said. "Tomorrow is going to be a trying day."

Hopefully, they'd all live through it.

CHAPTER 21

DANIA

DANIA LEANED on the edge of the sink in her room, letting the water she'd just splashed on her face fall into the silver basin. Quirky and Ty had left with Kile right after dinner, bringing food to the other enforcers. Cal had given each of the humans a personal bag containing what he'd called *their favorite foods* for snacking, so they wouldn't be tempted to take any of the food meant for her fellow enforcers.

She couldn't decide if that was very nice of him, making sure everyone got their own share, or very strange. Both Cal and Peter had seemed preoccupied, Cal remaining in his private kitchen to clean up, and the doctor running back to the med bay to work on something important.

They both seemed very jumpy. However, they had admitted there was a possible threat from the sync navigator, which could explain why they both seemed so distracted. Alexander and Ethan were in engineering now, reviewing the technology for any abnormalities.

She looked over her shoulder, through the sitting area, and stared at the door to her room, as if she could see clear through to engineering. She'd initially been avoiding the area to keep from drawing attention to the very much *still-alive* engineer. However, since Alexander was the only enforcer left on board, crossing the hall to engineering shouldn't pose any threat to Ethan, and it might quell the sinking feeling plaguing her gut.

She made her way down the stairs to lower engineering and tapped the panel on the wall, gaining access. Alexander and Alanna both moved together, forming a human wall.

Alanna released her breath and laughed, stepping aside to reveal Ethan behind her.

"Sorry," the navigator said. "I guess we're all a bit jumpy."

Dania didn't blame them. If she'd been an enforcer, Alexander would have been forced to make some uncomfortable choices if they had tried to execute the engineer.

"What have you discovered from scanning the problematic tech?" Dania asked.

Ethan turned from his screen. "Only that we can't see what we need to see with the camera angles we have."

On the screen, exterior lighting shadowed an innocent-enough-looking metal part. "Can you go out and look?"

"Cal's afraid of anyone suiting up and going outside with that cloud coming in like a meteor about to strike." Ethan glanced at the screen again. "But I don't see a choice. We can probably get out there before he finds out and then deal with his temper once we're back on board."

Alexander folded his arms. "This time, I happen to agree with the captain. The cloud has not shown hostility yet, but they are within striking distance for a singular, polarized shot. It wouldn't do enough damage to a shielded ship, but a man in a space suit would be far too easy to use as target practice."

Ethan paled. "I guess that kills that idea."

Alexander pointed at the screen. "All you need is to make sure that the tech is hovering above with magnets and not actually attached, correct?"

"Yeah."

Alexander's hair took flight. He held out his hands as the power of their prince filled him. His skin started to fade.

Alanna reached for him. "What's happening?"

"Don't touch him." Dania swiped her hand away. "Alexander, stop! Remember, you've been recovering."

His eyes met hers before he winked out, as if he'd never been there.

Alanna gasped. "What?" She turned to Dania. "Huh?"

Dania had projected herself from the *Star Renegade* months before, but Alanna had been in another part of the ship at the time. Dania needed to remember that many enforcer abilities were still foreign to her new friends.

She held up her hands. "He's fine."

At least, Dania hoped he was fine. Alexander needed to stop acting like he hadn't been suspended in a vat of liquid keeping him barely alive for weeks.

Ethan pointed at his screen. "Look at that. No spacesuit required."

Outside the ship, Alexander moved in front of the camera, inspecting the sync navigator.

Holding a bubble of air around you to breathe in space wasn't hard. Dania had been nearly out of pathogens the last time she'd tried. Of course, she'd ended up passing out at the time.

Alexander's voice eased into her mind. *'The magnets seem to be working. The apparatus is holding…'* His voice faded into a moan.

She tensed, staring at the screen. "Alexander?"

A suction sound filled the chamber, and Alexander appeared several feet off the ground before falling, slamming to the deck.

"Alexander!" Alanna ran to him, gathering him in her arms as he wheezed, clawing at his throat. "Breathe!" she shouted.

He continued to struggle, hissing like he was still in the vacuum of space. Dania knelt beside him as Alanna pulled him tight to her chest.

"Doc!" Ethan shouted at his communication panel. "We have an emergency. Lower engineering. Alexander can't breathe!"

"Coming!" Peter shouted.

Ethan came back to them. "Tell me what to do!"

That was the problem. Neither of them knew what to do.

Peter ran into the room with a small bag. "Always an adventure with enforcers onboard." He took Alexander from Alanna's arms and eased him to the floor. "What happened?"

"He projected himself into space to look at the hull." Dania held her chest, trying to will her heart to stop beating so fast. "He just popped back inside like this."

Peter shook his head. "What is it with enforcers not adhering to doctor's orders? By now, you should know you aren't invincible."

He listened to Alexander's chest with a stethoscope while Alanna brushed Alexander's hair from his eyes and held his head steady. "Come on," she whispered. "Breathe. You got this."

Alexander opened his eyes, coughed, then took a deep breath.

Peter sat back. "Well, that's convenient. I didn't even do anything yet." He shined a light in Alexander's pupils. "How are you doing there, spaceman?"

Alexander blinked at him, then looked at Alanna. "I got cold. I couldn't breathe."

"Maybe that's because you should be on light duty." Peter held an instrument over Alexander's chest until the lights on it blinked. "That means no space-walking."

Alexander sat up. "Projecting yourself into space is not difficult. I only looked at the hull. I wasn't doing anything strenuous."

Peter rubbed his eyes. "I don't know how to get through to you people. You need to act like humans once in a while so you can recharge." He showed Alexander the device. "Oddly enough, despite the theatrics, your pathogens are building up again. I wish I knew why." He stood. "Let's get you to the med bay so I can do a full scan. Can you walk?"

"I'll help him." Alanna held out her hand to hoist Alexander up.

Dania got on his other side, placing his arm over her shoulder. "Did you say his pathogens are building back up?"

Peter nodded. "Scientifically, this is driving me nuts." He walked to the door and opened it for them. "I'm going to run some scans, but I can't read them until later. I've got something time sensitive to figure out first." He grimaced, staring at Alexander, then walked out.

"What was that about?" Dania asked.

Alanna maneuvered Alexander to the door. "It looked like he had a thought about what might have happened, but he didn't like what that big brain of his came up with."

That didn't sound good.

"I can walk on my own." Alexander released Alanna.

He started to stumble.

"Whoa, there, soldier." Alanna grabbed him. "Let's take some baby steps."

"The doctor told you to stop being so stubborn," Dania reminded him.

"It's just walking. Humans walk everywhere." His brow furrowed when he saw the concern on Dania's face. "I'm fine."

He tried to stand on his own again but had to grab the doorframe.

"You know what?" Alanna said. "I've got him. I think he's trying to act all big and bad in front of his general."

"I am not! I'm fine." Alexander winced. "Oww."

Alanna chuckled. "Yeah, okay, you're fine." She turned to Dania. "Why don't you check on Cal? He's been acting kind of strange since dinner. I really thought he'd be out and walking around the ship by now."

Dania nodded. However, Alexander's need to impress her was far more likely than finding Cal still hiding in his kitchen. Cal had seemed agitated earlier though, which she'd chalked up to having so many enforcers onboard.

She helped get Alexander to the med bay and then headed back to the front of the ship and placed her hand on the access panel to Cal's dining room. The door was still set for automatic entry and slid open.

Cal sat at the table in his usual seat, staring at the

mostly empty plates. It didn't look like he'd cleared anything.

Dania stepped inside. "Are you okay?"

He startled, as if he hadn't heard her enter, before his head hung low again. "Have you ever felt trapped? Like no matter what you do, something terrible will happen?"

A few months ago she would have answered differently, but becoming more human changed things in ways she'd never dreamed possible.

But this seemed more like a rhetorical question, or maybe even a cry for help.

She straightened, her hands clenching as if preparing for battle. Cal had stood behind her, and she should do no less for him. Dania bit her bottom lip, looking around the room. What did humans normally do to help ease another's tension?

There were many things, but one seemed the easiest in this situation.

She moved behind him and rubbed his shoulders. "I think it's normal. There's a battle coming. You're worried about your people."

"They aren't just my people. This is my family."

Dania lowered her hands. She knew that. He loved this crew more than he cared for himself.

But he'd said *they*. Not *you*.

Did he think of her as one of that family, or still as an outsider?

He reached back and grabbed her right hand. "I won't let anything happen to you."

So, he *did* think of her as family? A smile played on her lips but turned to a frown as she stared at their clenched fingers. His touch seemed desperate. Needy.

What did he think might happen to her?

"I'm not getting on that Kever ship, Cal. This is my home now."

He nodded and released her.

Each day, the weight of humanity hung heavier over her head. If she were completely human, would the stress overtake her, like it had Cal? The others seemed to take things better, but maybe that was because they didn't feel responsible for the lives of their crew. Their friends. Their family.

"Tell you what." Dania grabbed a plate. "How about I help you clean up, and then we have a nice cup of tea?" She grabbed another plate and stacked it atop the first. "I believe I saw a jar of actual organic honey last time we cooked together. That's good in tea, right?"

He smiled. "My mom used to say that tea with honey was almost as good as a belly filled with pasta to ease a tired soul."

Well, Cal's soul certainly seemed tired.

Dania matched his smile. "Then I'd love to cuddle up on the couch and sip some tea. You can tell me more about your mother."

He stood, his gaze taking her in like some sort of tether reaching into the vast expanse of space. "That sounds nice."

"Good." She stacked another plate in her hand and headed into the kitchen. If nothing else, she could offer him one calm night before the battle that could very well change everything in their lives, either for good or for bad.

She slipped into the kitchen and rested the plates against her hip. The counters were strewn with cookware, like Cal had used two pots and two bowls for every part of the meal. True, there'd been more people at the table than they were accustomed to, but the extras seemed highly unnecessary.

She placed the plates in the sink and looked over the mess. There was a small amount of broccoli still left in a bowl beside the refrigerator. It was unlike Cal to be that careless with fresh food.

A small bowl of sauce sat beside the cupboard on the other side of the room, the same sauce he'd poured over the chicken. Dania smiled. It still smelled heavenly, even cold.

Grabbing a piece of broccoli, she dipped it into the sauce and popped it in her mouth. The sweetness mixed with the crunch of the vegetable and the flavors burst across her tongue. Alanna was right. Fresh food was so much more satisfying than vegetable pills. This would make a wonderful soup.

Dishes fell to the floor behind her. Cal stood in the doorway, gaping. "What are you doing?" He stared at her, oblivious to the broken plates on the ground at his feet.

She swallowed the rest of the vegetable. "I ate some broccoli. What's wrong?"

His lips moved like he couldn't find the words. "W-Which bowl did you get that from?"

"The broccoli?" She pointed to the bowl beside the refrigerator.

The color returned to his face. He breathed deeply, as if he'd been holding his breath.

She frowned. "Are you okay?"

He laughed. "Now I am. Sorry. I guess it's been a long day."

She supposed it had been for all of them.

She grabbed another piece of broccoli. "Have you ever tried dipping it in the sauce?"

His eyes drew to the bowl behind her. "T-The sauce?"

"Yes, it's delicious."

The color drained from his face again, like the world had just ended, and he'd been forced to watch. He fell to his knees.

"Cal!" She crouched beside him. "What's wrong?"

He covered his face with his hands, doubling over. "I can't do this anymore. I just can't do this anymore!"

"You can't do what anymore?"

He lowered his hands. His eyes were red and glassy. "I'm a horrible person."

What had brought this on? "Don't be ridiculous. Your crew loves you."

He flinched, like the words hurt. "No matter what I try to do, it goes wrong."

"That's not true." Dinner had been tense, but no blood had been spilled. After seating enforcers and known criminals at the same table, he had to realize what an accomplishment that was.

He pulled her into his arms, jostling the plates scattered on the floor. "I never meant to hurt you."

His hold seemed desperate, like his whole world was falling apart. She'd seen humans console each other. This kind of embrace was important, somehow.

She placed her arms around him, and some of his tension abated. Some. Not all.

However, a surprising warmth spread over *her,* as her own trepidations seemed to melt into Cal's embrace—until the sensation whisked away as soon as it had come.

Dania tensed. Was that normal? Or was this the effect

of the shunt Alexander had put inside her, stopping her from experiencing emotional connection?

Cal's breaths came labored as he continued to cling to her. "This is all my fault. I'm so sorry."

Had her eating the sauce from the meal triggered something? And why had he been concerned about which bowl she'd eaten from?

The conversation at dinner flashed through her mind. It had been mostly centered on Dania, and none of it good.

He must have realized what a hindrance her newfound humanity was. How she was less of a leader in her people's eyes, since she no longer held the power of an enforcer.

Yes, being onboard the *Star Renegade* had made her less in the enforcers' eyes, but in reality, she'd become so much more.

"You haven't hurt me, Cal. If anything, you saved me."

He scoffed, releasing her. "I really wish that were true."

Dania stood. This seemed like a recurring argument with him. How was it possible that a man so loved by his friends could have such a low opinion of himself?

She held out her hand to him. "Come on. I was promised tea."

He squinted as he looked up at her. "Tea? Really?"

"Yes." She grabbed his arm and hoisted him to his feet. "But first we need to clean up this mess. I believe you're the one who told me about the importance of a clean kitchen."

He lowered his head and laughed a mirthless laugh.

"Hey." She cupped his cheek, raising his eyes back to hers. "Tomorrow is going to be hard. Let's spend one nice, quiet evening together and forget all about it for a little while. Just you, me, and a nice honey tea."

His features softened. "I really don't deserve you." He drew her into his arms again. "Let's skip the dishes. The recycler will work just as well tomorrow."

His touch seemed tentative, maybe even frightened.

Was he really so worried about the attack tomorrow? And if so, should Dania be more concerned?

Maybe he was the one thinking clearly. She'd been programmed not to worry about her own mortality, but humans seemed to dwell on things like this. Maybe it would be a good idea to push duty aside, just this once, and simply enjoy each other's company.

She tapped him on the back. "Okay, how about that tea?" And maybe, if she got lucky, he would tell her what was really bothering him.

CAL WOKE to a weight on his chest and a slight snore. He blinked, finding Dania asleep on his shoulder with her arm draped over him. They'd never turned out the lights, and the soft illumination from above made her skin glow like an angel. Either that, or his mother's special blend of tea had done its magic once again and given her a restful sleep with wonderful dreams.

He dragged his finger along her forehead, pushing tangled strands of brownish hair from her cheek. Her hair seemed to be darkening every day—more signs of humanity sinking in. Cal's chest clenched. Too bad it hadn't happened sooner. More of the real Dania came out every day, and he'd loved being a part of that more than he'd ever expected.

Her eyes fluttered open. She blinked a few times, looking around. "I guess I fell asleep. I'm sorry."

"No worries. I did too. It was a long day." But he couldn't remember when a bad day had ended as nice as that one had.

He'd managed to push out thoughts of the sauce he'd

left in that bowl beside the sink. He'd thought it had been empty, but apparently not empty enough to ward off a dip of broccoli.

How could he have been so careless?

He took a deep breath, steadying himself. Doc was already working on an antidote. As soon as it was ready, he'd give it to Dania. He wouldn't let those pirates anywhere near her.

The comm pinged from Ty's station on the bridge. "Boss, sorry, we tried to give you guys as much time as we could, but we kinda need you two up here. The enforcers are starting to throw temper tantrums out there."

Dania eased off his chest. "How did he know I was here?"

Cal rubbed his eyes. "They always know."

Doc had probably scanned heartbeats and discovered that Dania had spent the night. This was going to be a little hard to explain.

He stood and tapped the comm. "We're coming."

"Again, boss, I am *so* sorry. I know that you…" He sighed. "You know what I mean."

That Cal rarely spent time with women? Yeah, *that,* Cal definitely knew. And Ty usually liked to ride him about it.

But today there were no quips? No lip? Things must be pretty serious up there.

Dania stood beside him, combing her hair with her fingers. "You have that look on your face like things are bad."

"I think they might be." He walked into the kitchen and grimaced.

He'd forgotten what a mess they'd left. He took the infected bowl of sauce and tossed it into the recycler along with the last of the enforcers' dishes. The rest of it could wait.

He grabbed a few protein sticks, vegetable supplements, and two canisters of water before returning and handing one of each to Dania. "Breakfast is served."

She opened the water and took a drink, then swallowed the supplements before taking a bite of the protein bar.

The room seemed brighter than usual. Cozy. The warmth they'd shared last night, Cal telling stories about his family and Dania sharing how she and Alexander used to drive the royal family nuts, had breathed a new life into these stark walls. It was amazing how company could change the overall mood in the room.

She took another drink and closed the bottle. "I'm ready. Let's go."

She headed for the door, but Cal grabbed her arm.

She spun toward him. "What?"

He pointed over his shoulder. "I have private stairs. The bridge is directly above us."

"Oh, okay." Her cheeks reddened as she followed.

Was she worried about what the crew would think?

"We can go the other way if you want to make it look like you slept somewhere else."

She frowned at him. "Why would I do that?"

A block formed in his throat. "In case, you know, you were embarrassed or anything."

"About sleeping on your couch? Why would that be embarrassing?"

Cal laughed. "I guess it isn't. Never mind." It was refreshing to be with someone not concerned about anyone else knowing their business.

The stairs opened to the upper hallway. Cal placed his

hand on the panel to enter the bridge, taking a slow breath to steady himself.

He stepped inside and took his chair. "What's going on?"

Ty tapped on his panel. "The cloud is twice as dense, and it will be here within a few hours. Kile has his people at the ready." He tapped on the screen in his console. "His poor pilots should be sleeping, but they're probably already in their ships waiting for orders."

Ty glanced over his shoulder, where Dania stood in front of Doc's station looking at the monitor. Her hair stuck out at odd angles rather than her normal soft waves. Cal should have offered her a comb.

A wide smile spread across Ty's face as he leaned toward Cal. "In case we don't live through this, let me just say, *It's-about-time.*"

Cal checked power readings throughout the ship. "Nothing happened."

"Nothing? Yeah, right." He smirked. "Her hairdo says differently."

The door opened and Alanna entered. She looked at Dania and the navigator's cheeks turned pink as she took her chair. She smiled and gave Cal a double thumbs-up.

"Nothing happened," Cal repeated.

Ty snorted a laugh. "I never pictured you as a hair-puller, Cal."

Cal held up his hands. "Stop. Just stop."

"What's wrong?" Dania asked, centering herself behind Ty and Cal.

"Nothing." He looked at Ty and Alanna. "We fell asleep on my couch while drinking tea."

Ty frowned. "Really?" He turned to Dania. "Really?"

Did he seriously just ask the woman who couldn't lie to corroborate Cal's story?

Dania nodded. "It was a long day, and it was nice. The tea was good."

Ty shook his head, spinning back to his console. "Well, that's boring."

Alanna smiled, tapping keys on the comm panel. "I think it's sweet."

"Can we please focus, people?" Cal flipped on the comm. "Ethan, are we good back there? Do you have that alien tech ready to save our asses?"

"All set, boss. Remember, it will only give us about thirty minutes of power for whatever we connect it to, so we need to be sure."

"Understood."

Dania reset her footing, somehow making herself look taller. "Can you patch me into my ship?"

"You got it Tea-Girl." Alanna tapped on her panel. "You are good to go."

"Kile?" Dania said to the image of her ship on the viewscreen.

"Finally!" His voice rang out. "I was beginning to think the captain had talked you out of doing your duty."

Cal glared at the screen. Hadn't this guy ever heard of sleep?

"Well, I'm here now," Dania said. "Can all ships hear me?"

Several pings came through the line.

Dania nodded. "Add names and ship callsigns to those pings so I can reach you directly if needed. Otherwise, I will speak to all ships at once." She took a deep breath. "You are all trained and have completed missions on your own. You are fully capable of fighting without me controlling your every move. Show me the skills I know you have and make our sponsor proud."

Cal wasn't so sure that blasted prince had it in him to be proud of any of them. They were tools to him, not his children. Still, her comment seemed to cool off the heat that had been ricocheting between the ships.

"It looks like that's all of them," Alanna said. "Do you want to send out any preliminary orders?"

Dania shook her head. "Not until I see the threat and observe how my people work on their own." Her lips thinned as she looked out into the stars. "This will be a very unique deployment for all of us."

That was an understatement. Cal was used to running away from danger. The *Star Renegade* was no stranger to being shot at, but they'd never been on the offensive. Their plan was not to escape this time, but to engage directly; and at the moment, they weren't even sure what they were about to engage.

"Any news on that cloud?" Cal asked.

Ty huffed a mirthless laugh. "Other than *it's huge*? No."

Huge was an understatement. There was no telling how many ships were in that mass of churning black space. They really needed help. Hopefully, everyone on Dania's ship ate their fill last night, and the enforcers were all showing as steady blips on whatever tracking system the pirates were using to confirm they had ingested the powder.

Cal closed his eyes as a drumming started behind his temple. This was no time to start with the headaches again. He took a guzzle of his water and a bite of his protein bar before hitting the comm.

"Doc, how are things coming with that assignment I gave you?"

It would be a hell of a lot easier if those enforcers were battling the slavers when this was all over so they could get Dania out of there. Still, she wouldn't be too happy with Cal if Alexander were taken again. Or any of them, for that matter.

"Still working on it," Doc said. "This isn't as easy as it sounds."

Cal had never thought it would be easy. That was why he'd asked the smartest guy he knew.

Best-case scenario, the slavers had seen the enforcers on their tracking equipment and were already on their way. And, hopefully, Dania hadn't eaten enough of that sauce to make a difference and the pirates wouldn't even know she was on board.

With the reinforcements, they would save the colony and then the slavers would start chasing the enforcers down. That would give the *Star Renegade* a chance to escape.

Then Doc would do his magic and all of the sudden the tracking would stop, giving the enforcers a chance to get home to daddy to recharge their batteries—and the slavers would already have done their part to save the colony.

All this would tick off the pirates, but hey, at this point, what was one more group of people chasing them going to hurt? And who was to say that the enforcers wouldn't figure it out on their own?

"Just do your best," Cal said before shutting off the comm to the med bay.

"The cloud is in range," Ty said.

"Still no way to break through the static?" Cal asked.

"There won't be," Dania said. "They will hide their numbers until they're right on top of us."

That didn't sound like fun.

"Your orders, General?" Cal asked.

Dania stared out into the cloud, her brow furrowed. She was supposed to be this amazing military leader, but she looked just as afraid as the rest of them. Maybe the pathogens suppressed fear as well. It would be a hell of a lot easier to command if you weren't afraid of dying.

Alanna adjusted the comm speaker in her ear. "Maybe we should contact them? You know, give them a chance to back off?"

Ty looked over at her. "You actually think that would work?"

"No, but it seems polite."

"I doubt they're going to be polite," Cal said.

"I agree." Dania looked at Alanna. "Will my voice activate the comm?"

Alanna nodded. "Turning on your voice commands now."

Dania took a deep breath. "I want all ships in flight. Let's make a show of force. Remote pilots at the ready."

"Remote pilots?" Cal asked.

Dania nodded. "If the enforcer pilots project themselves into space while flying, we need remote pilots available to take control of their ships. It will double our firepower, if needed."

Cal had seen enforcers float and fight in space once, and he'd hoped he'd never have to see it again. Luckily, this time, their power would be shooting *away* from the *Star Renegade*.

Ships shot out from the Kever cruiser, creating a wall between them and the cloud.

For some reason, he'd only expected sixteen ships, but there were more zooming in and out of the weave pattern they had created than Cal could count.

Still, they looked so small out there with the black menace coming closer. It was like a field of glowing star flies facing down a pulsing, black moon.

Now that the cloud was here, it had to be as plain to the enforcers as it was to him. Even with the extra pilots, they were ridiculously outnumbered. This was a fight that they couldn't win.

CHAPTER 23
DANIA

DANIA'S STOMACH clenched as her hand trembled on the back of Cal's chair. What was wrong with her? She used to look forward to the anticipation of battle. There was nothing like the thrill of charging toward an enemy and relishing in their annihilation.

Back then, she'd had nothing to lose, though, other than the love of her sponsor. Now she had friends. Family. People who she cared about.

Her chest tightened, considering Alexander out in his ship ready to do battle. How many times had she sent him to what could have been his death and not cared? His safety, and that of all her enforcers, had been secondary to their mission.

Not anymore. She wanted to save the colonies, but not at the expense of people under her command. Cal reached over his shoulder and squeezed her fingers. The gesture settled her, but only slightly. She now understood his trepidation in all things, all decisions. Lives hung in the balance, and the lives of the people you lead should never be taken for granted.

She closed her eyes and reached out, hoping Alexander was not too far away.

Warmth spread over her as his mind touched hers. *'Do you have special orders, General?'*

'Yes. Don't die.'

'I believe that's a given. Anything else?'

Eleven enforcer pilots held ranks, with normal Kever-piloted ships behind them. She'd never commanded mundane pilots. It was quite possible those who did not rely on their magical abilities may prove more beneficial than she would normally think, since they would be more reliant on their own skills, and less dependent on her.

'Keep watch over the guard pilots,' she told him. *'They may need your strength.'*

'You are looking to reduce casualties? That's very unlike you.'

'You've been saying that more frequently these days.'

A slight hum tingled under her skin as she awaited his reply.

'Saving the colony is our goal. Everything else is secondary.'

The link broke suddenly, but Alexander's ship banked out of formation and pulled alongside the guard ships. Dania wondered if they would appreciate the help or be insulted. She supposed it didn't matter as long as they had an extra level of protection.

"Something's happening." Alanna leaned closer to her panel. "The cloud is breaking up."

"Prepare for battle!" Dania's hands clenched into fists. She'd rather hover in space, destroying everything in her path, but she knew this battle would be different.

The cloud dissipated, parting like a gentle mist of galactic dust. But Dania knew better. The scattering fog was not composed of micro-particles, but hundreds of ships.

"Here we go!" Ty called.

The *Star Renegade* banked down, swerving over and around the ships, giving Dania the perfect view of the battle. Her people spread out, holding their lines in what would normally have been considered an impenetrable web, but not this time. Not with this many ships attacking them.

Three explosions flared and winked out in the vacuum of space. No, not three explosions. Three ships. Three guard pilots had lost their lives in an instant.

"Switch up!" Dania called. "Spiral for constant movement. Do not allow yourselves to become targets." Why would she even have to tell them that?

She cringed at the sound of her own voice. When she'd sent orders in the past, her commands would shoot into her enforcers' minds with precise images and exact directions. Rudimentary words seemed too simplistic. What if they didn't understand?

The enforcers fired, many breaking formation as she'd intended. But others hesitated.

Alexander's group of non-magical pilots shot through the ranks of slower enforcer ships, annihilating anything in their flight path. But for every one Cartek ship destroyed, two took its place. Sometimes three.

The *Star Renegade* spun up and over an attacking ship, raining laser fire across its bow. Fire burst from the ship's engines before the chill of space snuffed out the light.

"Got him!" Ty said.

Cal's hands flew over the controls on his panel. "Keep it going."

Three more Cartek ships exploded in Alexander's wake. But a fourth got through, and another one of her pilots died.

"Cover the holes in our defense patterns!" Again, these were things she shouldn't have to tell them.

Dania held up her palms, willing her power out to her enforcers. But then she drew her hands back. She had no primordial energy of her own to help defend them. No strength to add to theirs.

Another ship exploded and debris spiraled, hitting another ship. Her breath hitched as the cloud coated over them in a rush.

"Dania!" Kile's voice called over the comm.

Another explosion.

And another.

More lives lost.

'*There are too many of them,*' Alexander's voice remained calm, but she could sense his agitation as his ship rolled, spraying fire and death in his wake.

Dania wiped her eyes. "I want all enforcers out of their ships. Remote pilots, take their controls. There is to be no lull in the attack."

She glanced back to the mundane pilots. '*Except for you, Alexander. Stay with the guards.*'

'*Understood.*'

Thank goodness he didn't object. The last thing she needed was him leaving his ship and losing consciousness, hanging in space for the Carteks to incinerate at will.

One after another, her enforcers winked out of their cockpits and rematerialized in space. Fire shot from their hands, taking on the oncoming ships.

One Cartek ship went down, and then the one behind

it. Shivana attacked with her usual fury, leaving a line of drifting, lifeless ships floating past her from the momentum of the attack.

But they kept coming.

"Coordinate a single blow, right down their center, then another splitting the right flank."

They didn't react. Her enforcers kept plowing ahead, each taking on the ships directly in front of them.

"Can you hear me?" She looked at Alanna. "Can they hear me?"

She nodded. "Comms are sending fine. I think they're just too busy."

Too busy defending themselves, rather than fighting for the greater good.

She turned away from the screen, then looked back. They weren't linked. They were fighting alone.

"Whoa!" Ty twisted the ship around an explosion. "Getting a little hot around here."

"We need more room to fly." Cal wiped his forehead with the back of his hand. "Half of those explosions are impacts."

He was right. Some of those Cartek ships looked like they were hitting other ships on purpose. In some cases disabling their own ships.

Shivana pointed her hands toward the center of the advancing ships and shot. Then Miguel joined her, then another joined from behind them.

Three followed her orders, uniting their power into one decisive stroke. But they were the only three to comply.

Dania grabbed her temples. "I said, *a single blow!*" Dividing strength would not help them against such numbers.

But it was too late. The ships surrounded her people. A spray of fire shot through them from multiple angles. Miguel jolted back from his spatial axis and hung lifeless in space. The bubble still shimmered around him, the only sign that he was still alive.

"Someone get Miguel!" Dania whispered.

"I have him." Alexander's ship fired three rounds, clearing a path around the lifeless enforcer.

Several mundane guard ships surrounded Miguel. One skipper craft shot a cable and dragged him back toward the royal cruiser. A bolt of light hit Shivana. She grabbed her stomach but kept fighting with her free hand.

"This is not going well," Ty said.

No, it wasn't. Dania had no place standing on this bridge. Kile had been wrong. He would have been a better choice to lead them. Without her powers, she was incapable of controlling her people. They were working as small units, not a coordinated force.

They were being slaughtered, and it was her fault.

ONE OF THE ships with an actual pilot inside exploded. Cal slumped in his chair. Were those pilots human, or Kevers not powerful enough to project themselves into space? Not that it mattered. A life was a life, and the Carteks were cutting right through them.

Cal slammed his fist on the console. "Where are they?"

"Who?" Dania asked.

The proverbial cavalry.

Cal had kept his end of the bargain. Those enforcers must have been lit up on whatever tracking hardware the pirates planned on using. That was the only requirement for them to join the fight and tip the odds against the Carteks.

Unless they'd smelled a double cross. There was no way the pirates could know they were working on an antidote, though. Heck, Doc hadn't even figured out if it was possible to turn the things off yet.

A piece of debris hit the ship, and Dania grabbed the back of his chair to steady herself. Her gaze remained fixed on the battle, her jaw set and determined.

He'd never meant for her to touch those tracking devices, but now she may have them inside her, too. If Doc couldn't find a solution, they might spend the rest of her life running from not only the Banes, but from pirates as well.

A blast of energy lit up the area in front of the ship before a body in a white uniform with short, silver-white hair slammed against the viewscreen. Particles of frozen red crystals shimmered, drifting into space.

Dania cried out, covering her mouth, before the body slid off the viewscreen and disappeared.

"I think I'm gonna puke!" Alanna said, but she kept swiping her fingers across her panel.

Dania's hand moved from her mouth to her chest. It was pointless to ask if she'd known that guy. He'd been one of her men.

Cal reached for her. "You okay?"

She drew in a deep breath. "I've seen death before."

Of course she had, but from her pale complexion, this was probably the first time she'd been capable of processing the finality of it. The loss.

Cal wanted to hold her and give her the comfort he hadn't received after his father was murdered. But all he could do was grab her hand. Their eyes met, and he did his best to convey everything in his heart. Hopefully, it would be enough until she had time to grieve.

Taking a deep breath, she broke his gaze and straightened, looking out into the battle. The horror in her eyes melted into a grim, angry resolve. "Close the lines. Pilots, cover your enforcers' backs."

Those enforcers needed a hell of a lot more than a few more people to cover their backs.

Cal turned to Alanna. "Are there no other friendly ships out there?"

"You mean the colonists? They're all still fleeing and giving us a wide berth."

"I can't blame them," Ty said, banking the ship over a swirling, sparking vessel. "I don't want to be here, either."

Ethan came over the comm. "We can't take much more of this. The *Renegade* is a lover, not a fighter."

"Ideas?" Cal said.

"I got one," the engineer said. "It's crazy, but it just might work."

"I'm all for crazy."

Alanna's panel lit up. She stopped hitting buttons. "Ethan, what are you doing?"

"That program I just sent you will triangulate on all the Kevers and their ships."

Alanna frowned. "Yeah, okay, I could have done that myself. What's up?"

"Can you focus a jump on all those targets and pull us all out of here?"

Dania spun, staring at Alanna's comm as if she could see Ethan's face. "Leave the battle? Forsake the colony? Never!"

Cal stood. "He may be right. We can't win this."

She turned back to him, her eyes slicing him like daggers. "But neither can the planetary defenses." Dania pointed out the window. "The Carteks will cut right through them." She took three labored breaths before her shoulders slumped. She knew when she'd been beat, but she was probably too proud to admit it.

"We still have some time," Ethan said over the comm.

"Now that we know what we're up against, we can come up with another plan."

"Ephershia has three synchronous moons," Alanna said. "I can jump us behind them. It won't give us long, but maybe just enough time to figure things out and mount one last offensive."

"If we make the jump, how long before the Carteks catch up to us?" Cal asked.

Alanna held up her hands. "From what I can see of their maneuverability, two or three hours?"

"That's enough to do some repairs," Ty said.

That was a tall order for Cal's navigator, though. "Can you jump that many ships?"

Alanna looked out the viewscreen. "Umm…"

"Focus your energy through the nav panel," Ethan said. "I'll juice it up with the alien tech. It should make your jump ability better than the king himself."

"Are you sure?" Alanna asked.

There was a short hesitation. "Well, no, but does anyone have a better idea?"

No, they certainly didn't.

Cal nodded. "Do it." He hit the comm. "Hang on, people. We're in for a bumpy jump."

Dania watched him sit, but she didn't object.

He wanted to support her and tell her everything was okay. But at the moment, it wasn't okay. She was still relying on powers that she didn't have, and it would kill them all if she let it.

Still, the look of defeat on her face cut a hole into his chest. "I'm sorry I had to take over." Well, not really. He was sorrier that she looked hurt about it.

She touched his shoulder. "I'm okay. It's a good plan. Ty

is right. We need to regroup." She glanced over at Alanna. "I don't want them finding out about what you can do, though. For your safety, we'll pretend I'm the one jumping them."

Alanna nodded. "I'm all for staying under the radar."

Another ship exploded. The bridge rumbled.

"That was too close," Ty said.

Cal leaned back so he could see past Ty. "Alanna, sooner would be better than later."

"On it." The navigator stood, and a lighted dial spun in the air in front of her. A pink glow from the gears shined on her face as her lower lip trembled. "I can do this," she whispered to herself, rolling her shoulders. "I can totally do this."

Dania looked out over the screen. "Attention, Kever ships. You are about to experience a singularity. Do not fight it. Bring down your shielding on my mark."

Shielding. Good call. Kever tech may have bounced Alanna's power right back at the Renegade, for all Cal knew.

Alanna took a deep breath. "Ready." She spun the dial, hovering the gears over her console. "As usual, I love everybody!" She wiped her nose with her free hand. "Three. Two. One."

"Now!" Dania shouted.

The air inside the chamber turned purple. Reality shrunk and twisted before light scorched Cal's eyes. Stars blasted into their sights, and two moons appeared on their right.

"Three minutes!" Ty called.

Cal took a deep breath. If anyone managed to follow through Alanna's jump, they were cooked.

Ship after friendly ship appeared, followed by one enforcer hanging in space, still in an attack pose, like she'd tried to fend off their escape. As she floated, her arms drifted lax to her sides and her head lolled back.

"Shivana," Dania whispered.

"It looks like she's okay," Alanna said. "She's just exhausted." She flopped into her chair. "That makes two of us."

Dania closed her eyes, took a deep breath, and spoke to her people outside the *Renegade*. "The singularity is closed, and you are all safe for the time being."

Ice crystals leaked from two of the ships as their oxygen escaped into space. Several more hung at odd angles with laser marks littering their hulls.

"That's three minutes," Ty said. "It looks like we're clear."

Dania's cheek twitched as she addressed her people again. "We have only a few hours. Regroup, repair, and rest. This is not over. We *will* save this colony." She turned to Alanna. "Sever the voice comm."

Alanna nodded, tapped her panel, then slumped, lying across her station.

Dania ran to her. "Are you okay?"

"Everything is spinning." Alanna held her head. "That was *not* easy. I feel like I just lifted all those ships with my bare hands."

The outer comm pinged, and Kile's face appeared on the screen. "Dania, you skipped space? How?"

Dania returned to the center of the room, where Kile could see her. "We used an interesting piece of technology on the ship." She glanced at Alanna. "But at this point, it seems I've burned through the last of my reserves. We all need to rest."

Cal raised a brow. Those were some pretty exact words. Not really lying, but not telling the truth, either.

On the screen, Kile nodded before the transmission switched off.

"I hate to tell everyone this," Ty said. "But we're on the wrong side of the moons. We're out in clear sight. The Carteks know exactly where we are."

"Wait. What?" Alanna lifted her head from the console and looked into the screens in her console. "Omigosh! What did I do?" She grabbed the sides of her head, tears flooding her eyes. "I'm sorry."

"No worries," Ty said. "Nothing's changed. We still have just over three hours before they get here at their top speed."

"And we can still get between them and the planet?" Dania asked.

Ty nodded. "Yeah, but I'm not sure how the results will be any different than they were a few minutes ago."

Dania straightened, the fire returning to her eyes. "I know how." She opened a comm to the med bay. "Peter, how many pathogen treatments do you have prepared?"

"I have two full treatments. One for you and one for Alex, just in case he changes his mind. I also have the next round brewing and half done. Why?"

The determination in Dania's eyes matched the day Cal had first met her. She didn't like failure, and she'd do anything to fix this.

She nodded, staring into the comm. "I want you to give me all of them."

"What?" It sounded like Doc dropped something down in the med bay.

Heat flooded Cal as he stood. "Dania, no!"

She held up her palm to him and continued to stare at the comm. "Peter, I need you to turn me back into an enforcer."

CAL SHOVED into the med bay in front of Dania. "Tell her this is crazy."

"This is crazy." Doc watched Dania walk in. "We can barely keep you stabilized with a regular treatment. I have no idea what a double hit will do to you."

She lifted her chin. "Neither do I, but I *do know* what will happen if the Carteks get here and I can't connect my soldiers."

"Human generals command troops without any kind of mind control," Cal said. "These enforcers have been doing fine on their own without you the whole time you've been gone."

"Because they have not been in a battle like this. Linked, enforcers are nearly unstoppable. Separate, they can make mistakes."

Cal grabbed her hands. "*This* is a mistake. I don't want to lose you."

"If the Carteks get here, we all lose."

The determination in her voice was enough to stop Cal's next retort.

She was right on far too many levels. But the cost was too great.

Cal tightened his grip on her hands. "This is Alexander's battle. We were only supposed to drop him off and then disappear. We can still do that."

"And leave all those people to die?"

He pointed out the window. "I can't help them. But I *can* help my own crew."

Dania looked down. "I have spent my whole life executing people in the name of the law. So few times have I had the opportunity to protect the innocent from true horrors." She squeezed his hands. "I need to do this."

Cal leaned down and rested his forehead against hers. Somehow, he knew she'd say that. He wasn't sure if trying to stop her was more for her, or for him.

He looked at Doc. "What are her chances of surviving?"

He shrugged. "Fifty percent?"

They both gaped at him.

"You all expect me to have all the answers, but I keep reminding you that I'm the first person to ever treat a living enforcer." He sighed. "The truth is that I have no stinking clue what will happen. But my guess from her previous treatments is that this will stop her heart."

Dania smiled sweetly and jumped onto a gurney. "I trust you."

Doc rubbed his face. "Well, thanks for the vote of confidence, but..."

"But nothing." Dania shifted on the gurney. "That cloud is coming, and millions of people are going to die. If you have a better idea, I'll listen, but this is all I have."

Cal's hands trembled as he moved closer to the gurney. Was that really all she had? He reached for her but lowered his hand. Why couldn't she see what kind of effect losing her would have on this crew…on *him*?

A machine in the back of the med bay beeped three times. The door opened, and Quirky stepped in. She stopped in the middle of the room and looked at each of them. "Umm, hi. Am I interrupting something?"

Dania looked small on that gurney, but she had a power about her that was far stronger than any strength she could obtain from pathogens, either real or synthetic. Cal wished she could see that. "Please reconsider."

"There's nothing to reconsider. If the Carteks get here, and nothing has changed, we'll all die." She reached out and held his hand. "You're all my family. I can't let that happen if I can do something about it."

Quirky stepped between them. "Okay, so, I definitely think I missed something."

Doc grabbed a pair of gloves. "You actually have good timing for once. We need to give Dania a pathogen treatment."

"Already? There's like an armada of nasties out there. Can't it wait?"

"No." Dania lifted her chin. "It definitely can't wait."

The door opened again.

"Hold on!" Alanna limped in, Ethan helping her. She sat next to Dania on the gurney. "Please don't do this. You're my best friend."

"Hey!" Quirky put her hands on her hips. "What am I, meteor dust?"

Doc pulled Rachel back and handed her some gloves before walking to the refrigeration cabinet.

Dania adjusted her weight on the gurney. "I gave up all

my power for freedom and for the love of this ship and her crew. If I can save you all, it will be worth it."

Alanna hugged her. "But what if you don't make it?"

Dania closed her eyes and smiled. "I'll just have to live so we don't have to find out."

Alanna sniffed and nodded, wiping her damp cheeks.

Doc closed the refrigerator and returned, handing Alanna a cup. "Drink this. The electrolytes will give you a boost."

She gulped it down. "Can I help with Dania?"

"Yes, by resting and getting better."

"Come on." Ethan helped Alanna onto the other gurney.

There were far too many people in this room. "Ethan, thanks for bringing Alanna down, but you should probably stay in engineering in case Ty needs you."

He saluted. "On it." He pointed at Alanna. "Get better." Then he pointed at Dania. "Walk out of here alive or I'll be mad at you."

Dania grinned. "I wouldn't want that."

Ethan laughed and slipped through the door.

Quirky rolled an IV bag up to Dania's bed. "It's okay. I got this. Me and Dani are like the treatment team." She leaned toward Alanna and pretended to whisper. "They told me this was chemo, but I know it's something special about her enforcer-ness. I let them think I'm fooled, though. It makes it more fun." She turned to Doc, clapping her hands. "Are we ready?"

Dania reached for Cal. "Will you stay?"

He grabbed her hand, taking the chair beside her bed. "Always."

Doc held up a syringe. "Here we go."

Dania held Cal's gaze as the first syringe passed through the liquid in the bag and traveled down into her arm. There was a defiance in that gaze. A certainty.

Cal wished he felt the same assurance. He squeezed her hand. "I have a few more recipes I'd like to try with you. Some old-world favorites."

She smiled. "Like what?"

Doc prepared the next syringe. He glanced at Cal before inserting the needle into the bag.

"Well," Cal said. "There are a few simple things, like mac and cheese, that I think you'll love. But I also have my mother's lasagna recipe."

Quirky snorted a laugh. "You sure do make a lot of Italian food for a guy with the last name Espinoza."

Cal laughed. "That's my dad's last name. My mom's maiden name was Bertoni. She grew up in Italy before meeting my dad."

Doc's skin blanched when he checked the readings. He mouthed the words *keep her talking*.

"I'd love to learn more about your mother," Dania said. "And I'd really love to learn more recipes."

Cal nodded. "It's a date. I just need to find somewhere with cheese that hasn't expired."

Dania's skin paled. She frowned. "I feel odd."

Doc appeared at her side with a stethoscope. "Define *odd*."

"The room is spinning, and it just got really hot in here."

Quirky put a cloth on Dania's forehead. "Wow, she's burning up." She walked over to the panel on the wall. "Oh, boy."

"I don't like the sound of that," Cal said.

"Umm, Doctor Pete? Remember those red bars you told me about? The ones that are not supposed to go over five hundred?"

Doc blanched, looking up. "Yeah…?"

"Well, they're about to hit six hundred."

Dania's face twisted. Her breathing became erratic. "Cal!"

"I'm here." A ball lodged in his throat, but he choked it down.

"Shit!" Doc cried.

Cal gritted his teeth, clasping Dania's hand as her nearly vacant eyes fixed, like she could tell he was there but couldn't quite see him. "Doc! What do we do?"

Peter stood with his hands at his sides, staring at the floor.

Dania's body started to convulse. The gurney rattled beneath her.

Alanna appeared at the head of the gurney and grabbed the sides of Dania's face. "Come on, girlfriend. You got this. Stay with me!"

"Doc!" Cal shouted.

Peter backed away, holding his head.

"No!" Cal stood, still gripping Dania's hand. "Don't you dare blank out on us, Doc. She needs you."

He blinked, gaping, as his gaze fell on each of them. "I-I don't know what to do."

"Don't give me that shit. Think it through. What's wrong with her?"

Doc blinked, looking at Dania. "There are too many pathogens in her blood. Her body can't handle it."

Dania cried out as her back arched.

Alanna continued to hold her palms on Dania's temples. "Come on, Dania! Fight!"

Cal steadied himself. "Okay, too many pathogens… So how do we get them out?"

Doc pulled at his hair. "I don't know. We have to flush them out of her blood somehow."

A chill settled over Cal's skin. That sounded complicated, but Doc's brilliance had never let him down. "Then do it!"

"I've never done anything like that before. Too much can go wrong."

Quirky pushed past him. "Oh, come on. It's not that hard. We just have to bleed her out first."

Cal and Doc gaped at her.

"Bleed her out?" Cal shook his head. "Are you out of your mind?"

Doc's hands fell to his sides. His lips parted and he looked at the floor, his eyes widening. "Maybe not." He looked up. "Well, not completely bleeding her out, but if we remove enough tainted blood, we can replace it with clean, pathogen-free blood. It would be exactly what I said. A blood flush."

Quirky folded her arms. "Well, yeah. That's what I meant. What did you think, I was gonna drain her dry or something?" She rolled her eyes. "Kill her to save her? What kind of med tech do you think I am?" She rushed to the other side of the room and pulled a square medical device on a rolling cart toward Dania's bed. "Back on Hedonaii, we did this all the time for guests who'd injected lethal amounts of Zolurian hallucinogens into their blood. It works like a charm."

Cal cocked his head. "You've done this before?"

She put her hands on her hips. "Why do you sound so surprised?"

Doc slapped his own cheek, then shook his head like he was trying to clear away a fog. "Okay, it's actually a good idea."

"Do we have everything we need?" Alanna asked.

"Yeah," Quirky said. "We just need someone with Dani's blood type."

Doc groaned. "She's an enforcer. No one has her blood type."

"Maybe not, but a substitute might work." Cal took off his jacket. "I'm O negative. My mom told me that meant I could donate to anyone."

Quirky nodded. "He's right. I mean, Dani's not like a normal person, but it's the safest bet we have."

Doc pulled up a gurney alongside Dania. Cal got onto the mattress and stared at her. This could go bad. Very bad. But he'd do anything for his crew. Anything for *her*.

"I'm ready," he told them.

Alanna stepped away from the gurney, but Dania started to scream again.

Doc held up his palm. "No. Stay with her. For some reason, you seem to be keeping her calm."

Alanna placed her palms back on Dania's temples. "Are you sure I won't get in the way?"

Doc shook his head. "It definitely won't be worse than her squirming in pain."

Quirky ran from one bed to the other, checking a million different things. Doc just kept nodding at her, probably just as impressed as Cal was with her med tech abilities.

Dania grew pale as Doc drew blood from her other arm,

running the fluids into a recycler. He seemed determined. Focused. Which probably meant things were going well.

Alanna crouched at the head of Dania's gurney, whispering as she massaged Dania's temples. For now, it seemed to keep Dania calm.

Rachel adjusted the tubes in Cal's arm. "Okay, Captain O Negative. Here we go." A line of red traveled down a thin string of tubing from Cal's arm to Dania. Doc grimaced on the other side of Dania's bed, but he remained focused on her, checking her temperature and readings on the machines for what seemed like hours.

Rachel looked down at Cal. "You still with me?"

"Yeah."

She nodded. "Impressive. Most guys pass out by now." She looked at Doc. "I'm not sure how much Cally has left to give if we want him to be able to get out of that bed anytime soon." She looked at Dania's machines and clapped her hands. "Hey! I think it's actually working!"

"Was there ever a doubt?" Cal asked.

She shrugged. "Well, you know, things happen."

Cal closed his eyes and laid his head back. The room started to spin.

"You okay?" Quirky asked.

Maybe. Maybe not. It didn't matter as long as Dania made it through.

CHAPTER 26

DANIA

DANIA'S LASHES FLUTTERED OPEN. Bright lights stung her eyes.

"Oh, sorry!" Rachel's voice said, before the lamp over Dania's face turned off. "That should be better."

Dania blinked. "What happened?"

Kile leaned into view. "The doctor tried to kill you. That's what happened."

"Oh, shut up." Rachel slapped his arm. "Will you please get over yourself? He only did what Dani asked him to do."

On the other side of the bed, Cal smiled at Dania as he rubbed her shoulder. "How are you feeling?"

He sat in a chair while everyone else stood. He was pale. Ghostly pale.

A flood of heat swept over her. "You look ill. What happened?"

"They put the smuggler's tainted blood in you," Kile said. "Disgusting."

Rachel slapped him again. "Stop being so melodramatic." She looked down at Dania. "He isn't wrong. Well, he was about the tainted part, but not about the blood part."

Dania rubbed her head. "Would someone please translate Rachel-speak into English?"

"Blood transfusion," Peter said. "The pathogens were too much. We used Cal's blood to flush them out."

"You should not have tried to pollute her blood with your unethical treatments in the first place."

Dania sat up. "Kile, stop."

"Whoa there," Peter said, grabbing Dania's shoulders. "You've been through a lot. You need to take it easy for at least a week."

She tilted her head. "A week? How long until the Carteks get here?"

"A little over an hour," Cal said.

"An hour?" Dania stood. The tubes attached to her arm pulled at the bag beside her bed. "Take this off."

Peter held up his hands. "I looked for ways to speed up your recovery, but there aren't any. Sweetie, you just need to rest."

Had he lost his mind? "I do not need rest!" An immense heat swirled within her, circling in her chest before blasting out.

A flash of light filled the room. All of the beds lifted from the floor several feet and then slammed back to the tiles. A machine somewhere screamed with a solid, annoying tone as everyone gaped.

A slight hum emanated from within her. The tingle was both familiar and completely foreign at the same time.

Kile took a step toward her. "Did you do that?"

Had she? Dania looked at her palms, opening and closing her hands.

She called to the resonance pulsing in the room, and the

energy came back to her, swirling neatly in her chest, warming her from within.

She looked up. "I think maybe I did." She scanned the room and found a small handheld device she'd seen Peter run over a patient. She held out her hand, and the instrument flew across the room into her grasp.

"You did it!" Kile shouted.

Dania turned the device over in her hand. "So it appears."

Peter removed the tubes running to her arm, covering the site with a small bandage.

Cal moved beside her. "Do you feel okay? Are you still *you*?"

There was pain in his eyes. Sadness, fear, and maybe regret. But mostly fear.

She tossed the medical instrument on the bed and placed her palm on his cheek. Her fingers felt so cold on his warm skin. She wanted to draw him closer—to go back to his study and sit close on the couch together. Maybe even fall asleep.

But she was an enforcer again. Her life was no longer hers.

"I'm fine." She forced herself to smile. "You're not trying to get out of mac and cheese, are you?"

Cal laughed, a beautiful sound that warmed the entire room. "Definitely not." He shivered. "After today, I think we could both use a little comfort food."

Dania wasn't sure how sustenance could equal comfort, but she definitely looked forward to another night on his couch.

"As delightfully revolting as this is," Kile said, "I need to remind you there is a fleet of enemy ships coming." He pulled them apart. "I am willing to overlook the doctor's crimes this once, if he somehow managed to fix you." He turned Dania toward him. "Can you link us? Can you make us an army again?"

A valid question. All of this was for naught if she couldn't become the general she once was.

"Can you feel me?" she asked him. "Can you sense my presence?"

He grimaced, shaking his head. "No, I cannot."

"Maybe try something else?" Rachel said. "You made stuff move. Maybe you can still do the linky-thingy even if the Big Guy can't feel you?"

Could it be possible?

Dania closed her eyes and reached out through the ship, past the walls, and into the cold of space. She could sense her people, but no more so than yesterday. Drawing in all the strength she had, she pulled on the tendrils of primordial energy connecting them. Her power drummed within her, not as strong as before, but more than she'd touched in far too long. She drew the energy in, warming the center of her being, before forcing it out.

'Come to me,' she ordered.

The drum continued, lulling in strength.

'Dania?' Alexander's voice came back. *'What's wrong?'*

Only Alexander…the one connection she'd never lost.

'Is anyone acting differently? Do you see any sign our people can hear me?'

Her skin cooled as her friend's attention left her, then returned. *'No. If you tried, I don't think they even noticed.'*

Dania sighed and broke the link.

Kile's face darkened. "Failure."

"We can try again." Dania turned to Peter. "Give me more pathogens."

Peter backed away. "Like hell I will. Look at Cal. Do you want to take a chance at needing more of his blood to save you?"

Dania closed her eyes. She didn't have to see Cal's pale skin again to know that she couldn't ask more of him.

"I kinda gotta side with Doctor Pete on this one," Rachel said. "'Cause back on Hedonaii, this was a last resort. I mean, it all worked out, but what we just did was kinda a big deal. I'm not even sure why you look so good, and Cally looks like he's about to vomit and keel over."

Heat radiated off Kile as he advanced on Dania. "Are you happy with your choices now? Was this pitiful human worth losing millions of lives?"

A ball built in her throat. He was right. Her happiness was not worth so much loss. "I never meant for this to happen."

He walked toward the door. "This is what happens when you forsake your sponsor." The door seemed to close unnaturally hard behind him.

Dania cringed. She wished he was wrong, but he wasn't. Her duty was to protect the innocent from those who would do them harm. Now was her chance to save millions, but she'd failed them.

Cal placed his hand around her waist and pulled her toward him. "We'll figure it out."

No, they wouldn't figure it out.

This was her fault, and all those people on Ephershia were about to die.

QUIRKY PLACED her hands on her hips, glaring at the door Kile had just walked through. "You know, if I didn't love him so much, I wouldn't like him at all. He's kind of a jerk sometimes."

Too bad Rachel's love life wasn't the worst of their problems.

Cal leaned on the edge of a gurney, steadying himself, trying to look strong when he felt like he might fall over. "I hate to say it, but Kile is right." They all stared at him. "Not about Dania. About the Carteks. If we're going to fight, we need to regroup and get ready."

Dania rubbed her face. "I usually control my enforcers with my mind. They're an extension of me. I'm not sure how to do this." Her face reddened. "Seeing them fail like that... Seeing them die..."

"I said once before that human generals command their soldiers without mind links. There's no reason you can't too."

"But humans are more autonomous. Enforcers are not trained to think on their own in battle."

Cal shook his head. The more he learned about enforcers, the more ridiculous the whole Kever culture sounded. Why have an army that implodes if their leader is struck down? It made no sense.

"I think you need to give your people more credit. They've watched you command them for years. Some of your training must have rubbed off on them."

Quirky nodded. "That's true! My guy told me that he became the leader he is today by watching Dani." She shrugged. "He also said that she'd become the biggest disappointment of his life. But hey, the first part was pretty good, and probably as close to a compliment as I've ever heard from him."

Doc gave her a gentle tug back. "I don't think you're really helping, sweetie."

"No, she is helping." Cal stood, grabbing onto the edge of the gurney when the room spun. "If Kile was able to learn, the others will be, too." He turned to Dania. "You just need to give them direction."

"I *was* giving them direction, but most of them didn't listen." She rubbed her face with her palms. "Some may have been insubordinate, but I think most didn't get my orders fast enough."

"I think that's my job," Alanna said. "Ethan's tech is supposed to supercharge us for about thirty minutes. We didn't use it that long. Maybe I can tweak the comm to use the rest of the power to send Dania's messages faster."

Cal gaped. When Ty had first discovered Cartek signals in free space, they figured there must have been some sort of instantaneous transmission technology. Maybe Alanna was onto something. "Why don't you find Ethan and get to work on that?"

"On it." She headed for the door.

Dania dragged her fingers through her hair. "I'll still have to voice the words. That takes seconds. The delay can kill them."

"All we can do is our best."

Quirky rubbed her own shoulders, hugging herself. "Please try, Dani. I don't know if my family got away. For all I know, everyone I care about is still on that planet." She lowered her arms. "I know backing out of that treaty thing was bad, but I'm sure they realize that now. None of us ever dreamed we'd be attacked."

Ty's voice pinged overhead. "Please tell me everyone is awake, rejuvenated, and ready to start their day, because we've got incoming."

Cal hit the comm. "How much time?"

"Maybe twenty, thirty minutes. It looks like Alexander is scrambling the fighter ships out there."

Cal turned to Dania. "Isn't he your healer? Is he the most qualified to be leading the fighter ships?"

"Alexander is one of our strongest. It's true he's coded to look for a peaceful alternative, but if there is none, he's more than capable of taking action."

Cal nodded. Hopefully, Dania's people respected that and didn't have issues about taking commands from a man who was basically a doctor.

"We're on our way," Cal said.

Quirky held up her hand. "I hate to say this, Captain, but you look like you're gonna fall over. Maybe you should go back to bed and let Dani handle this?"

Cal walked to the doors—*both* of the doors. He blinked a few times before the hazy image became a single exit, then walked through.

He really didn't need anyone to tell him he should sleep. That was brutally obvious, even to him, but he'd commanded in worse condition. When this was all over, they'd find a safe place in a friendly outlier colony to hole up and sleep for a few weeks, if needed.

Ty had already put the *Star Renegade* between the colony and the advancing cloud by the time Cal entered the bridge. The enforcer and guard ships were flying in a looser pattern than what they'd tried last time. It might allow for maneuverability, but the real problem was numbers. Back on Earth, ants had been known to take down creatures a hundred times their size just with sheer volume. The black cloud was no longer a cloud, but an uncountable number of ships flying in erratic patterns toward them.

The sad truth was that while Prince Geron's heart may have been in the right place for the first time in his life, he simply had not sent enough enforcers to make a difference.

Dania moved behind him. "Sit. It will give your body some time to recover."

Cal was pretty sure his body needed a little more than sitting.

Ty handed him a bottle of water. "Doc made me promise to keep you hydrated."

Cal took the bottle. "And what happens when I have to pee right in the middle of battle?"

"You're the lucky one with a personal bathroom right downstairs."

Alanna ran through the door and took her seat. "Ethan's making final adjustments, but it looks like we don't have time to test anything." She frowned, looking at her console. "How long has this light been flashing?" She smacked Ty. "Why didn't you tell me this light was flashing?"

"Whoa there, princess. I've been a little too busy over here to watch nav and comms."

Cal leaned back. "What is it?"

She reviewed her screen. "An encrypted message was transmitted and then set to repeat."

"Repeat? Where was it sent from?"

"It looks like lower engineering."

Cal hit the comm. "Ethan, did you send out an encrypted message?"

"I'm working on projecting the comm for Alanna. When would I have time to send a message?"

Alanna rubbed her face. "Cal, the message was sent through space like a laser. I'm not even sure how."

"Do I want to know where it went?"

She paled. "Keveron."

Cal spun to Dania.

"You know it wasn't me," she said.

"Then who?"

She looked down. "Kile did look perturbed."

"Mad enough to turn you in?"

"Yes," Alanna said. "The message gives our exact coordinates. It's addressed to anyone who wants the honor of killing Dania DuBane."

Traitor!

Ty tapped on his controls. "I hate to tell you this, but we've got a bigger problem."

Cal rubbed his face. "Are you serious? Worse than the cloud? Worse than the whole Kever Empire knowing where we are?"

"Maybe." Ty grimaced. "We got incoming, but not from in front of us. It's coming from Ephershia."

"The colonists?" Dania asked.

"I doubt it," Ty said. "They're using stealth tech, and we're being hailed."

The screen blinked, and Chris Columbus appeared, smiling through his scraggly goatee. "Hey, buddy. Looks like you could use a hand."

Cal gasped so hard, he coughed. "Where have you been?"

Chris shrugged. "You know me. I go with the flow."

This, Cal knew. He was just never sure if that flow could be trusted.

"I got a friend of yours here who'd like to chat," Chris said.

His connection winked out and static appeared before Victor's smiling face filled the screen. He looked just as smug as he had when he'd given Cal the tracking devices to put into the enforcers' food. "Well done, Captain Espinoza. Sorry we're late, but we needed to get our nails done for the occasion."

"Not funny. We lost some good pilots back there."

"You lost some *Kevers*. Not a big deal." He looked like he was tapping a panel beneath the screen. "We've analyzed the Cartek flying patterns. We're moving in, adding to the puny little wall you've formed. Let the enforcers know we're friendly so they don't pick fights with the wrong side." The comm winked out.

"Pirates?" Dania asked.

"This is a story I gotta hear," Ty said. "Afterward, though. Right now, it looks like things are about to get messy."

That was probably true, and maybe good. He had no idea how to explain why the pirates were suddenly willing to help.

Cal glanced back to Dania. "Tell Alexander and the others not to engage the pirates." Maybe, if they got lucky, this would all be done before the Kevers found them.

"This would be much easier if I could force them to comply." Dania looked at Alanna. "Are we ready?"

The navigator nodded.

Dania turned to the viewscreen. "This is Dania. As difficult as this will be, you will stand down on all previous directives concerning the pirate ships. The pirates are fighting alongside us. Do not engage."

There was an odd taint to her words that hinted at the word 'yet,' which was probably the most he could hope for. All the people on those ships were criminals, and the enforcers were bound to uphold the law, but their first order was to save the colony. If they were successful, all hell would break loose, and the enforcers would probably snap and turn on everyone—including the *Star Renegade*. By then, Cal planned on flying dark and being halfway to a secluded planet.

Alexander's voice came over the comm. "Many of these are slaver ships."

Cal tensed. He'd hoped the enforcers would be too busy to notice just how hardened the felons fighting alongside them were.

He checked the comm tracking on Victor's transmission and traced it back to a heavily fortified skipper craft...one scratched and pock-marked to make it look like it had seen heavy battle.

Sweat touched his brow. It was one of the ships

Alexander had called up when he'd been tracking down the pirates who'd kidnapped him on Opanus. Victor had mentioned that they'd captured Alexander, but Cal hadn't realized he was one of the actual men involved.

Dania leaned closer. "When were you able to contact these criminals, and why would they help?"

Cal swiped the data closed and checked the forward shields. "I'd like to think some of them have family down there, and maybe some are here out of the goodness of their hearts."

"But that isn't true." Dania looked out to the new ships taking places among their own.

"No," Cal admitted. "They're in it for profit."

"Mercenaries." Dania grimaced.

"Does it really matter?" Ty said. "Because our chances just got a whole lot better."

The screen flickered, and Alexander appeared from within the cockpit of his fighter. "My general will not force you to answer, so I'm asking directly, Mr. Espinoza. Why are they here? What did you offer them in return?"

Cal gripped the edge of his chair. "Can we not get into this right now?"

Ty and Alanna glanced at each other. Ty paused before returning his attention to the screen.

The enforcer's eyes darkened. "I recognize several of those ships, Mr. Espinoza."

Cal closed his eyes. He'd dropped the title 'Captain,' just like Kile did when he wanted to belittle Cal.

Alexander's expression darkened. "At least three of them were involved with...with Opanus."

He hesitated on the last part of the sentence, and with

good reason. Victor and his friends had encased Alexander in an oversized fish tank, sold him, and hung him on a wall like a hunting trophy. Alexander had every right to be pissed.

The enforcer's gaze remained fixed on Cal. "You've betrayed us, haven't you?"

Alanna walked into the sights of the viewscreen. "Cal wouldn't do that."

Alexander stared at her for a moment. "I seriously hope you're right."

The comm winked out.

"He'll follow orders," Dania said. "The good of the colony is still his first concern."

Maybe, but the guy sure wasn't happy about it.

"Here we go!" Ty called.

The Cartek cloud split apart, raining fire on the wall of ships. The pirates attacked with abandon, weaving in and out. The enforcer ships gave the mercenaries the first run and then moved forward, taking out any enemy crafts that got through. The alien ships lit up, then disappeared—or floated dead in space.

"Squad two, move below the wall. Make sure they don't try to slip by," Dania said.

Three enforcer ships dropped out of formation and out of the viewscreen's sights.

A blast lit up the room, and the *Renegade* shook.

"It's okay," Ty said. "She's a tough little bird."

"Something is wrong." Alanna's fingers glided over her console. "We're being tapped."

"A data breach? Are they after your communications?" Cal asked.

"No," she said. "Memory feeds."

Cal cursed under his breath. "The Carteks?"

Alanna shook her head. "It looks like the pirates. Two of them scanned the enforcer ships, pinged their command ship, and now they're scanning us."

"Block it!"

"You don't have to tell me that, but they keep getting a step ahead of me." She frowned. "I-I secured our main computer, but they didn't go after that."

"What *did* they go after?"

She glanced at him. "The med bay."

"Why would they want medical records?" Ty asked.

It wasn't medical records they wanted. It was Doc's research. Depending on how well Doc had encrypted his files, they may have just gotten a whole lot of data that Cal didn't want anywhere near Victor's eyes.

"They just cut off the connection," Alanna said. "I guess they got what they wanted."

Cal pinged the med bay comm as Ty banked the ship down, avoiding a Cartek fighter.

"Doc, you may have just gotten hacked."

"I see it." He cursed under his breath. "My security bounced them away from all the pathogen experimentation and information about Dania and Alexander. But—" The sound of tapping keys carried over the line before he cursed again. "Cal, they know what I've been working on for the past few days."

Cal's head lolled back. That meant they knew Cal planned on screwing them.

Alanna held her finger to her ear. "Hey, umm, this is weird. The Carteks are scanning the pirates now. They're slicing right through their tech." Her eyes widened. "It looks like they're downloading entire ship systems."

"What?" Cal said.

"They must have anticipated such an offensive," Dania said.

"Cal?" Alanna turned to him. "Now they're talking. The pirates and the Carteks."

"Please tell me they're threatening each other."

"Doesn't look like it."

They were sharing notes. That couldn't be good.

Dania leaned down to him. "Your temperature and heart rate are spiking. What's going on?"

There was no use trying to deny it. Things were probably about to get really ugly.

"Both the Carteks and the pirates tried to cut a deal with me. I was going to screw them both. If they're talking, they're about to figure it all out."

Ty swerved around another ship. "Not cool, Cal. You should have warned us."

This, he knew. Now more than ever.

His private comm went off. He hadn't seen that code in years: Chris Columbus's encrypted tag. Cal tapped *receive*.

The ships outside banked up, turned, and came straight for them. Not just the Carteks, but the pirates, too.

"Are they *all* mounting an offensive against us?" Dania asked.

"That's certainly what it looks like," Ty said.

And now their odds just got a million times worse.

Alexander's voice came over the comm. "Dania, what are your orders?" A ship exploded somewhere near him.

Dania stared out into the frenzy outside. "There are too many."

"Your orders?" Alexander repeated.

She stared out the viewscreen. The light of an exploding ship ignited in her eyes.

There was nothing left to do, and they all knew it.

Cal hit the comm. "Retreat!"

CHAPTER 28
DANIA

DANIA WISHED there were another answer, but there wasn't. She approved the retreat. The enforcer and guard ships arced away from the combat, throttling toward Dania's former cruiser. They were retreating, as ordered, but they'd been directed to protect the colony. Chances were, they wouldn't comply with the retreat for long.

"Alanna, can you get us out of here?" Cal asked.

"I can try, but—"

"But what?"

Sweat glistened beneath her eyes. Her skin seemed a shade paler than normal. "I don't know why, but I'm not feeling great." She wiped her face with her sleeve. "I think maybe jumping everyone last time was too much for me." She pointed to the screen. "Anyway, right now, there's no clear path."

She was probably right. It would be like trying to jump in an asteroid field.

Alanna's breaths seemed shallow. She held on to the edge of her station like she might fall over.

"Are you okay on the nav and comm?"

She nodded. "Yeah. I got this. No worries."

But Cal always worried, and this time, he'd been right. A few moments ago, they'd had a small chance, but now they were fighting two armies.

Dania pulled at her hair. She didn't want to sacrifice her people, or the *Star Renegade*, but there were still thousands of civilians on that planet.

She touched Cal's shoulder. "We can't abandon the colony."

"I don't want to but dying here won't save them. I gotta hope that those pirates have some sort of honor and do the right thing once we're gone."

Dania rubbed her eyes. That was unlikely, but Cal was right. Their chances were slim fighting the Carteks, but they were close to nil fighting the pirates as well if she could not link her enforcers into a battle unit. Without her, they were no more effective than a well-fortified human squadron.

A blast of lasers lit up the viewscreen. The ship rumbled.

"Are we okay?" Cal asked.

"Yes." Ty adjusted the instruments on his panel. "But we're already banged up. We're not going to be okay for much longer."

Another jolt hit them. The lights winked out, then came back on as Dania stumbled to the floor, catching herself just before slamming her head into the deck. She tried to call up her strength, draw on the hum she'd felt in the med bay, but the resonance no longer flowed through her. Was it gone already?

Ethan's voice came over the comm. "We can't take much more of this!"

Dania pulled herself back up. Just a few months ago, she would have been able to throw a shield around this ship. She would have laughed at this attack and then annihilated their enemies. How could there be nothing left in her? How could everything simply be gone?

In space, a single enforcer had left their ship and hung among the stars. Alexander's long, silver hair drifted about him as bolts of swirling energy shot from his fists. Behind him, the friendly ships raced for the protection of the cruiser.

Dania gulped. Last time he'd floated in space, he'd passed out.

"Alexander," Dania whispered. "What are you doing?"

The answer was simple. He was protecting the mundane pilots, as he'd been instructed to do, no matter the risk to himself.

An ear-shattering tone blasted through the hull. Dania covered her ears in a vain attempt to stop the pain.

Around the deck, Cal, Ty, and Alanna did the same until the tone stopped.

"What was that?" Ty asked.

Cal blinked, shaking his head as if trying to clear the last remnants of the sound. "Did that come from outside?"

"From space?" Ty rubbed his temples like his ears still rung. "That's impossible. There's no air out there to carry sound."

Dania shivered like space had reached into the ship and chilled her. It wasn't impossible. Not where she came from, at least.

The stars before them rippled, and a massive cruiser appeared. Several smaller pirate ships exploded up against the ship's enormous hull, unable to escape in time.

"What the hell?" Ty tried to swerve and ended up flying alongside the behemoth.

"Royal insignias," Alanna announced, but that ship needed no introduction.

"It's the high prince," Dania said.

"As in the future king?" Ty asked.

Another, slightly smaller, ship appeared, then another, boxing them in.

"We're in trouble!" Ty called, swerving the ship again.

Alexander appeared in front of them, hanging in the space between the *Star Renegade* and the largest cruiser.

"What's he doing?" Alanna asked.

"Protecting me," Dania said. "It's in his coding. He has no choice."

Alanna stood, turning to Dania. "But last time he was outside, he couldn't breathe."

This, Dania knew all too well.

Kile walked onto the deck. His eyes widened on Alexander through the screen. "Fool!"

Cal stood to face Kile, but the enforcer disappeared, reappearing outside to grab Alexander. A second later, they reappeared on the floor beside Dania.

Alexander coughed, wrestling with his commander.

"Getting a little crowded in here!" Ty said.

Dania started to kneel beside Alexander, but her friend pushed Kile off and stood.

"They're going to execute Dania." Alexander's breaths were labored. His brow furrowed slightly.

Alanna had been right. Alexander shouldn't have been out there. Whether he wanted to admit it or not, he was starting to feel the drain of his distance from their sponsor.

Kile got to his feet. "She's committed a crime against the crown. Of course, they want to execute her."

Alexander's gaze grew even colder. "You brought them here."

"I did."

Dania cringed.

So, it was true. She'd hoped spending time on the *Star Renegade* had softened Kile, but his programming still held. The law was the law, and laws could not be broken. She'd betrayed her sponsor, maybe the worst crime an enforcer could commit. This crime was not something she could hide from. Be it now, or weeks from now, they would find her, and she would pay for what she'd done.

Alanna tapped on her console. "There's a ping coming in from that really big ship."

Cal gripped his armrests. "Block it."

"I'm trying. It's like it's alive. It's working around our systems."

"You cannot disregard a communication from the high prince," Kile said.

"Why not?" Ty angled the ship around a smaller craft. "He's not the king."

"He might not be king," Alanna said. "But I don't think he cares. The communication is breaking through now."

Kile said something under his breath, then grabbed Alexander's arm. "Tap into your power."

"Why?"

"Just do it."

Alexander's hair began to drift about him. His gaze flicked to Dania, more unsure than she'd ever seen him.

Kile turned to Dania. "I'm sorry."

Before she could question why, his hand shot toward

her, grabbing her by the neck. Her throat constricted, her breath leaving her.

"Hey!" Cal shot from his chair.

Kile glanced at him, and Cal jolted like the air around him had solidified. He lifted from the ground and drifted to the right of the room, where Doc's and Ethan's empty stations were.

"Get off me!" Cal shouted at Kile.

Dania's commander barely glanced at him. "You'll thank me later."

Dania doubted that was true.

The screen wavered into a picture of a male enforcer, sporting the shimmering white uniform and long hair floating about his head as if the strands were alive. Levin… the high prince's general. That ship was second in power only to the king's. There was no escaping this, for any of them.

Kile lowered his head slightly. "General."

Levin's long, silver hair swayed as his gaze lanced Dania and held. She'd stood by this man's side once, each protecting their prince during a visit to their father. At the time, he'd treated her like an equal, which she was. Or at least she had been.

He broke her gaze and looked at Kile. "I see you have her under control."

Kile shook Dania. "Completely."

She whimpered. It wasn't a lie. She couldn't move. Kile could snap her neck if he wanted to. She'd known they'd catch up with her one day. She'd just never expected to die at the hands of her own commander.

THE GENERAL ON the screen nodded. "You can keep her secure?"

Kile's lips thinned. He raised her off the floor, holding her by the back of the neck. Dania didn't even struggle, but tears streamed down her cheeks.

Heat flushed through Cal. Kile had lived on this ship. Shared meals with them. And now this?

Cal struggled against the air holding him. The enforcer wasn't keeping anybody secure. Cal wasn't letting anyone on his ship be captured.

Ty held up his palm and mouthed, *'Calm down.'*

Calm down? How could he be calm when this guy had Dania completely at his mercy?

Levin's gaze carried over Dania. He didn't even seem to look at her eyes. It was more like a butcher eyeing up a piece of meat.

A smug smile spread across the general's face. "Excellent. After we deal with this minor illegal skirmish, the high prince has directed us to the planet. The humans have asked to reinstate their treaty with our king."

"A wise choice," Kile said.

Levin nodded. "Yes. It's amusing how humans change their minds once threatened. Prepare to rejoin the fleet."

Kile seemed to stiffen. "I will have to…" He glanced at Cal. "I will have to secure the remainder of this ship first. Alexander and I have control of the bridge, but there are a few other highly adept members of this crew to deal with."

Wait. A lie?

Well, maybe not. Two enforcers were more than enough to take control, and Cal and Dania couldn't move. At the moment, Doc and Ethan were Cal's ace in the hole. Heck, even Quirky might be resourceful enough to help. Hopefully, they knew what was going on and had figured a way out of this mess.

A beam of light flowed across the ship.

"They scanned us," Alanna whispered. "Standard heartbeat search."

They were looking for the rest of the crew. They'd better not be planning on boarding and taking them out. Not that Cal could do anything about it at the moment.

Levin's nose flared, his eyes looking down like he was reviewing the readings before returning his attention to Kile. "Very well. Secure the ship and return to your duty." He looked like he was grinding his teeth. "I find the lack of cohesiveness in Geron's guard inconvenient."

Kile lowered his head. "As do I, General."

The screen winked out, and Cal could move again.

Kile released Dania. Her feet hit the floor, and she took a deep breath.

Cal ran to her, cupping her face with his hands. "Are you all right?"

She nodded.

"I'm sorry," Kile whispered.

"*Sorry?*" Cal raged. "You nearly killed her."

Dania touched his arm. "He didn't, Cal. I think he may have saved me."

"What?"

She grasped his hands. "The high prince would grant me no mercy, Cal. I'm nothing to him."

Alanna's fingers tapped across her console as she typed, calling up several screens. "Cal, that big enforcer ship just spit out a bunch of little ones. Most are chasing the pirates, but a few are heading straight for us."

Lovely. Cal turned to Kile. "Can that enforcer tell that you just let Dania go?"

The commander shrugged. "I don't know." He looked out the window. "But that is far more ships than would be required for an escort if he didn't consider this ship a threat."

Cal returned to his command chair and opened a secure comm. "Chris, if you can hear me, get out of there. Those enforcers are going to obliterate everything in their path. No prisoners."

One of the ships spun, lit up, and then darted to the right.

"Give him cover," Cal said.

Ty frowned. "Are you serious? After all he's done to us?"

"Consider this payback for the one or two *nice things* he's done."

Ty tapped on his console and a spray of firepower throttled over the bow of one of the ships chasing Chris. The attacking craft spun and then headed for the *Star Renegade* as Chris Columbus disappeared into the stars.

"Good luck, buddy," Cal whispered.

"Is anyone else worried about the ships headed for us?" Ty asked. "Because I'm pretty sure after helping a known pirate escape, they've figured out the *Star Renegade* is no longer secure."

Lasers shot out of the massive royal cruiser, destroying three pirate skipper crafts. Cal grimaced, a small part of him hoping that Victor was inside one of them, but he had a bad feeling he hadn't seen the last of the slaver.

Cal tapped Ty on the shoulder. "Keep us alive."

"You make it hard sometimes."

Cal sprayed laser fire out toward the attacking ships as Ty rolled the *Star Renegade* out of the Kevers' range.

Five more ships turned and headed straight for the *Star Renegade* as two more large Kever cruisers shimmered into existence, blocking the last of their escape routes.

"Excellent," Kile said.

Cal looked back at him. "Are you out of your mind?"

"On the contrary. I am the only one thinking clearly." He pointed through the viewscreen. "If my calculations are correct, the Carteks..."

"They're leaving!" Alanna shouted. "The Carteks are scattering like comet flies in an asteroid field!"

Dania massaged her neck. "They're running."

Kile nodded. "They never expected to face the true might of the Banes. They have never shown themselves to be anything but cowards."

Another pirate ship exploded. Three of the Kever cruisers started firing on the last remnants of the cloud.

"That's why you called them," Dania said to Kile.

Explosions outside lit up the commander's face. "Without intervention, our mission would have failed. I, for one, would rather die than return to my sponsor in defeat."

Cal stood, filling the last bit of space in the room. "Well, next time you'd rather die, do it without putting Dania, or anyone else on my crew in danger."

"I did what I needed to do to save that planet as well as our enforcers."

Ty shot the forward turrets, and one of the attacking ships started venting crystals into space. That would buy them at least a few minutes.

Cal glared at Kile. "If you couldn't find a solution that didn't involve selling us out, then you didn't try hard enough."

Kile's hair started to drift. "You think I sold you out? You think I turned in my own general?"

"That's exactly what you did."

The ship rumbled as Ty banked them down.

Kile's face reddened. "What did you offer the pirates, Mr. Espinoza? What made them so interested in fighting alongside their king—alongside the enforcers of the very laws they spend their entire existences challenging?"

Cal's stomach twisted. He couldn't argue with that. He had to admit, Big Bad was no worse than Cal.

The ship jolted. Cal nearly fell back into his chair. "Ty?"

"Sorry to bother everyone's pissing match, but I'm trying not to get us killed over here." He spun the ship down.

He was right. Cal sat and looked over his shoulder at Kile. "We need to table this. Let's get out alive first."

Kile looked out at the cruisers bearing down on them. "Agreed."

"Can you help us?" Cal asked.

Kile frowned at him. "Against the high prince's enforcers? Are you insane?"

"He couldn't even if he wanted to," Dania said. "It would be like raising a weapon to the king."

Cal turned to Alanna. "Are you feeling up to a jump yet?"

She frowned at her screen. "I don't think I have a choice. I don't think I can jump far, but I can get us somewhere safer. I'm looking for a clear avenue."

"If you see one, take it."

The colors of Alanna's screen flashed in her eyes. "Where do you want to go?"

"Somewhere that's not here. Any direction you can take us, just make the jump."

Alanna tapped the comm. "Everyone hold on to something."

Doc pinged back. "Do *not* jump."

"I'm fine," Alanna said.

"Don't jump!" he reiterated.

Alanna's lips parted. She looked at Cal, but he had no idea what was wrong, either.

The doors split open. Doc pushed inside, squeezing between Kile and Alexander. "Don't jump!"

The ship rumbled. Cal fired a spray of blind artillery from the lower turrets, hoping they'd get lucky and hit something.

Cal called over his shoulder. "Doc, we need to get out of here. What's the problem?"

"If we jump, the pirates will be right behind us."

The trackers! Dammit! He was right.

"Heads up!" Ty ducked reflexively as a ship exploded, sending debris cascading over their viewscreen.

A spray of sparks shot from the panel over Alanna's head.

"You okay, princess?" Ty asked.

"Yeah, but I'd prefer *not* getting my hair singed off."

Doc opened a container and handed one vial to Alexander, and another to Kile. "I need you to drink this."

Kile handed it back to him. "I'm not drinking anything from you."

Doc rubbed his face. "You both have tracking devices inside you. If we jump, the pirates will follow and attack. We'll only be marginally better off than we are now."

Kile snarled at him. "I am an enforcer. No one can track me."

Doc ran a scanner over him. It started to beep over the commander's midriff.

He showed the enforcer the device. "Well, guess what, sweetheart? They can track you from pretty much anywhere in the galaxy. And believe it or not, we don't want you dead."

The deck rumbled. A tone sounded and the lights dimmed before brightening again.

Ethan's voice came over the comm. "We're okay! I'm keeping ahead of it, but it would be helpful if we stopped getting hit!"

Another spray of sparks shot over Alanna's head. "He's not kidding!"

Cal stood. They needed to get out of there, but Doc was right. They couldn't jump to safety if they could be tracked. It was time to own up to what he'd done.

He turned to Kile. "It's true. There are trackers in all your people."

Dania inched closer. "Cal?" Her voice sounded small, and he hated that he was the cause of that.

"It was the only way the pirates would agree to help. And while I'm admitting to being the biggest ass in the universe, I might as well tell you that the Carteks are still threatening to implode the *Star Renegade* if I don't hand them all of your enforcers on a titanium platter."

Kile's eyes narrowed. "And you were angry at *me* for selling Dania out, when I had no intention of giving her up in the first place?"

Cal held up his hands. "I had no intention of giving you up, either. That's why Doc made an antidote."

"Which I just finished." Doc pointed at the vials. "And I'd really appreciate it if you both drank that so we can get out of this war zone."

Alanna screamed. Fire shot out of the panel beside her.

Alexander held up his hand, but she'd already stripped off her jacket and covered the flames.

"That one hurt." She rubbed the top of her head, returning to her seat.

Kile's face reddened as he stared Doc down. He looked at the vial and then to Alexander. A question hung in his eyes. Or maybe defiance. Probably both.

"Are you sure it's safe?" Alexander asked Doc.

Doc's expression softened. "I need you to trust me."

Alanna smothered another small fire with her coat. "Please, Alexander. You have to know by now that we wouldn't intentionally hurt you."

Alexander glanced at her and nodded before he tossed back the vial like a vodka shot.

Doc held up a scanner. It started to beep, just like it had with Kile. "Come on. Come on. Come on. Come on. Come on!" The beeping stopped and he threw his fist in the air. "Yes! It worked!" He faced Kile and pointed at Alexander. "See? He drank the antidote, and he's not dead."

Alexander took the medical device and scanned himself. "I'm fine, Commander. And there is no sign of a tracking device, either."

Another explosion lit up the bridge before space obliterated the flames. The ship rattled, and Doc, Dania, and the two enforcers stumbled. They needed to get out of there before the *Star Renegade* suffered the same fate.

Ty banked around the wreckage. "Hurry up, people!"

Kile's nostrils flared. "Very well." He drank the vial.

Dania inched closer. "Do I need to take that, too?"

Cal sighed. "I didn't want to infect you, but it was in the sauce."

She frowned. "The sauce I ate after everyone had left?"

Doc scanned her. "You must have gotten lucky. I'm not reading anything, but let's treat you, just to stay on the safe side." He opened the package and handed her a vial. "Luckily, I brought extra in case Big Bad threw one at me."

Dania glared at Cal before drinking down the serum.

Her expression was far too reminiscent of the woman they'd dragged onto the ship in handcuffs so many months ago. He didn't want to go backward with her. They'd come so far.

Cal's eyes started to burn. "Dania, I'm sorry. I never would have done that to you intentionally."

Her eyes flashed. "But you could do that to my friends? To Alexander?"

Ty called over his shoulder. "How about I promise to hold Cal down so you can beat him up later, and right now we concentrate on getting out of here?"

"Agreed." Cal took his seat. "Alanna, if you see an opening, take it."

"On it!" Coordinates flashed across her screen, lighting up her face.

Dania looked out into the battle. "Can you save my people?"

"They won't be harmed," Kile said. "They will be taken back to Geron."

She turned to him. "But the tracking devices were in the food."

"They're too scattered," Alanna said. "We're just not close enough."

Kile was right. Dania's enforcers were the prince's problem now.

"Leave them. Get us out of here." Hell, they already hated Cal for selling them out. They could hate him for this order, too.

"Okay." Alanna stood, and the blue gears appeared at the ends of her fingertips.

"What is that?" Kile asked.

Alanna grimaced. "Oh, shoot. Would you please pretend you didn't see any of this?" She pressed her fingers in the center of the gears, and a soft, purple haze fell over the room. Alexander and Kile both stumbled, while Dania grabbed the back of Cal's chair before they burst back into space.

"Where are we?" Cal asked.

A blast hit the ship. The walls rumbled.

"What the hell?" Cal said.

"Shoot. Shoot. Shoot!" Alanna tapped on her panel, holding her head with one hand. "We're only on the outskirts of the battle."

"Can you jump again?" He turned to her.

A clang reverberated through the hull, and a hunk of metal flew past them.

Alanna's eyes were red and teary when she met his gaze. She held her chair with one hand and rubbed her forehead with the other. "I'm sorry. I-I think I'm sick."

Alexander moved toward her. "What's wrong?"

"I don't know. My head is swimming."

"Dammit!" Ty spun the ship. "They're coming after us again!"

Alexander placed his hands on Alanna's temples. "I can try to keep you strong." He leaned closer to her. "Can you try again?"

"No way," Cal said. "Take her to the med bay."

Alanna spun back to her console, still holding her head. "You need me."

"You can barely sit up."

The ship jolted again, and the deck rumbled beneath their feet.

"I can't jump, but I can navigate." She tapped the comm. "Ethan?"

"Yes, my love?" he answered.

Alanna rolled her eyes, then blinked like she was having trouble focusing. "Reroute the alien tech from the comm to propulsion. Sync to my station."

"Not liking that idea," Ty said.

"Only the tech. You'll still be in control until I take over."

"What are you thinking?" Cal asked.

"I'm going to jump with the tech."

A low growl eddied up from Kile's throat, but he didn't

question what they were planning to do. They'd all probably get an earful about this later.

If they lived.

Cal tapped the comm. "Ethan, will it work that way?"

"It's worked on everything else I've attached it to." Something clicked on the other end. "All right, beautiful. Give it all you got."

Alanna took a deep breath. "Here we go." She waved her hand above her console and the gears appeared.

Alexander held her shoulders. "I'm here. I'll keep you steady."

Her eyes grew heavy as she placed her fingers in the center of the gears. Cal hated asking her to do this, but she was right. Alanna, as usual, was their only way out.

The ship hummed as the stars before them turned to long lines of light.

They hung, weightless. The lights blinked, lowered, and raised again.

Cal's head spun. Pressure built, and pain lanced his skull, pounding in a slow drum as if his heartbeat had slowed.

The ship jimmied, a low rattle shaking his seat. The air about him thickened, and he struggled to get in a breath before the lines of light sucked back in, becoming pinprick stars again before the ship jolted to a stop as if it had hit something.

"Clear!" Ty called. "Three minutes!"

Doc cursed behind Cal.

Dania moaned. Cal was aware of her falling and tried to reach out, but she seemed to slip through his fingers in a hazy, blurred, slow-motion until she hit the floor beside Ty.

"Whoa!" Ty leapt from his seat and leaned over her.

"Breathe," Alexander whispered, somewhere off to Cal's right…probably still with Alanna.

The light of each star in the viewscreen reached across space, lancing Cal's pupils. Pain exploded from his eye sockets as the drumming throb in his temples deepened.

"Cal?" Ty's voice raked through his skull, severing the last bit of hold he had on reality.

The ship may have made it, but Cal had left part of himself back in the star fight. He fell from his chair, retching.

DANIA FOLDED HER ARMS, staring down at Cal. The lights of the med bay left a slightly green sheen on his skin, although it was entirely possible that color was real.

On the opposite wall, Alexander sat beside Alanna, holding her hand. The woman had also passed out shortly after they'd returned to regular space. Rachel put an extra pillow under Alanna's head, whispering to Alexander that she just needed to rest.

Kile entered the med bay and stood by Dania's side.

He grimaced, glaring at Cal. "He betrayed us, yet you still stand over his bed."

Dania closed her eyes. If Cal were anyone else, she would have executed him in his sleep for his crimes and been on her way. At least, a year ago that was what she would have done. "I'd like to give him a chance to explain."

Peter adjusted a drip going into Cal's arm and glanced at Kile. "It's not like he *wanted* to put those trackers in you any more than you wanted to bring that angry prince down on top of Dania." He ran a scanner over Cal's forehead.

Kile's nostrils flared. "I told you I had no intention of allowing anyone to harm Dania."

Peter pointed his light pen at Kile. "But you knew it was a possibility your plan might backfire."

"Of course. But to save the colony, it was an acceptable risk."

"Exactly." Peter slipped his light pen into his pocket. "The first thing Cal did when he got back to the ship was give me a sample of the tracking devices. I was working on an antidote before any of you had even been infected." He shrugged. "Was it a good plan? Maybe not, but he had no time to come up with anything else. He did what he could to save the colonists *and* keep all of your sorry asses out of Palian steel handcuffs." Peter walked to the far side of the room and started packing vials into a small metal container.

Kile watched him go before lowering his eyes.

Did he feel remorse for calling the enforcers down on her?

Most likely not. Even if he were capable of feeling guilt, he shouldn't. It had been a well-executed plan. He probably didn't hesitate. Such a decision was easy to make when you were an enforcer.

Dania shivered, imagining Cal in a similar situation, weighing his options. He could have infected her as well. He was probably supposed to. But he hadn't.

She remembered dinner that night… Cal had pulled her plate away from Kile and given her commander a different one. Her meal had never contained trackers.

Her stomach churned. If she were in that position, would she have betrayed people she cared about for a greater good?

A year ago, yes. She would have had no choice, especially if under orders. But now? What would she have done in Cal's place?

Humanity was confusing. Humanity was...*hard.*

Cal's brow furrowed in his sleep. No doubt he was still experiencing the pain that had caused him to vomit coming out of the jump. Peter said Cal's headaches were getting worse and harder to treat. She wondered if Cal would allow Alexander to examine him.

Of course, Alexander had not even looked at Cal since finding out what he'd done. Whatever trust had been gained between them had been lost, maybe never to return.

What other choice did Cal have, though? Was he supposed to say no to an extra mass of ships that could have helped save the planet, when alone they were nearly destined to fail?

Peter handed the metal box to Kile. "This should be more than enough of the antidote to clear all your enforcers. There are thirty extra just in case anyone else on the ship ate the food Cal sent over."

Kile tilted the box so the vials shifted inside and drummed his fingers on the container. "That is very generous of you." He looked up. "Thank you."

Dania gaped. Had he just said *thank you*...to a *human?* Let alone to the 'utterly incompetent illegally practicing doctor.'

Peter smiled. "You're welcome, Big Bad." He tapped his shoulder. "It's what friends do."

Rachel inched closer, bereft of her normal bouncy abandon. She placed her hand on Kile's arm. "You're gonna leave again, aren't you?"

He looked straight ahead, maybe avoiding her eyes. "Yes."

Her eyes flooded with tears. "Please stay. I know Cally did something really dumb, but that's Cally. You even said so yourself, that he's a complete waste of air and all."

Kile placed his hand on her cheek. "Quirky, you know I want to stay, but I can't." He held up the box. "My people have been tagged. If I don't get this serum to them, they will be tracked down and captured…drugged and put on display like they did to Alexander." He lowered his hand and looked away from her. "I cannot let that happen."

She punched his shoulder. He barely moved. "You big softie. Doing the right thing always takes you away from me, and I hate that."

He leaned down and whispered something in her ear.

Rachel smiled, her whole face lighting up. "Well, that sounds like fun!" She grabbed his arm, tugging him to the door. "See you guys later!"

Peter laughed as the door closed behind them. "Having her as a med tech is like working with an emotional tornado inside my lab."

Across the room, Alexander's hair floated about him as he stood beside Alanna's bed. Dania held up the ends of her own lifeless hair. She missed that sense of power always swirling about her. It was strange, though, that even after all this time, and all Alexander had been through, he still held Geron's primordial energy.

Doc followed her gaze. "You okay, sweetie?"

She shook her head. "Look at his hair."

"Yeah. I'm still trying to figure that out. It doesn't make any sense."

If Peter couldn't make sense of it, the chances of Dania figuring it out were slim. Still, she dearly wanted to.

Peter frowned, walking over to Alexander. "Hey, maybe you should let her sleep."

"She's sleeping fine," Alexander said. "I'm trying to heal her."

"Is it working?"

Alexander pursed his lips. "Not as well as I would've hoped."

Peter nodded. "I know my girl here. The only thing that works for her is sleep. And being alone. Her mojo doesn't realign when there are too many people in here."

Alexander tilted his head to the right. "*Mojo*?"

Peter placed his hand on his own chest. "There's something I know that you don't? Allow me a minute to soak this in." He breathed in, then out in a way Kile would have called theatrical.

Alexander's cheeks flushed. The doctor was probably making fun of her friend. It *was* odd, though, that Alexander's extraordinary healing abilities were not helping Alanna.

Dania walked over to the woman's bed and touched her forehead, hoping to give her the same sense of calm she'd given Dania. Her temperature seemed level but slightly low.

"Now *you're* acting like a doctor, too?" Peter asked.

"No." Dania just hated seeing her new friends look so beaten.

Peter pointed to the door. "Then get out. You could both do with some sleep yourselves."

He was probably right. "Come on." She tugged Alexander toward the door, taking one last look at Cal. His chest rose and fell in a gentle cadence. He looked so peaceful.

"He betrayed us, Dania," Alexander said.

She knew that. She should hate him.

"Yes, you should," Alexander said as they stepped into the hall.

But did that mean that she should hate Kile, too? Didn't he also betray her?

"You cannot begrudge your commander for doing his duty. The outcome was positive. The colony was saved."

True, but Peter was right. Kile's plan could have gone very wrong.

"But it didn't."

She looked back into the med bay, watching Cal as the doctor pulled a sheet up to his chin.

Alexander tapped the controls, closing the door. "Any human who betrayed us once will do so again."

She knew that. Once a criminal, always a criminal.

He was a smuggler.

He lied.

That was part of who he was.

Alexander's breathing slowed, and a slight smile touched his lips before he covered it.

Dania closed her eyes and pushed her friend out of her mind. Alexander couldn't understand human reasoning. Not yet at least. It would be some time before he learned or was even capable of understanding that not all things are as simple as right and wrong.

Yes, Cal had betrayed her. Yes, he was a smuggler. Yes, he'd lied. But should he be treated differently than Kile, simply because of who he was?

Alexander would say *yes*.

A year ago, she would have agreed with him.

But now?

She glanced back to the med bay door. Cal had seemed so helpless on that gurney. So frail. He'd taught her so much about what it was to be human.

And that made it even harder to walk away.

CAL STARED at Dania's door. This close to engineering, he would have expected pits and pockmarks, but oddly enough, her door seemed the cleanest out of the entire ship.

It was strange, what you noticed when you were procrastinating.

When Cal had woken up, and after Doc had confirmed he wasn't in immediate danger of his headache rebounding, he'd discovered they were halfway to Kirato. They needed somewhere to lie low for a while, and he couldn't blame them for heading to the one place they all felt safe.

What his crew hadn't taken into consideration, was that interplanetary merchants had stopped all supply runs to colonies on the Cartek border. This forced Kirato into the illicit goods trade just to stay alive. Enforcers never cared why a person did something illegal, just that there had been a crime. Cal just needed to figure out a way to keep Alexander and Kile on the ship or find a place to drop them off before they got anywhere near the planet.

The shiny metal skewed his reflection, leaving him in a

slight haze. That seemed fitting, since he wasn't even sure how to see himself anymore.

His eyes drew to the floor. Doc told him Dania had been there while Cal had lain unconscious. But he'd still woken up alone.

He couldn't really blame her. He'd sold out her friends and even considered selling out her. He shook his head. He was kidding himself if he thought he had it in him to put a tag on her. He'd never put her at risk. She knew that.

Well, he *hoped* she knew that. But even if she did, that probably wouldn't be enough for her to forgive him for putting her people in danger.

She wasn't their general anymore, but the slight pinch in her brow, the sad set of her eyes when she'd found out what he'd done, had been enough to tell him that she still cared about the men and woman who'd been under her command.

He wished he'd been awake to explain things to her. Who knew what Kile and Alexander had said to her while he'd been unconscious? Worse, who knew what they'd talked her into?

The door slid open, and Dania stood in the archway. "Are you going to keep staring at my door, or are you going to knock?"

He smiled. He'd caught her lingering outside his own door, once, and he'd said the exact same thing. "Touché."

She frowned. "Doesn't that word mean to strike someone?"

"Yeah, but it also means..." He wiped his eyes. "It's kind of hard to explain."

"You don't want to hit me, right? Or do you want *me* to hit *you*?"

He held up his hands. "None of the above. Can we please start this conversation over?"

She moved into the hallway and closed the door behind her.

Cal's gut twisted. He supposed he deserved her not inviting him inside. That was her personal space. The place where she invited friends. It wasn't a place she'd invite someone who'd betrayed her.

Dania leaned against the wall. "How's Alanna doing?"

Alanna? "She's fine, I guess. She basically has two doctors. The best we both had to offer."

Dania smiled, looking down. "Peter threw Alexander out."

Cal laughed. He wished he'd been awake to see Mr. Perfect put in his place.

He chewed the inside of his mouth. This ridiculous small talk wasn't why he was here. He needed to get this over with before he went insane. "Listen, I'm not even going to try to dance around this. I was an ass. I made a bad decision. It was wrong, and I'm sorry."

She looked up. "You are?"

Her eyes were steely. Direct. Very much like an enforcer's.

Cal's chest clenched. "Yeah. Of course, I am."

Her gaze seemed to cut through his eyes, lancing straight back into his brain. If she still had power, he'd be afraid she was rooting around in there, searching for his darkest secrets.

Well, she wouldn't find anything worse than what she already knew.

He did his best not to look away, but she was making it damn hard. She wasn't a general anymore, but that didn't mean the woman didn't still have a commanding presence. That was not the kind of thing that diminished pathogens could take away.

She shifted her weight. "What would have happened if those pirates hadn't started fighting alongside us?"

Cal blinked. That was probably the last question he'd expected. "What do you mean?"

"If we were left alone, just the *Star Renegade* and my ship to protect the planet, what do you think would have happened?"

That was an easy one. They'd been exponentially outnumbered. "We would have been annihilated."

"And the colony?"

Wasn't that obvious? "Ephershia would have been a total loss." Was there a trick question hiding in there? What was she trying to get at?

She cocked her head. "So, you're sorry that we saved the colony?"

What? "No. Of course not."

"Then you aren't sorry that you placed tracking devices in my people."

Cal looked down. "Okay." He hated it when she made things hard on him. But he didn't deserve her going easy on him, either. "I'm not sorry about that, I guess. But I am sorry that I didn't tell you."

She nodded. "Me too. Because I probably would have helped you."

Cal startled. "What?"

"The mission was to save the colony. If you had told me, and then I'd told my people, they would have weighed the odds. In the end, they would have ingested the trackers voluntarily."

He gulped. The idea of telling them what was going on…of *asking*… It had never even occurred to him.

He rubbed his face. "I don't know what to say."

She folded her arms. "You didn't trust me enough to do the right thing."

"No! That's not it." But maybe it was. He shook his head. "I really screwed this one up." How could he have been such an idiot? "Dammit!" He turned and punched the wall.

"Did your ship do something to offend you?"

He spun back to her, expecting a smile. There was none. She was still a general, standing in a hallway with a man who wasn't worthy to stand in her presence.

He lowered his eyes. "I'm not a very good leader. I never have been."

"That's not true, and we both know it. The *Star Renegade* is on every enforcer's kill list. You don't get that kind of attention if you're a bad captain."

Cal scoffed, shaking his head. "You do if you have a good crew capable of digging you out of your own idiocy."

She laughed. "You were good in the battle. Probably better than me. I'm good at thinking what needs to be done. I relay those thoughts with my mind and use my enforcers like extensions of my own arms. That's what generals are trained to do." She pursed her lips. "I don't lead my people like you lead this ship. And my people don't love me like your crew loves you."

"*Love* is a pretty strong word."

"They wouldn't be here if they didn't adore you."

Cal sighed. "Why do I feel like you're trying to cheer me up? I'm the one who did something stupid behind your back."

She took a step toward him. "Don't lie to me again, Cal. I've lost some trust in you. I hope you can earn it back."

He steadied himself against the wall. Was she actually giving him a second chance? "I'd sure like to try."

"Good. And I look forward to the day that you trust me as well."

"I already trust you." That sounded incredibly robotic. If he'd trusted her, he would have told her. She'd already made that clear.

Her gaze continued to penetrate him. "I'm glad you trust me. When we get to Kirato, I'm bringing Kile to the surface."

Cal's jaw dropped. "What?"

"This is not going to be a quick visit. We all know that. You can't keep him and Alexander on the ship."

Cal shook his head. "I'm not betraying Stanley and Mel. They took me in and hid me from the enforcers. I'm not bringing two of them right on top of their heads."

It was bad enough that he'd taken Dania there once before. Taking two fully charged enforcers would be like setting a bomb to explode and then hoping it wouldn't go off.

"Then I suggest you call Stanley and make sure everything on the planet looks perfectly legal."

Cal rubbed his forehead. "Wow. I'm not even sure that's possible."

She closed her eyes and sighed. "I'm programmed not to lie, and I promised Stanley I would tell Geron about their plight."

"Yeah. So?"

"I'm not going back to Keveron. Ever. I need to show

Kile what I saw so he can get those people the help I promised."

Ahhhh. Now it started to make sense. But Kile was still an enforcer, and every bit the problem Cal was worried about. "Can you order him not to see anything illegal?"

"No. And we'll have Alexander to worry about as well."

Cal rubbed the back of his neck. "This doesn't sound like a good time."

"You're a smuggler. You hide things for a living. You'll figure it out."

Sure, he would. But how was he supposed to hide the entire colony?

CHAPTER 32

DANIA

HEAT BLASTED Dania's face as Cal opened the door to the cargo bay.

"Home sweet home," Ty said, already mopping the sweat from his forehead.

Alanna tossed him an over-the-shoulder bag. "You love it here, and you know it."

"Only because Mel is a better cook than Cal."

"I find that hard to believe," Dania said.

Cal held up his hands in defeat. "I'll bow down to Mel's culinary artistry any day. The woman could make rock soup taste good if she tried hard enough."

Rachel dragged Kile toward the door, stopping near the edge. "That's Kirato?" She frowned. "It's disgusting."

"It's a little beat up," Ty said. "But *disgusting* is a bit harsh."

Alexander moved beside them and frowned. "*Beat up* is an inadequate description. Those buildings are crumbling." He turned to Cal. "Have they been attacked?"

"Only by time and neglect. The king cut them off. They

don't see any trade. They've been on their own for far too long."

"Impossible," Kile said. "This is a loyal world. Our king sees to all under his protection."

Dania shivered despite the heat. She'd thought the same thing. "That's why I wanted to show you. I didn't believe it, either."

Doc and Ethan joined them, passing a few containers to Cal. Warmth spread around the crew that seemed to have less to do with the weather and more to do with the location. While Ty was the only one born here, this planet seemed to have become home for all of them.

Sand whisked around the base of the ship as Cal looked at the broken exit ramp. "Damn." He turned to Ty. "Your job is to get that fixed while we're here."

"Already ahead of you, boss." He pointed out the door to a small skipper ship approaching. The ship hovered, stabilized, and then sent out a ramp, attaching the skipper to the *Star Renegade*.

Ty bowed, motioning to the ship. "Our transport awaits."

Kile folded his arms. "You do realize we can simply jump down."

Quirky looked over the edge. "Thirty feet? Not all of them have a big, strong enforcer to carry them to the ground."

Ethan pushed past them. "Would you two stop being so gross? Food is too scarce to make the rest of us vomit our breakfast."

They boarded the skipper ship and Ty fist-bumped the pilots and began chatting about technology and circuitry he'd seen on some of the inner-rim planets. The others remained oddly silent. Even Rachel.

A small crowd had gathered by the time the skipper craft settled on the ground. They cheered as the crew got out, many shouting, "Espinoza!"

Kile glanced at Cal. "They act as if they respect you."

Cal laughed. "Is that really so hard to believe?" Cal didn't wait for an answer. He stepped off the platform into a crowd of happy faces.

Dania stayed back, smiling as the people greeted the crew. These colonists had endured such poverty, yet their laughter filled the air with joy, even though this time, the *Star Renegade* hadn't come bearing a fortune in food and supplies.

"Excuse me, ma'am?" A small girl in a soiled, patched dress tugged on Dania's leg.

"Yes?" Dania knelt to the child's eye level.

The little one scratched her nose. "Are you the magic flying lady?"

Dania cocked her head. *Flying lady?*

A woman and man moved behind the girl, smiling and holding hands. The woman seemed familiar, although the smile seemed foreign on her lips.

The little girl threw her arms around Dania's neck. "My mama says you're the magic flying lady who saved me." She squeezed Dania into a hug. "Thank you."

Dania tensed, but then her shock wore off. This was the tiny girl who'd nearly died in her mother's arms. Dania had given her oranges and used her power to force the vitamin C into the girl's bloodstream, speeding her healing.

Dania returned the hug. "You're very welcome. You've gotten so big."

"And I go to school now, too."

Dania smiled. "And I bet you're very smart."

The father reached out his hand to shake Dania's. "You saved her. We never had a chance to properly thank you."

Dania worked to hold back her tears. "That's not necessary." She watched the little girl run into the crowd and greet several more children of about the same age, all wearing tattered clothing. "Seeing her well is all the thanks I need."

They bowed their heads slightly and backed away, a touch of fear in their eyes. Dania sensed Alexander behind her before he spoke.

"It looks like you've been here before."

She nodded. "These people need help."

He frowned. "So I see."

"Calvin Espinoza!" A voice boomed through the crowd.

The people parted for a tall, stout, dark-bearded man wearing faded striped robes and material wrapped around his head to ward off the heat of the sun.

Cal beamed. "Stanley!"

They embraced, Stanley slapping Cal on the back.

A woman pushed through the crowd behind them. "Where are they? Where are my boys?"

"Mel!" Doc and Ethan shouted.

Her long, billowing black skirt and white apron blew in the breeze as she pinched both their cheeks. "Look at you two." Her eyes widened, seeing Ty. "And you! Don't they feed you?" She spun toward Cal. "Calvin, you promised to feed my Tyler." She poked Ty's stomach. "He's skin and bones."

"I'm fine, Mel," Ty said.

"You are not fine." She waved her hands in the air. "I

need to cook! I can't have you all starving to death!" She grabbed Ty by the collar and dragged him into the crowd. "You need to eat before you drop dead!"

"I'm fine, Mel!" he repeated before the crowd closed around them.

Stanley shook his head. "My Amelia does not change."

"We wouldn't want her to," Peter said.

Stanley bowed to Dania. "And the pretty lady returns."

Dania lowered her eyes as she approached. "I'm sorry. I wasn't able to keep my promise."

Stanley held up his pointer finger. "Yet."

Dania stared at him. "Yet?"

"You have not kept your promise *yet*." He grabbed her shoulders.

She flinched again, unaccustomed to the familiarity.

"You made a promise from your heart. I know you will help us. We are far from expecting miracles, or expecting all this to be fixed overnight."

Kile moved forward. "Why is this colony in such disrepair?"

Stanley smiled. "Well, hello there, my large and assuming friend." He motioned to the buildings around them. "Welcome to Kirato. What little we have, is yours."

Alexander stepped beside Kile. "What happened here?"

"We have not seen a trader in over a year." Stanley turned to Cal. "The last ship we've actually seen was the *Star Renegade*."

Dania gaped. That had been well over six months ago. The *Star Renegade* had come with a fortune in citrus and other goods, but nowhere near enough to last so long.

Cal frowned. "How's your food supply?"

Stanley tapped Cal's back again. "We get by. We always get by."

"It's impossible that you haven't seen a ship," Alexander said. "You're on the trade routes."

Stanley held up his hands. "That may be, but they do not stop."

"I promised them help," Dania said. "I was going to inform the king." But she'd never gotten home. Now she couldn't go back.

Kile scowled, scanning the decrepit buildings. "This is unacceptable. This is a valuable trade stop. An important colony."

She was glad he didn't think differently. That meant that he'd expected the colony to be thriving as well. The question still was…did the king know?

A group of artisans set out to repair the *Star Renegade*. Interestingly enough, Cal didn't leave anyone behind to watch the ship. He had such trust in these people.

"Weren't you afraid of someone calling in a bounty last time?" Dania asked.

"Yeah, I was. But this time, I arrived with two enforcers. The colonists may have questioned who you were last time we were here, but there's no mistaking them." He pointed his thumb at Kile and Alexander. "Anyway, I trust anyone that Stanley sends me." He smiled. "And Ethan and Doc are running surveillance."

Ahhhh…so maybe he wasn't *entirely* trusting.

Cal hadn't evaded capture this long by being foolish. Luck had a lot to do with it, but they'd also learned the art of strategic caution.

Within an hour, they were scattered around a table with

plates filled with odd vegetables and strange, small cuts of meat.

"Do I want to know what this is?" Ethan asked.

"Probably not," Doc whispered.

"Who cares?" Rachel said, her cheeks full. "It's delicious." She gave Amelia a thumbs-up.

Stanley's wife smiled. "I like this girl. She knows good food when she eats it." She pointed her fork at Ty. "Now you eat."

Ty pointed to his full cheek. "I'm eating, I'm eating!"

The crew's smiles grew as they cut into the odd food. The texture was unusual, but Rachel was right. The flavors burst through Dania's mouth.

Mel watched with pride as each guest cleaned their plate and reached for more from the pile in the center of the table.

"Oww." Ethan looked under the table. "Did someone just kick me?"

Rachel set down her fork and knife. "I-I did."

Ethan frowned at her from the far end of the table. "You kicked me from all of the way down there?"

Rachel stood. "Shut up." She grabbed a roll, throwing it at Ethan and hitting the engineer on the forehead.

"Hey! What gives?"

"Oh. Sorry." She grabbed two more rolls and threw them over Ethan's head.

One hit the wall and slid down. The other bounced on the floor and settled on the ground beside the door.

Rachel smiled and sat. "Okay, then. Now we can eat." She started spooning vegetables into her mouth, keeping her face down.

Everyone stared at her, and Dania was glad that she

wasn't the only one to notice the erratic behavior. This was odd, even by Rachel standards.

Amelia seemed to force a smile before she folded her hands along the edge of her dish. "May I ask why you threw the rolls? Were they not to your liking?"

Rachel swallowed. "Nah. They're delicious. But I didn't want to be rude."

Amelia tilted her head. "You threw food so as not to be rude?"

Rachel's eyes darted around the table, as if just noticing everyone was staring. "Yeah. Doesn't everyone?"

Cal took a deep breath and let it out slowly. "Rachel is a little unique, Mel. We've kind of gotten used to her."

"We have?" Ethan chuckled, and picked up his fork, Rachel's outburst apparently forgotten for the much more interesting food.

Dania's gaze drew back to the floor. The rolls were gone. Had someone picked them up when she hadn't been looking?

Alexander glanced at Rachel. His lips thinned slightly, probably disapproving of her outburst. He continued to stare, and his temperature wavered slightly until a slight smile spread over his lips—the same smile she'd seen when they were younger and he'd figured out the codes used to seal the doors to the armory.

Alanna handed Alexander a plate of blue, orange, and red vegetables. "Do you want some more?"

He frowned before looking at their hosts. "You have a significant amount of food here for a planet that seems to be in need." He glanced at Rachel, still stuffing her mouth with food, and then turned back to Stanley and Mel. "Is this an unnecessary extravagance?"

Stanley snorted, covering his mouth. "We have learned to utilize what the planet gives us."

"What does that mean?" Kile asked.

Stanley pointed at the vegetables. "Casa weed is a nuisance. We used to try to kill it. It grew up the walls and ruined foundations. But it also has similar properties to spinach and kale." Then he pointed to the meat. "And some native animals breed in excess. They are not normally palatable, but you can live on them. My Amelia is a master of hiding their unusually bitter aftertaste."

Kile looked down. "You should not have to eat rodents and weeds."

Rachel's eyes widened. "Rodents?" She looked at her plate, shrugged, and took another bite. "Oh, well. Tastes good enough for me!"

"Once again," Stanley said. "We make do. You do not survive in the outlier colonies if you cannot adapt."

Kile grimaced at his plate. "Prince Geron will hear of this. He sent us to protect Ephershia, even though they'd withdrawn from the treaty. He'll certainly send a good, loyal colony the aid it needs."

Stanley placed his fork down. "We do not blame the king or your prince. They have other things to worry about. We are far from other colonies, but we do hear what's going on in the galaxy."

"What do you mean?" Cal asked.

"There are skirmishes everywhere. The Cartek numbers are multiplying like the beetles in the south dung caves. The Banes are fighting back, but no one expected the sudden show of force."

They crew flicked glances at each other. This, they knew all too well.

Stanley held Mel's hand. "We have considered ourselves lucky. Yes, we are forgotten, but we seem to be forgotten by the Carteks as well. We sit on their border, but their ships fly right by us."

Probably because there were so few people here. Not to mention the desert-like heat. The humidity-loving Carteks probably looked at this planet as a wasteland. But maybe not for long. If no one stopped them, they'd eventually swarm over everything. And when that time came, Dania wasn't sure even the enforcers would be able to stop them.

CHAPTER 33

DANIA

DANIA WATCHED the double moon rise from the horizon. A chill touched the air, but the stone wall in front of her and the sand beneath her still radiated heat.

Dust swirled on a light breeze as Kile approached.

"Did you enjoy the meal?" she asked.

He seemed to consider his answer. "The woman is surprisingly adept at cooking rat."

Dania suppressed her laugh. It probably hadn't been actual rat meat, but the Earthan rodents were known to escape from trading ships and had already infested almost every colonized planet, so it was quite possible.

"I'm not here to talk about food," he said.

"I figured not." She steeled herself for the inevitable fight to keep her humanity. But alone, without her powers, she would be helpless if he chose to drag her back to Keveron.

The breeze shifted Kile's hair as he stared at the horizon. He wasn't normally so pensive. She supposed living on the *Star Renegade* did that to people.

"The navigator skipped space," he finally said.

Dania tensed. Alanna was the last thing she'd expected him to bring up. "Yes, she did."

"You've seen her do this before?"

"Yes."

His cheek twitched as he continued to stare into the distance.

"It's not illegal," she said.

"No. It's not."

His silence started to press in on her chest. What was going through his mind, and why mention this now?

Finally, he turned to her. "With the exception of possibly the engineer, I find the navigator to be the least guilty of anyone on that ship."

"I agree."

He nodded, looking back to the horizon. "If I mention this to the Banes, they'll show interest."

Dania flinched. She could order him not to mention it, but would he listen?

He sighed. "However, if I do say anything, they may be more concerned about this oddity than that of a vassal planet falling to ruin."

This was a sad truth. The Kevers had an odd sense of priorities at times.

"Not mentioning Alanna's abilities is not a lie, unless they ask directly," Dania reminded him.

He nodded. "And I would not expect them to ask directly."

"What if they ask how this ship tends to disappear?"

He seemed to consider the question. "I witnessed the engineer hook a piece of Cartek technology to the engines. Afterward, the ship skipped space." He shrugged. "It would not be a lie."

Dania released her breath, finally relaxing. "Thank you."

"However, that leads us to the second matter at hand." He turned to her. "I'm sure you realize that if the Carteks are attacking at multiple points, and in great numbers, Geron may be called to offer his enforcers to support the king in a military capacity."

The cool air chilled Dania's lungs as she took in a deep breath. "You're probably right."

"We were far too disjointed while unlinked. The battle for Ephershia showed us we're worthless without you."

"You aren't worthless."

"Without you, Geron will need to go into battle directly. He will see war firsthand while his brothers and sisters direct their enforcers from safety."

Dania closed her eyes. She hadn't considered that. "Geron is not a military leader. He knows nothing about battle."

"Which is why he needs his general. I cannot take your place, Dania. You know this. I'm not coded to link them."

She took a deep breath and held it. All the other princes and princesses had multiple generals. It was a failsafe so a second could take command should another fall. Geron had never seen the need. He had enforcers because he was required to have a guard. No one had expected the war with the Carteks to become so widespread.

But she seemed so distanced from that now. Like she had the memories of another person. "I love my sponsor and would never wish him harm, but I cannot go back to that emotionless existence."

He nodded. "I didn't expect you to react differently." He lowered his eyes, and his disappointment cut through her.

His feelings shouldn't matter, though. He was part of her life *before*.

The *Star Renegade* was her life *after*. Her *now*.

All Dania wanted to do was forget who she *had been* and discover who she *could be*.

Kile looked up and stared at the moons, as if he were appreciating their beauty. That was odd in itself, but no odder than him allowing their conversation to end in what Kile should most likely consider a defeat. Even though she was technically still his general, his programming should not have allowed a defeat of any kind.

Unless he hadn't been defeated.

Dania flicked a glance at him, then took in the wispy clouds approaching the moons. "Whatever your orders from Geron were, they've been fulfilled, haven't they?"

"Yes."

How could that be? "What were his orders concerning me?"

"As I said when I first arrived, he requested that you return."

"In time. Not immediately."

"Yes."

The caveat of *in time* left a large amount of leeway for interpretation. Which was probably why he wasn't dragging her back kicking and screaming.

Kile's gaze centered on her. "He asked me to make sure you were safe."

Dania gaped. "Safe?"

He nodded, looking back to the moons. "Our host made some interesting points at dinner." He held up his palms. "This planet has been forgotten by both sides. It is a place in-between." He lowered his hands. "I, for one, cannot think of anywhere safer for you. At least until you come to your senses."

Her tongue grew dry as she continued to stare. He was actually going to leave her here. Geron had worded his orders as a request, and Kile had made that request of her, thus fulfilling his duty.

Until Geron changed his orders, she was free.

She closed her lips and looked at the sand beneath her boots. Was this real? Was she really free?

Behind them, Alanna led Alexander out of Stanley and Amelia's modest home. Rachel stepped out with them, hugging herself as if it were cold.

"Isn't it pretty?" Alanna said, looking at the moons. "I never get tired of a Kirato moonrise."

Kile met Alexander's gaze. "We need to get back to Geron. We need to do what we can to prepare our people and keep our prince safe."

Alexander glanced at Alanna, then back to Kile. "I'm not going with you."

Dania startled. How could Alexander say that? Kile was right. Geron needed protection. How could Alexander refuse?

Kile's temperature spiked by nearly a half degree. "Don't be foolish."

"My orders are to protect Dania. If she is staying, then so am I."

The commander's lips thinned. "You're one of our strongest. We'll need you."

Alexander shook his head. "Geron's orders were clear."

Kile closed his eyes, taking a deep breath. "You're making me return alone?"

Dania touched his arm. "You are more than capable of leading them, Kile. You did it for many years."

"Not in war." He stormed off, the sand whisking up around his feet.

"Big Guy?" Rachel sprinted after him, but it was doubtful even her unique form of distraction would be enough to center Dania's commander.

Alanna inched closer to Alexander. "I can't believe you're staying."

He didn't answer, but Dania's stomach clenched when Alexander took Alanna's hand in his. Maybe Dania wasn't the only reason he'd decided to stay.

Dania's cheeks heated. The air seemed stifling, despite being cool. Alexander had said he'd stayed to protect her, and he was unable to lie. In the end, he would return to Geron, though. And the chances of him leaving Dania behind were still zero.

That would leave Alanna just as broken as Rachel had been, and was about to be once more, as soon as Kile left. And there'd be nothing Dania could do to help either of them.

CAL STOOD on the edge of the landing platform as Kile inspected the ship Stanley had offered him. It wasn't long before the old trader shook the enforcer's hand and joined Cal as Kile continued to search the ship.

"What's he looking for?" Cal asked.

"I don't think our new friend quite trusts me. He's searching for explosives."

"Will he find any?"

Stanley chuckled. "If I could only afford explosives, maybe I could coax more traders here."

"Which makes me ask: How do you even have a ship here to give him?"

"Same as the *Star Renegade*. It was a wreck, and the local artisans fixed it as the days passed just to keep their skills fresh. What we didn't have was fuel to fly her."

And Cal had given them just enough to get Kile back home. There was no need to be overly generous, with war and the chance of supply shortages coming.

"That's a heck of a nice ship, though. I hate to admit it,

but it's nicer than the *Renegade*. You been holding out on me?"

"You wouldn't give up the *Star Renegade*." Stanley looked back to the ship. "Even if you considered it, Tyler wouldn't let you."

Cal nodded. His friend was right on both counts.

"Besides, my understanding from your beautiful flying lady is that she and our enforcer friends cannot lie." Stanley pointed at Kile. "Your very tall and assuming friend said he will get us help. He needs a good ship to get him home. I consider this an investment in Kirato's future."

"I'd like to hope he'll bring back help, but I'm not sure the king will really give a damn if the rest of the galaxy is in chaos."

Stanley shrugged. "A small chance is better than no chance at all. Hope is better than despair any day."

Dania approached from the other side of the platform. She hugged herself, watching her commander prepare for departure.

Stanley placed his hand on Cal's back. "If anyone ever told me the young man who'd hidden in my storage lockers would try to befriend, let alone *save* an enforcer, I would never have believed it."

Cal laughed. "I don't think I would have believed it, either."

Stanley watched Dania pace. "You did good there, Calvin. I'm sure it wasn't easy."

It still wasn't easy. Dania would probably have to fight against her past for the rest of her life. She was definitely more trouble than he'd bargained for.

Stanley nudged him. "Whatever you are thinking, she's worth it."

"You have no idea what I was thinking."

Stanley smiled. "I'm an old man, but I'm not *that* old." He tapped Cal's back with his palm before walking toward the houses. "It's good to have you home."

Cal took a deep breath of the still-hot air. "It's good to be home."

DANIA GLANCED at Cal as he approached, then redirected her gaze to Kile as her commander walked onto the ship Stanley had provided for him.

Once Kile returned and deactivated the tracking devices their people had ingested, her enforcers would be called to battle one way or another.

She'd seen a lot of skirmishes while on board the *Star Renegade*, but nothing like a battle in the name of the king. Dania missed the sensation of her sponsor's power coursing through her, the feel of the energy discharging as she destroyed those in violation of the law.

This new life, though, this interesting existence where she had *choices*, had become far more important to her. Power meant losing herself again. It meant becoming a tool of law once more, rather than the person she had become. No amount of power was worth that.

"It's a pretty nice ship he's got there," Cal said.

Dania nodded. "It's adequate."

She cringed, hearing Kile's words come out of her mouth… The same words she would've used if she were still under Geron's influence. Maybe some of her reactions were habit, rather than Kever control.

"I'm sorry," she said. "I meant, it's a good ship. It should get him back to Bane space safely." And hopefully, Geron and his father would be receptive to the plight of this planet and send Kirato help.

Cal's jaw tensed as he looked back to the ship. "I'm glad he's taking the message for you. I don't want you anywhere near the Banes."

Dania nodded. She wanted to stay far away as well. The draw to the power was still there, whether she wanted to recognize it or not. If faced with a Bane—if faced with her sponsor—she wasn't sure if she'd be able to resist the nagging in her gut, the empty place longing to be filled with her prince's primordial energy.

The moons loomed high overhead. A chill touched her skin, despite the heat still radiating from the sun-scorched sand. No matter how badly she wanted to avoid the Banes, she knew Geron would eventually find her. And if the Carteks kept pressing their advantage and kept attacking Earth's holdings, there may be nowhere to hide from this war.

A low hum shook the ground as Kile's ship lifted from the surface, wafting up dust in its wake. A small funnel formed, skewing her vision and casting small pieces of debris across the sandy surface. The dust settled quickly, concealing the traces of the ship that had once stood there, leaving the ground clean and unmarred.

Kile's departure didn't feel so much like an end, but a new beginning—maybe a beginning none of them were prepared for.

Her stomach fluttered. The newness and uncertainty of

it all was both horrifying and exhilarating, and she wasn't sure how to feel. Deep down, she knew the ongoing conflicts in the galaxy might lead to this…to a war against an enemy no one would be able to hide from.

Her life had just begun, but now the end seemed to loom closer than ever. She leaned her head on Cal's shoulder, and his tension seemed to ease. She was glad she could do that for him, even if it was only temporary. Because she feared the oncoming storm may overcome them all.

Cal laced his fingers with hers as Kile's ship ascended toward the stars.

"This isn't over," he said.

She gripped his hand tighter. "I know."

CHAPTER 36
ALEXANDER

ALEXANDER'S BOOTSTEPS echoed on the *Star Renegade*'s flooring as he strode toward the center of the ship. The hall seemed compressed, almost stifling after spending a few days in Kirato's open air. Still, a sense of warmth filled him as he drank in the familiarity and the odd sense of safety inside the dented and scratched walls. Espinoza, for all his shortcomings, had created a sense of family here. Something that Alexander had lost when Dania hadn't returned from her last mission. He could almost understand her attraction to this ship and crew, and her overall desire to stay.

Stopping at the stairway that led to the lower levels, he ran his fingers over a scorch mark in the wall. The weapon that had caused this had been calibrated to kill, and in this confined space, either someone had died or the shooter had been firing a warning shot. He'd have to ask the crew about the details one day, if they'd be willing to tell him.

He climbed onto the ladder and descended to the crew deck below, passing another spray of scorch marks. In some ways, the battle scars were not unexpected. The crew engaged in illegal activities nearly every time the ship made port.

Oddly enough, Alexander didn't care. Dania had made it plain that everything this crew did was to support the colony on Kirato. As an enforcer, Alexander had also been forced to break the king's law if the law was in contention with a mission. What this crew had done to save the colony was no different.

Alexander closed his eyes and took a deep breath. Even considering that this crew might not be guilty showed him how badly he needed to get back to his sponsor. But his mission—to protect Dania—was clear. He'd remain by her side until he could bring her home, no matter how conflicted he became.

Until then, he needed to confront the one member of this crew who *was* guilty of a crime. Reaching the crew quarters across from engineering, he stopped at the doorway to the left of his own quarters and knocked.

"She's not home!" Rachel called from within.

Did that actually work with the rest of the crew? He knocked again.

"I said, I'm not here!"

He shouldn't have expected her to be compliant. Alexander held his palm to the access control and sent a slight burst of power into the mechanism.

As the door opened, Rachel spun toward him. "Hey! Breaking and entering is a crime!"

He stepped inside. "So is lying to an enforcer."

"When did I lie to you?"

"You are here, are you not?"

"Yeah. So?" Her eyes widened. She covered her mouth before she lowered her hands, her face returning to a mask of confidence. "Well, yeah, okay, I lied, but so did you. You lied to Dani."

Alexander gritted his teeth. "I would never lie to my general."

"No? No?" She leaned toward him. "Really? Then what's with your hair all swirling around like crazy, huh? You've been away from dear old princey-poo for a long time." She poked him in the chest. "Why do you have powers and Dani doesn't?"

Alexander's gut clenched. This was a valid concern. Dania was incredibly encumbered in her current state. There was no reason she hadn't benefitted from the same trickling of power he'd received. Then again, if his hypothesis was correct, then it made perfect sense.

Rachel leaned back, gaping. "Wait a minute. You *do* know! You know why you have power and Dani doesn't? And you're keeping that from her? How could you do that? How could you not tell her?"

Alexander held up his palms. "I *will* tell her, once I'm certain what's going on."

A triumphant look flashed across her face.

He narrowed his eyes on her. "You're quite adept at deflecting attention from yourself. I came here to talk about *your* crime."

She folded her arms. "Oh, please. The only crime I've committed was breaking into a creepy old castle to rescue your sorry butt from an eccentric collector. You're welcome, by the way."

He took in a deep breath, then released it. "You, Ms. Quirky, are harboring a stowaway."

Her skin grew pale. "I-I am not!"

"Another lie?"

"No." Her temperature spiked a tenth of a degree as she held up he arms and motioned to the room. "Do you see a stowaway?"

"If your friend were here, I wouldn't be able to see him, and you know it."

"So, now you're seeing people who aren't there? We do have a doctor on this ship if you want him to give you an exam." She walked over to her communication panel. "I can call him if you want. The med bay is just upstairs."

Alexander took another calming breath. "Your friend has a penchant for rolls. He steals food from the lounge. He gets caught in automatic doors, making them look like they are malfunctioning, leading to unnecessary repairs. Not to mention that his constant triggering of the recyclers in the med bay is making our doctor question his sanity."

She laughed. "He does love playing with the recyclers. He thinks they're great fun." She gasped and covered her mouth again.

Alexander folded his arms. "Harboring a stowaway is illegal."

"It is not! I-I mean, he's not a stowaway."

"You're hiding a passenger on this ship that the captain does not know about."

"He's not hurting anyone. They can't even see him."

"Any stowaway is illegal."

She looked to her left, then right, before grabbing a small box from her bed table and holding up a coin. "I'll pay his passage."

"That would mean telling the captain."

She shook her head. "Don't tell Cally. With Kile gone, they might just kick me off the ship, and I couldn't bear it."

She was worried about losing her place on the *Star Rene-*

gade? This was an interesting reaction he hadn't expected. "Why is that a concern? My understanding is that you had a good life before coming here."

She shrugged. "I don't know. I just like it here. They treat me nice."

"So you return their kindness by lying to them?"

She looked at the ceiling. "I was lonely, and he needed a place to stay." Lowering her eyes, she rubbed her face. "It was just fun at first. I didn't think it would be a problem."

"The crew isn't only questioning the machinery. They're questioning *you*. If you check the files, you'll see they've scanned you for space sickness."

She lowered her eyes. "I know."

For some reason, she didn't seem to care that the crew questioned her sanity. Loneliness, he'd seen, could be a powerful induction to crime. "Tell the captain about the stowaway, or I will tell him for you."

She looked up, her eyes ablaze. "If you tell Cally, I'll tell Dani you know how to recharge your power and you're keeping it a secret."

His veins heated. He took another steadying breath. "That is *not* what's going on."

"Oh, I think it is. Dani is my friend, and she misses all that power stuff. It kills her to see you walking around with your hair all swirly and alive-looking, and you being able to do crazy stuff like break into people's rooms like you just did." She lifted her chin. "Keeping that from her is wrong, and you know it."

The problem was, he wasn't certain why his powers weren't fading. He only had conjecture, no facts. He needed to do more research to see if his hypothesis was right.

She folded her arms again. "It looks like we both have

secrets."

"I'll tell Dania in time." If his guess as to the source of the power was correct, the ramifications could be significant. He needed to be sure.

"And I'll tell Cally in time, too. Just not yet. You know Cally. He'll overreact."

That was probably true, on both counts. The stowaway would certainly make him angry, but Alexander's information could likely put the *Star Renegade* on the run for the rest of their lives, even more so than they already were.

"So, deal then?" Rachel held out her hand. "I keep your secret, and you keep mine?"

A deal with the least trustworthy member of this crew? It probably wasn't the best idea, but until he knew more, a few more days of the recyclers going off on their own wouldn't hurt anything.

Alexander took her hand and shook on it, but he knew time was running out for both of them.

———

Ready for the next adventure? Book 4 is only a click away.
Pick up Renegade Legacy now at your favorite retailer.

Want to hear updates on future books and a few odd meanderings here and there? Sign up for my newsletter here.

www.jennifermeaton.com
Or
https://www.subscribepage.com/s2b4f1_copy4

ACKNOWLEDGMENTS

I always laugh when I have conversations with people and they listen, wide-eyed, as I explain all the steps there are to creating a book.

"I thought you just wrote it and that was all!" I hear over and over again.

There's a lot to bringing these stories to life. A series takes planning and time, not only to write, but to come up with characters and plots and worlds for the adventures to take place in.

While I'd love to say that I write a single draft and send it out to the world, the truth is, I'm not *that good*. What you just read was probably close to a 20th draft.

Through the process the novel has been read by beta readers, developmental editors, a copy editor, and a proof-reader. Each one of these people provide feedback, and the edits begin anew. Each polish gives it more action, more scenery, more emotion, and hopefully a more satisfying experience for the reader.

I'd like to thank my beta and developmental team: Shaila Patel, Jenna Standage, Amy McMullen, Melanie Comb, and Emilee Garriss for going through the story with a fine-toothed comb and pointing out everything that I could strengthen. It always amazes me how a different set of eyes sees something new.

Thank you to my patient copy editor, Amy McNulty, who knows better than anyone that I love commas far, far, far too much.

And my final line of defense, my proofreader Tandy Boese, who always catches something, even though six editors reviewed the novel before her.

I'd be remiss if I also didn't thank my family for their support. They are always in the background, waving Pom Poms, cooking meals, and doing laundry to help me make it to the finish line of each novel, and I greatly appreciate it.

And, of course, THANK YOU for reading. Your smuggler's heart and great reviews keep me going. I really appreciate you jumping onboard the *Star Renegade* and traveling the galaxy with Cal and the crew.

ABOUT THE AUTHOR

Jennifer M. Eaton hails from the eastern shore of the North American Continent on planet Earth. Yes, regrettably, she is human, but please don't hold that against her.

While not traipsing through the galaxy looking for specimens for her space moth collection, she lives with her wonderfully supportive husband, three energetic offspring, and a duo of poodles who run the spaceport when she's not around.

During infrequent excursions to her home planet of Earth, Jennifer enjoys long hikes in the woods, bicycling, swimming, snorkeling, and snuggling up by the fire with a great book; but great adventures are always a short shuttle ride away.

Read more from Jennifer M. Eaton

www.jennifereaton.com
Blog: Jennifermeaton.com

facebook.com/Jennifereaton.author
twitter.com/jennifermeaton
instagram.com/jennifermeaton
goodreads.com/Jennifermeaton